THE
SHADOW
COURT

WILDE JUSTICE, BOOK 4

JENN STARK

Books by Jenn Stark

Wilde Justice Series
The Red King
The Lost Queen
The Hallowed Knight
The Shadow Court

Immortal Vegas Series
Getting Wilde
Wilde Card
Born To Be Wilde
Wicked And Wilde
Aces Wilde
Forever Wilde
Wilde Child
Call of the Wilde
Running Wilde
Wilde Fire
One Wilde Night (prequel novella)

Demon Enforcers Series
Demon Unbound
Demon Forsaken
Demon Bewitched
Demon Ensnared

For Sara.

THE MOON.

CHAPTER ONE

Time was, I'd go anywhere, find anything, if the price was right.

Times hadn't changed all that much.

"Bats," whispered the man in front of me. I could smell the fear oozing out his pores, along with half his body weight in sweat, as he pushed aside a thick, heavy strand of vines to reveal the cave beyond. Though it was night, the humidity in this section of the French Guiana rainforest was clocking in at approximately two hundred and thirty-five percent, and the sweltering heat of the day hadn't diminished much. It was like being trapped in a wet wool sock. With mosquitoes.

"You know that for sure? Or were you told?" I peered into the dark, slightly cooler space beyond the makeshift hole he'd just created. I'd already learned that a great deal of Alonso's knowledge of this blighted section of South America was from hearsay and ghost stories. Some of which was helpful, most of which was not. Still, I needed the guy.

Here in the armpit of South America, nobody knew or cared that I was Sara Wilde, mighty Justice of the Arcana Council, dedicated to righting the wrongs perpetrated against the psychic underdogs of the world. They only knew I was a treasure hunter with money to burn. Sadly, not enough of them cared about that either. Even after I'd laid down an impressive number of euros in the shambledown café in Kourou, Alonso was the only guide willing to set aside his rum-soaked Ti' Punch and take me into the jungle.

His terms had been specific and nonnegotiable. We could travel only at night under a clear and star-filled sky, alone, and as silently as possible. He didn't necessarily believe in the old gods of his people, but that didn't mean he wanted to piss them off.

Fair enough.

"I don't know firsthand," he confessed, surprising me. I appreciated honesty in my petrified guides. "But the men who survived Île du Diable and found this cave said the bats *here* were worse than *there*." He left the implications of that hanging like the bats themselves, and I fought the instinct to flinch.

French Guiana wasn't known for a heck of a lot besides being hot, sticky, and the site of one of the world's nastiest penal colonies ever conceived, built on a cluster of three islands just off its coast. Devil's Island had been closed in the 1950s and was now a tourist attraction, of course, but the stench of despair that still radiated from the very rocks of the place reached all the way to the mainland. It'd been a very bad place for very bad men...the guards even more so than the inmates.

The stories of the vampire bats were part of that lore. Hovering above prisoners who were tied to the point of virtual immobility, the bats would wait until the men drifted asleep, then swoop down and feast, sinking in sharp fangs and, true to their name, lapping up the blood. It was only one of a host of tortures the prisoners endured, and very, very few men survived the place. Of the eighty thousand souls condemned to Devil's Island by the French government, mostly for crimes against the state, all but two thousand had ended up as food for the sharks that circled the island like it was free sandwich day at Chick-fil-A.

A tiny fraction of those two thousand had actually escaped Devil's Island and survived to tell the tale. One of those tales had brought me here tonight.

"Let's go in," I said.

"You go in," Alonso countered. "I will keep watch here to protect you from the wrath of Guabancex."

I leveled a stare at him. "You've seen Indiana Jones, right? You know the guy who stays behind is the one who gets impaled by a million arrows?"

"I stay here." His dark eyes shone with terror in the moonlight, terror that seemed completely out of proportion to the threat of flying things with sharp teeth. Not that I was a huge fan of getting bitten by bats, but we were both wearing sturdy cargo pants and long-sleeved shirts, despite the staggering heat. Our heads were covered with mosquito-proof burka-style hoods, and a veritable arsenal of bug, bat, and crawly-thing repellant hung from our belts. Or hung from mine, anyway, and I was more than happy to share.

Alonso remained resolute. "I watch the gate to the underworld, where the Sun Lord dwells until morning. You disturb the Goddess of Storms at *your* peril, not mine. I am but a humble guide."

"You're a humble guide who's been paid a thousand euros for a walk in the woods, buddy," I pointed out, but it was clear this battle had already been lost. I turned and surveyed the cave. "How deep is this, according to the stories you've heard?"

"Three levels," Alonso said quickly, relief rushing his words. "The first is an ordinary cave with an unstable floor and many holes, close together. Only one hole is the right one. The others drop you to your death.

The second, it is little more than a ledge. Below that, the treasure rests in a hole off the side of the ledge. The treasure is too heavy to move. The men who fell into the chamber could not take it out, but they saw it, reached for it, and that was enough to curse them. They all died."

"We all die eventually." I squinted into the hole, which looked very hole-like, as Alonso's words devolved into a low muttering. I could speak the local language credibly well, but I couldn't decipher mumbled prayers. Though my client had warned me to expect this, I hadn't believed local superstition would still be so strong sixty years after the last attempt for the treasure. Clearly, I'd been wrong. Virtually no one outside Kourou even knew this hoard existed, which was probably why it was still here. *If* it was still here.

"You go in, you go in," Alonso announced, his gaze shifting to the sky. "There is no wind. You go now? Now is good. There's no wind."

He brandished a long machete and, with a few short, decisive whacks, had cut the hole large enough for me to slip into the cave—but not so big that it would be difficult to camouflage.

"Right, right." I stepped in. No sooner had I cleared the opening than I heard Alonso carefully moving the vines back into place. I gave him about a thirty percent chance of still being there when I came back out, but I didn't worry about that as much as I used to. I had better built-in navigation these days for getting out of tight spots than when I'd started hunting artifacts six years ago.

Six years ago. Time sure did fly.

I straightened and pulled my penlight from my belt, keeping the beam low and covered while I peered upward. Sure enough, there was a host of bats wedged into the eaves of the cave, which meant that the vine-covered entrance wasn't the only opening into this area. The air wasn't as dank as it should have been either, especially considering the thick layer of guano covering the floor. I panned the flashlight over the floor and confirmed that yes, there was a ton of batshit on the floor and no, it hadn't been disturbed recently. As in not in years, from the looks of it. My client hadn't been lying about this part either. This was about as virgin a find as you could hope for.

Which begged the question, why?

Not moving from where I stood, which I knew was sturdy by the simple fact that I hadn't fallen through the floor yet, I stuck the penlight in my mouth and fished my deck of Tarot cards out of another pocket. While most people wouldn't interrupt their treasure hunt for a quick game of cards, this wasn't your usual treasure, I wasn't your usual hunter — and this wasn't your usual card game.

Since learning to use Tarot cards at an unreasonably young age, I'd gone from being a celebrated child psychic to a barely-legal arcane artifact hunter in only a handful of years. I'd been good at finding things — a little too good. I'd caught the attention of the most powerful collection of Tarot-based sorcerers on Earth, the Arcana Council, and one job had led to the other until I'd joined their ranks.

And then I'd gone and fallen in love with the biggest, baddest Council member of them all.

I tightened my jaw, inhaling a potent mix of bat poop and rotting vegetation to keep my senses sharp. Because the powerful, enigmatic and brilliant Armaeus Bertrand, Magician of the Arcana Council and yin to my yang, didn't know who I was anymore. In the midst of fighting off a cabal of gods attempting to breach Earth's borders, he'd recently jettisoned an entire swath of his memories—including everything to do with me. Now he wanted to find those memories, and I'd been voted the girl most likely to help him get that job done.

The icon buried deep in this cave would buy me the information I desperately needed to get started on that quest. More than enough reason for me to fall down the rabbit hole again, even if I had a creeping feeling of dread at what I might find at the bottom. *Why had Armaeus forgotten me?*

Unfortunately, there was no answer to that question. I refocused on the task at hand.

Shuffling Tarot cards in a rainforest was a fool's game, but I did the best I could, then pulled out three cards in quick succession. I didn't know this cave, I didn't know this idol I'd been sent after, I didn't know a lot about these people, the Arawak, or the superstitions they held about their storm goddess. But I did know the cards. Back when I'd first joined the artifact-recovery racket, they were the only thing I had to give me an edge over all the other treasure hunters out there, and they'd very rarely failed me.

They weren't going to fail me now either. Even if they made no sense right this particular second.

"Asshats," I muttered around the flashlight, scanning the cards before I stuffed them back in my pocket. I retrieved my penlight and swept the space again. I needed to know how to get down to the next level, ideally without falling and cracking open anything vital, so I'd expected one of the cards to deal with a floor of some sort. *Nope.*

I'd pulled the Three of Swords, Six of Pents, and Tower. The first was interesting enough, a heart pierced by three swords, and I obligingly pulled my own narrow machete free of my belt. The Three of Swords was the card of necessary cutting, so maybe the trick wasn't stepping on the right section of guano-covered rushes, but hacking into it. The droppings had the consistency of cement, after all, so it wasn't completely unreasonable. Maybe I'd need Alonso to man up and help me after all.

The Six of Pents was more problematic. It showed money raining down from the skies, but the only thing likely to fall on my head in here was a bunch of disgruntled bats. *Gross.*

Most troublesome of all was the Tower. That was the card of things exploding, foundations being ripped apart, and general kabooms. I didn't want kabooms. I didn't want so much as a jump scare while I was down here. I wanted to cut my way into the second level, find the hole where the treasure was, grab the storm goddess totem, and get the hell out. I wasn't too picky about how I managed that last part either, though I was trying to keep a low profile here.

It was one thing to show up in a run-down aboriginal bar looking for treasure as a no-name, scruffy-looking bounty hunter. Far different to shout out my exact identity by lighting my hands on fire and poofing into nothingness, skills I'd recently developed since meeting the Magician and his friends. If anyone was paying attention, I'd telegraph exactly who I was, and that wasn't a good idea for this job. Nobody could know I was here.

My client had been very clear on that part. He'd been jonesing for this icon for the better part of thirty years, but he'd never gotten up the guts to go after it, mainly because he'd *also* needed to keep a low profile about obtaining the icon, though for a very different reason. Anyone who knew he had it apparently would come after him with everything they had. And if they knew it had been picked up by me, same problem. Because my client and I had done work together—a lot of work. The upper echelons of the arcane black market were a very small community. If I wanted the information I'd been promised, I'd have to be very, very subtle.

I could do subtle. I'd spent a lot of years being subtle. Reckless too. But mostly subtle. I could do it now.

"Necessary cutting," I muttered, scanning the floor again. It all looked the same—a carpet of dung. Above me, the bats shifted, emitting a weird, alien chittering noise that snaked through the shadows as I took an experimental step forward.

"You find it?" Alonso's voice surprised me, and I half turned, glancing back to the opening he'd redraped with vines. Then I saw the bodies.

They were little more than skeletons, actually. Three of them, right at the mouth of the cave, all clearly caught midscrabble, with thick, rusted swords shoved into what had been their torsos. Their legs were buried under guano, so they had the illusion of being sucked down into a hole, but I stared at them a long second before I heard the guide's voice again, drifting through the thick foliage. "Miss Croft?"

My lips twisted. Alonso wasn't much up on his American pop culture, and sometimes, I couldn't help myself.

"I'm good. You say no one's come after this treasure for a while?"

"Not since the Space Center was built, no. They asked a lot of questions then, but no one told. No one wanted anyone to look. Guabancex would come and kill us all."

"Right." I moved forward to the pile of bodies and took a closer look. There was nothing left of clothing, barely any meat left clinging to the bones, but the swords looked old. Then again, most swords did. These were long and straight, just like in the Three of Swords card. So either these guys had been killed climbing out of the right hole, or they'd been killed trying to clamber out of the wrong hole. Either way, the swords pierced their shattered rib cages. Right through the heart, which fit the Three of Swords to a tee. This was my spot.

I rehooked my penlight to my belt, moved to the side of the skeletons, and kicked the skulls out of the way. These guys wouldn't be needing them. Then I squatted down and studied the swords. They were buried halfway in the guano, and they were wide bladed, sturdy. I stood again, leaned my weight on the nearest one, and pushed.

The ground beneath the sword resisted for a half second, then gave way. I pressed a little harder, and the sword dropped until the hilt connected flush with the dung-covered floor—but it didn't press all the way through.

Okay…

I turned to the next sword and shoved that down as well. It also dropped after a momentary resistance, but it also didn't go all the way through the floor. The third blade was more at an angle. I took a step toward it—

And bats exploded above me.

Easily two dozen winged monsters burst forward in a flurry of movement, each of the creatures seeming much bigger than when they'd been tucked up into the ceiling. Mindless of the heaps of guano, I flung myself to the floor, covering my head as they whooshed over me. Tiny claws wrenched at my hat and along the back of my shirt, and damned if I didn't feel the bite of tiny feral teeth into my shoulder. That alone was enough to make me flail, and I screamed, leaping to my feet again and reaching back to knock the thing off me, my hands sparking with heat in my panic.

"No, no, no—!" My own self-admonition was cut off as my next problem struck me, literally. The shower of rocks from the ceiling cascaded down over my head and shoulders, some as small as pebbles, others as large as baseballs. Very *heavy* baseballs, and I yelped with pain and surprise as I danced from side to side, trying to avoid the shower. I stepped right in the center of one of the bodies, cracking the rest of the poor guy's ribs…and my foot kept going straight through the cave floor.

"Alonso!" I howled as the soft surface gave way beneath me, but my voice was lost under a hundred years of batshit and death.

I fell into open space, screaming.

CHAPTER TWO

The fall was short and painful.

I crashed to the floor, every bone in my body bouncing with extreme prejudice. The machete was jarred loose from my hand and skidded across the stone surface before the sound of its progress ominously cut off a few seconds later, only to be followed by the clank of metal hitting stone once, twice, three times. The sounds progressed deeper and deeper into the belly of the earth until finally—there was a splash.

A splash?

I rolled over on my back, gasping. What was this place? From Alonso's stories, there was supposed to be a ledge broad enough for three or four people to stand on, the treasure dumped into a third hole beside it. But this ledge was barely wider than I was, and the hole on at least one side dropped way the hell too far to be useful. I sat up as I heard Alonso's terrified bleats above me and called out, but he didn't respond. The odds of him waiting around for me had just dropped to a cool fifteen percent.

That wasn't my only problem either. I unhooked my penlight and flashed its beam up to the ceiling where I'd crashed through, and realized the cave fall-in had not only sent rocks crashing down on my head, but several dead bats as well. Worse, the hole was now almost completely blocked by rocks, dirt, and a few stray, still-wriggling bat bodies. I made a face. That exit strategy had become seriously nasty. Not going to happen.

Yanking a couple more cards from my jacket pocket, I raked the penlight over them. Six of Swords, Five of Wands. A water journey ending in a fight? A fight with what, the bats?

The faintest sharp, quick exhale was my only warning.

A second later, a long, slender projectile pinged onto the ledge beside me, and I stared at it. The dart was exactly the last thing I expected to see on the rocky outcropping, second only to the next dart that landed right beside it. In the narrow beam of my penlight, I could see goo glistening on the tip of the wicked-looking projectile. Not just any old dart, then, but a poisoned one. *Neat.*

More to the point, *hello, Five of Wands.* Apparently, the fight portion of my day would be hitting sooner rather than later.

Another volley of blow darts soared toward me and I scrambled back from the edge of the shelf, into the more or less sheltered lee of the cliff. When the next barrage of darts clattered against the rock face, I managed a credible yelp as if one of the darts had struck home. Immediately, I heard the chatter of excited voices below me, the language still indistinct to me, but its murmurs echoing against the rocks. Then came the sound of a paddle being dipped in water. *Okay, then.* The water in the pool below was definitely deep and wide enough to allow for boats, but who were these people? And how did they know I was here? I mean, yes, there was the little detail of the noisy cave-in, but that'd happened mere minutes ago. The blow-dart brigade couldn't have assembled that quickly.

Unless Alonso had tipped them off that I was coming.

I grimaced, suddenly understanding why my guide might have been in such a hurry to get me into the cave and barricaded. Had he also set the rockfall into play somehow? I couldn't see how, but there was a lot about this situation I didn't understand. More to the point, a new sound insinuated itself into the relative quiet of the cave, above my half-assed whimpering: the sound of human exertion. Not the scrape of hands and feet, but the grunts of breath that would be required by someone silently climbing, say, a cliff wall. Which meant some of the intrepid boaters from below had taken to the rocks. This kept getting better and better.

I exhaled slowly, weighing my options. I understood my client's need for me to keep a low profile here and, if I was honest, there was a stubborn part of me that wanted to succeed without any skills but my own natural-born human abilities—and my ability to read the cards, of course. That skill had been a part of me so long, it was as natural to me as breathing.

Speaking of, it was time for another hit of oxygen. The cards had certainly set up the problem, but I hadn't gotten much in the way of a solution yet.

I fished out another card and stared at it for a long second, before stuffing it back in my pocket. It was the Star. Normally a card of hope and good fortune, except for when I was reading cards literally, the way I did when I was trying to get out of, say, death by blow darts. For that kind of reading, what was most important was the fact that the card depicted a woman leaning over a pool with one foot in the water. In other words, I needed to get into the water. I had to do that anyway if I wanted to get my hands on the goddess totem, so it seemed like there was no time like the present to get that started.

Moving as quietly as possible, I gathered my feet beneath me until I was on the balls of my toes in a crouch. I waited another second more until I fancied I could hear the breathing of my assailants enough to know that the climbers were only a few feet below the edge of the ledge. Then I lunged forward and jumped high, sailing into the open space. I didn't know how far the water stretched, but it had to be at least thirty or so feet to accommodate multiple canoes. I also didn't know how deep it was. To avoid breaking anything that mattered, I tucked my knees to my chest and flailed my arms, trying to make my mass as broad as possible and praying that the water was deeper than a few inches.

For once, my prayers were answered in the affirmative. Accompanied by a chorus of startled cries, I crashed into the water and sank a fair distance before my fingers grazed an uneven surface. Unwilling to open my eyes despite the fact that I'd glimpsed a flash of gold in the water, I had far less compunction about opening my third eye, an act that surely wouldn't be noticed this far underwater, given all the flailing going on above me.

The force of psychic energy that blasted back at me from the bottom of the cave pool nearly shot me out of the water and up against the cliff wall. I gasped, arguably not my best move underwater, but managed to remember where I was in time to avoid sucking in a lungful of ocean as I broke the water's surface. And it was definitely ocean I'd landed in, or at least partly ocean, which meant — once again — there should be a way out.

My brief foray above the water's surface was not entirely to my advantage, as another blast of blow darts assaulted me from all corners of the cavern. In addition, the cave divers above me peeled themselves off the wall and dropped into the water one by one, making five distinct plops. Five of Wands, five guys in the water.

I appreciated the symmetry of the cards, but I had a goddess to catch.

Diving down below the water again, I opened my regular eyes and kept my third eye to a mere slit. Much easier to manage the blast of energy that way. There was a pile of gold as I suspected, but a few pieces lit up as bright as the sun. A cup, a squat and angry-looking bull, several iterations of what looked like a fertility goddess—not the goddess I was looking for—and a handful of discs with spiraling circles etched into their surface. All of them pretty common, none of them what I needed, so I dug deeper, my lungs burning with the effort of holding my breath underwater. I hadn't even been down here all that long, but there was definitely something about being forced to hold your breath that made everything so much more difficult.

Then I found it. The tips of a flailing hand, unquestionably a part of the symbol I'd been primed for. I eagerly reached for it—

And was blasted to the side by a small, heavy human body, a virtual cannonball in the water. The force of the blow took me by surprise, and I went spinning through the water, my fingers wrenched free from the icon even as I barely grazed it. A slash of pain in my left arm galvanized my senses. *Crap*—one of the bastards in the water had a knife. If one of them had a blade, chances were all of them had one, which just made my evening that much more complicated.

Scrambling away from my attacker, I exploded upward, clearing the surface and sucking in precious air. I whirled around as another slash of pain seared across my shoulder, and I realized I had a knife sticking out of me. It was a nice knife, and it certainly wasn't the first time I'd been skewered, but the sudden pain nearly took my breath away. I felt my hands crackle to life, the supernatural ability for self-combustion I'd recently acquired struggling to be put to use, low profile or no.

I quelled the fire quickly. These men were only trying to protect what they believed was theirs, which probably *was* theirs by rights, and I was there to steal it. I certainly wasn't going to give up my bounty now that I was so close, but I didn't need to take them out at the same time. I also could only imagine the tales that would result about a goddess come down to Earth to steal their sacred relics. I needed that like a hole in the head.

I dodged to the side, barely missing another blow dart. If I didn't act fast, I was going to get that hole in the head whether I wanted it or not.

I treaded water for a precious few seconds, trying to get my bearings…and, sure enough, more darts whistled through the darkness, one of them planting in my other shoulder. "Hey!" I gritted out, yanking the projectile free before — hopefully — any of the poison on its tip could seep into me. Regardless, I needed to move.

Diving back down into the water, I kept my eyes open while I angled for the biggest mound of gold. That was what the escapees from Devil's Island had seen from the ledge, after all. Those were the tales that had survived through the decades until my client had finally heard them. The prison runners had shared the story of the goddess totem, so it had to be the same one I'd seen sticking out near the top. I'd disrupted it when I'd crash-landed into the pile, but it had to be close.

I slit open my third eye again as I kicked toward Mount Goldenstuff, and once more had to brace myself for the beam of energy. *Yup,* that was it. There was something else too. Spectral light, pouring in from beyond the pile, as if a train was racing toward the pool of water from the cavern wall. I shook my head as a wave of dizziness overtook me—was I really seeing that, or had some of the blow dart's poison started to affect me?

I had neither the time nor the oxygen stores to contemplate that possibility. I reached out and grabbed all the treasure I could in one swipe, including the flat, pounded-gold icon of the thrashing storm goddess, and kept moving. I broke the surface only long enough to draw in a lungful of air, then dropped again, kicking as hard as I could. I didn't have to look back to know I was being followed. I thrust on and on, but the truth remained that as strong as I was, I was not a good swimmer, and I was not making up the ground I normally would running. I believed I could run fast. I didn't believe I could swim well, and the old saw of "fake it till you make it" wasn't helping me out so much. As my lungs began to burn and my sight began to fade, the dark, cold stain of poison seeping through me from my left shoulder, I realized that all the supernatural powers in the world weren't going to help me if I died at the bottom of a cave.

Angling myself upward, I broke the water's surface for only a second before I cracked my head on the low ceiling of the cave. Delirious with pain, I reached out mentally for the only person I knew could help, remembering a fraction of a second later that I was wrong on that count too.

Armaeus Bertrand couldn't connect with me. He couldn't even remember me. Everything he'd pushed me to learn, everything we'd shared, every hope, every fight—every glance and touch and sigh—might as well have never happened. He was gone from me. Vanished in plain sight.

I sank down in the water again, my heart thudding with panic. The whole reason I was even here in this fucking hellhole was to *fix* that problem. I couldn't fix it if I *drowned*.

Impotent fury scorched through me, and in a flash, my debate was over. I was out of here. But while I wanted nothing more than to get as far away as I could as fast as possible, I couldn't leave Alonso behind if he hadn't actually betrayed me.

Hell, even if he had. Times were hard in French Guiana these days.

I crackled out of existence in that underground waterway and flashed back to the vine-strung cave opening...

No Alonso.

"Dammit!" Spinning around unsteadily, I unstuck the various blades the locals had sunk into my skin as a parting gift, then stashed those, the golden relic, and random bits of treasure into the steaming pockets of my jacket. Then I turned to run, panicked and confused.

I'd taken only three steps away from the opening when I saw Alonso. What was left of him, anyway. Pinned to a tree with half a dozen narrow handmade arrows sticking from his body, and a blue dart buried in his neck. Just like Indiana Jones said would happen.

I hated being right sometimes.

I tried to focus enough to whisk myself out of this death trap once and for all and back to the client who'd give me the precious information he'd promised, but with the cold drip of poison fouling my bloodstream, I couldn't...quite—

Just then, a hail of blow darts came soaring out of the trees. I yanked Alonso's machete free from his clenched fingers and ran forward, cursing as I raced blindly through the brush. Flicking my third eye open, I

23

could once again see a bright light leading me on. I hoped it was taking me in the right direction, but honestly, I didn't have much choice. I didn't know these trees, I didn't know these paths, and everyone around me did.

Wielding Alonso's machete, I slashed my way through the underbrush, picking up speed. My brain might be jacked up, but my feet still worked. I no longer cared about maintaining natural speed as much as getting the hell out. Then the trees broke in front of me, and the bright light of my third eye was replaced by the bright light of moonlight and open space.

I went hurtling out over the cliff to the ocean far below. I didn't know if there would be sharks there, but sharks weren't a problem for me. They couldn't tell my tale.

With a last surge of energy seconds before I hit the water, I burst into flame and crackled out of sight.

CHAPTER THREE

Y ou look like complete *merde*, eh? Worse than usual."

There was something ineffably elegant about getting insulted by a Frenchman that always managed to soften the blow of their disgust, but I still skewered Jean-Claude Mercault with a squint-eyed glare. "You never cared what I looked like when I worked for you before."

"Before? Before, bah!" he said, doing a flicky thing with his fingers as if he could shoo the words away. It was a gesture that worked for him, right along with his expensive deep-navy-blue suit and crisp white shirt, open at the neck. Mercault was a small, fastidiously put together man with slicked-back hair and a ruddy complexion, an eternally genteel expression on his face. You would never know that he had killed a significant portion of his family after they'd betrayed him, or that he'd suffered the loss of still other members of his family far dearer to him in an attack on his sprawling fortress of a home. He was no saint himself, of course. He'd double-crossed me more than a few times, when the price was right. For his sake, I hoped this wasn't going to be one of those times.

"Before, you were a tool. An excellent tool, well forged, whom I trusted to do her job and nothing more than her job," Mercault continued. "Now I am the tool, and you are the master."

"I'm not at all comfortable with this analogy," I muttered.

It also wasn't exactly true. A few days earlier, Mercault had reached out to me at an exceedingly opportune time, as I'd been reeling around in a state of both confusion and depression in the aftermath of my most recent assignment in my role as Justice of the Arcana Council. The assignment had ended pretty well — bad guys defeated, peace on Earth — but everything else had gone to complete hell. The Magician now no longer recognized me and was, by all accounts, not operating with a full deck. He was weak, and as the strongest sorcerer on the planet, weak was not his jam. The Arcana Council was being run by stand-ins, none of whom were me, and there were rumors of factions of opposition around the world thinking that now might be a good time to take the Council out entirely, or at least deal it a leveling blow.

I was in no mood to get leveled.

Then there was the personal fallout I was experiencing in the wake of Armaeus's memory lapse, a thousand variations of the same tune all played in the key of Why. Why had he forgotten me — and why only me, and not anyone else on the Council? Why, as arguably the most powerful sorcerer on the planet, couldn't he snap his fingers and regain his memories? And why did I feel so personally bereft at being forgotten? It wasn't like he thought I was expendable, or, well, easily forgettable…right?

In the midst of all this dithering, getting an urgent artifact-hunting request from Jean-Claude Mercault had been a blessing. Nevertheless, I wasn't foolish enough not to suspect the man of having ulterior motives.

Mercault could barely tie his shoes without considering all the angles to get it done better, faster, or cheaper.

Now the Frenchman grinned, but the expression of concern didn't leave his eyes as he tilted his glass of gin toward me, ice clinking. "Tools aside, you are many things now, eh, Sara Wilde? You come to me as a bounty hunter, responding to my plea as you did in the days of old, offering to find that which cannot be found. You say it was for money — but you do not need money, I think."

I shrugged. "I always need money."

"Ah, no. With your position now as Justice of the Arcana Council, you have access to the Council's great troves of treasure. You also have the ability to blast me into the next lifetime with a wave of your fiery hands. I know this to be true. And so I ask myself, why? Why does she agree to do this task for me?"

"I could ask you the same question. Why ask me to hunt down some trinket in the South American wilderness? Surely you have other people you can tap to find you gold."

At the mention of gold, Mercault's gaze shifted slightly, avarice making his pupils dilate. It was almost comforting, seeing his reaction. Like old times.

Still, he didn't allow himself to get fully distracted. "Perhaps I know you better than you know yourself, Madame Wilde. Money tempts you, but it is information you need. And it is information I have. Only the warnings, the rumors, the tales I have heard, I cannot tell you those in any ordinary way, lest I myself pay the price, eh? And so, instead of me sharing information that can get me killed, I am merely meeting with you to use your well-known services for my own gain."

My brows lifted as he spoke, his caginess pricking my current relentless, low-grade anxiety. "You afraid of someone, Mercault?"

"Afraid? Bah," he said, flicking his fingers again. "I merely know more than I should comfortably know about those who would seek to harm your precious Council."

A shiver trailed down my spine. If I was honest, I'd suspected this was Mercault's game when he'd reached out to me days earlier. Mercault was one of the most looped-in members of the worldwide Connected psychic community, and his intel was usually top-notch. He'd also played in the game of trafficking illicit psychic-enhancing drugs known as technoceuticals, so he had his finger on the pulse of the wealthiest and most brutal Connected criminals.

These days, Mercault constrained himself to technoceuticals that weren't sourced from human body parts, but most of his colleagues weren't so delicate. It was these kinds of people who I'd stumbled across as an artifact hunter that'd made me commit to protecting the most vulnerable of Connecteds, the young psychics whose parts were being harvested for these drugs. But if these black-market players had shared with Mercault some intel about a threat to the Council—and especially to Armaeus—I was damned well going to listen.

"I have no allegiance to this Council to which you have attached yourself, this web that has snared you as surely as any fly. It makes you weaker than you should be, Madame Wilde." Mercault leaned closer. "Because no one needs to fear the Council anymore if they are careful, eh? And the world has become very, very careful of late. Too careful. I do not trust it, and neither should you."

I narrowed my eyes. "I know you're just dying to tell me something, Mercault. Go ahead and spit it out. What do you know?" Mercault was being obnoxiously evasive, but I got the feeling he needed to be. Despite his posturing, he *was* afraid of something. For a man who'd made his bones as the head of the House of Pentacles, one of the largest and most profitable Connected syndicates working in the arcane black market, the fear didn't sit well.

"What do I know, what do I know… Everything and nothing, I am afraid." He waved his drink and settled back in his seat. "First, show me the idol."

I reached into the neckline of my shirt and pulled out the long leather cord I'd used to suspend the flat gold totem, then drew the gold artifact over my head. I handed it to Mercault, but he gestured with his gin toward the small table between us, where a velvet-lined tray sat. Obligingly, I dropped the icon onto the tray.

He leaned forward leisurely and took a closer look without touching it.

"Guabancex, bringer of storms," he mused, his voice, low and resonant. "Anything else?"

I set down my own glass of scotch and pulled another small bag out of my pocket. I'd kept a few of the disks, shipping them to places where they were needed more than in either Mercault's or my pockets, but I still had nearly a dozen to drop with a clink onto the tray. This time, Mercault didn't hesitate. He picked up the bag and poured the disks into his palm, whistling with appreciation. "How much of these were there?"

"Piles of them. And other totems too, mostly fertility goddess types. I didn't see another one like your totem, though. And I didn't have a lot of time to look around."

"Yes…" His gaze slid again to the storm goddess totem. It was a remarkably stylish piece executed flat in plate-thin gold, almost abstract, with the wide-eyed, wide-mouthed howling face surmounted by a crown of curls, and the sinuous, S-like curve of the goddess's arms that bisected the head, giving the impression of constant, thrashing motion. The ancient Arawak tribe from whom the locals were descended believed that Guabancex ruled over the hurricanes that pummeled the coast of Central and South America, and their totem to her looked exactly like what they feared — an enraged face in the center of a swirling hurricane. "There were guardians?"

"There were. Well-informed guardians. Which I hadn't been expecting, frankly."

He flicked a glance to me. "Not too well informed, though, eh? They attacked you. You think they would have done that if they'd known what you were capable of? They would have revered you as a new goddess."

I grimaced, remembering my own concerns along those same lines. "Well, my plan for keeping a low profile didn't exactly survive the experience. I had to get out using more than just my wits. I don't think anyone noticed, but if they did…"

He grunted. "If they did, I would already have heard about it, and we both would likely not be sitting here enjoying our drinks. The guide?"

"He definitely won't be telling anyone. I assume he was the one who tipped off the locals, but I don't know why. I paid him well enough."

"There is no price that fear cannot outstrip, in the end," Mercault said, the soul of reason. "But he is dead, you disappeared into the water, and any tales that come out of that godforsaken hole in the ground will get swallowed up as well. No one knows this acquisition has been made, and they won't unless it appears for sale. There would be many hungry bidders for this prize, but I have other plans for it."

That made me sit up a little straighter. "What kind of plans? You acted like this was a prize of rarest beauty for you, a personal quest you'd longed to complete."

He winked. "Oh, it is, Madame Wilde. It is. But we will get to that. You have delivered — *more* than delivered with these extra treasures as well. You have earned my honesty, and if anyone should ask, I will have received great value for sharing the information I know. Unfortunately, I cannot share it unasked. But if you ask, I will happily tell you."

I squinted at him. "Um…say that again, but coherently this time?"

He sighed. "Madame Wilde, in my position as head of the House of Pentacles, there is much that I see, much that I know. Much that I have been paid not to share with the Council. All to the good, I have no allegiances there. But now, now you are a member of the Council, and I have already betrayed you enough in this lifetime, while you have always tried to deal with me more fairly than I deserve. I have come to admire you, I am sad to say. And so I would offer you this information if you ask me for it. I simply cannot go running to you with it, eh? That would violate all that is true and good in this world."

"Oh-kay." I considered the Frenchman. I'd met Mercault early in my artifact-hunting days, knowing him only as a fringe player of the arcane black market. He was Connected — possessing psychic skills — but only in the most minor of ways, and most of the artifacts he sought were those that were rumored to have psychic-enhancing abilities. From the beginning, he'd wanted more than anything to have greater psychic skills, in whatever flavor he could manage. Oddly enough, I hadn't thought all that much about my own skills back then. I could read cards and I could find things. That'd been enough.

Then I'd met the Magician of the Arcana Council, and everything had changed.

The Magician, whose inconvenient memory lapse had occurred just as a growing level of disquiet was stirring throughout the Connected community — the threat of psychics going rogue, and of governments and multinational organizations starting to oppress the psychic community in force. Not a good time for the head of the Arcana Council to take a powder.

And here was Mercault, acting as squirrelly as a meth head in a Sudafed factory. "How do I know what you're so eager to tell me is the truth, or merely a fabrication to get you in with whoever it is you're afraid of?" I challenged.

Mercault made a face. "You do not trust me."

"I don't."

"Excellent." The grin that crept across his face was heartfelt. Despite his penchant for expensive clothes and overwrought homes, Mercault, at his core, was a thief, a rogue, and an outlaw. A grudging bond with an adversary would warm the cold rock of his heart far more than the handclasp of a dear friend. "But you see, you have bought my cooperation with this totem, which is worth far more than anyone else could pay. As a result, whatever information I give you is duly paid for. No one can fault me."

"And I can trust you to keep your mouth shut to anyone else?"

He pointed again to the totem. "Bought and paid for."

I left that alone for the moment. Instead, I plunged in. "Okay. Is this information you have about, ah…the Magician?"

Mercault's eyes shot wide. "Then it's true," he murmured, and the hair on my arms stood straight up. *Crap, crap, crap.* Clearly, I'd guessed wrong, though it seemed like the Magician's challenges weren't completely unknown to Mercault.

"I didn't believe the rumors, had discounted them entirely given the threats the Council faces," Mercault continued. He shifted his gaze to stare at some of the priceless art on the wall. "But you, here, now... No. That is not what I have to discuss with you. But I do know perhaps more than you think about your Magician, lore stored within my family for centuries. This information I will give you as well, bought and paid for with the extra treasure you brought from the cave. You will accept it?"

"Of course." Mercault's mood was confusing me tonight, but if he was willing to dole out information, I was more than willing to accept it.

He nodded, settling back in his chair. "Armaeus Bertrand has served as the Magician of the Arcana Council for over six hundred years, constantly spouting his insistence that the world of magic should remain balanced, balanced, balanced, and that humans and ordinary Connecteds should fend for themselves in nearly all matters of magic."

I barely suppressed a smile. Though the Magician no longer remembered me, I'd worked with him now for years. Mercault's family, a long line of scoundrels who preferred to operate on the dark side of the arcane black market, had doubtless interacted with him much longer than that. And he was French, much like the Magician himself. So it was reasonable to expect him to know Armaeus Bertrand very well.

"What most people do not realize," Mercault continued, "is that the Magician was not always quite so modulated in his approach to magic. According to my family history, which I have brought up to His Mightiness when the need serves me, Bertrand meddled with the best of them in the early centuries of his work on the Council."

"Really," I said, genuinely surprised. "That doesn't sound like him."

"It does not, not anymore," Mercault agreed. "But the Magician came to his role in a very turbulent time and spent the first few hundred years amassing all the dark knowledge he could obtain. He was convinced that if he learned it all, he could then sort out what is suitable for mortals to claim and what should be destroyed."

"That…does sound more like him. How do you know all this? You guys meet for neighborhood barbecues once upon a time?"

"You must understand, Madame Wilde, my family has been at the forefront of political and social power far longer than the Magician has been alive. We have endured our trials. We have survived our own revolution. We understood the value of secrets, particularly the secrets of the most arcane operators on the planet. Of which the Magician is merely one. Some would argue he is not even the strongest operator alive, at this late hour. And if the rumors are indeed true…"

He took another drink of his gin, watching me over the rim. I knew what he was thinking—that I was stronger than the Magician. Since I'd begun working with Armaeus a few short years before, my ability to access greater magical powers had shocked everyone around me, except for, perhaps, Armaeus himself, who constantly thought I should reach further. Part of the reason I'd agreed to the role of Justice of the Arcana Council was to impose some limitations on my abilities, reining myself in as Mercault aptly pointed out, though that wasn't really working out all that well so far.

But setting aside the question of who was the grandest sorcerer of them all, a small part of my mind had begun worrying over my abilities and their effect on me. Though I'd never admit as much to Mercault, the incident in the caverns of French Guiana bothered me more than a little. I'd gotten out alive with my artifacts intact, exactly like the old days. But unlike the old days, I'd had to rely on my newfound psychic skills, my magical powers, and I could easily see the danger in that. How long before I grew to rely on them exclusively, losing the sharpness of focus that had kept me alive during my early years as an artifact hunter? While there was no denying the convenience of being able to crackle out of a dangerous situation, how soft had I gotten? And what would happen if I was ever pushed too hard?

"Okay, what else do you have other than the Magician used to be an asshat?" I asked, refocusing. "That's not exactly breaking news."

"Did you know he has a home here—in Paris? One he has not visited since, bah…" Mercault did the finger flick again. "The mid-1800s. A pity, that. It is a beautiful home. He maintains it, but it's as if—poof!—it is gone from his thoughts. He has forgotten his memories before, like that, though not for a very long time. And it has always been by his choice, which is important, especially if the rumors are true, and it has happened again."

Alarm snaked through me. Exactly how many times *had* Armaeus banished his memories? And what sort of an effect would that have on a person over time? "Why is the question of his choice important?"

"Well, that is obvious, no? The Magician only gets rid of that which he does not need."

I winced, my heart wrenching a little at the cold assessment. Was that true? Had Armaeus considered his memories of me expendable, a tool to be leveraged for the higher good? Surely not, and yet…he *had* mentioned before that I could eventually become a threat to him, to his power. What if by forgetting me, he was protecting himself? What if he really did know too much about me, and that knowledge was harming him in some way? Should I leave him to his ignorance?

Should I leave him, period?

Oblivious to my growing dismay, Mercault kept going. "By the same token, once the Magician has discarded a memory, it is gone. Or, that is what used to be the case. If he is actually *looking* for his memories, there is a reason for it, and that reason bears watching. What has he forgotten this time?"

With Mercault's abrupt question, my chagrin flashed over to irritation, which was fine by me. Irritation and I went way back. "Why don't we focus on what you wanted to tell me about him?" I asked pointedly.

"Very well." Mercault shrugged, though his eyes glittered with interest. "There were two significant pockets of information, collections of spells, you could say, that the Magician wiped out of existence. Presumably, he did so by eliminating them from his memory, which effectively eliminated them from the memory of the world. Do not ask me how. The first was in Spain in 1478, but my family history is silent on the nature of the spells he employed. As of course it would be, since they have been forgotten. The fact that there is any information at all about the actions of the Magician is a miracle. But we are an old family and he was…an upstart. It chafed."

I raised my eyebrows. I had to hand it to Mercault, his intel was good. The Council had learned of this first breach of memory already, though the Magician could not yet pinpoint what he'd forgotten. "Fourteen seventy-eight," I said. "Right around the time of the Spanish Inquisition."

"The very same," Mercault agreed. "Arguably, the Magician was concerned that some of arcane lore might get discovered by the wrong group of anarchists and oppressors, and he took steps to make sure that did not happen without tacitly getting his hands dirty in the process."

I nodded in tacit agreement. That sounded exactly like something Armaeus would do, with his continual — and preferably anonymous — quest to ensure the balance of magic in the world.

"The second incidence of his lost memory was less than a hundred years later, during Queen Elizabeth's reign and likely occurring on English soil," Mercault continued. "The year was 1571. Once again, there is no indication of what was forgotten, only that a disruption in the historical record had taken place."

I fought the thrill of excitement. I hadn't known the date of the second occurrence, only that it had occurred. "And those were the only two times mentioned in your family's history?"

"The only two we knew about, yes." Mercault nodded. "But both times, he fell quite ill, however, and *that* happened a third time, without explanation. In the 1850s…coincidentally, around the time he stopped visiting his house in Paris."

I frowned. This hadn't been on my radar. "Ill in what way?"

"In the 1850s he was bedridden and frail, beset with a wasting sickness from which there was a slow and broken return. There is likely no connection, as his recovery the first two times was far swifter. He was a changed man all three times, however, not necessarily for the better. Then again, not necessarily for the worse either."

Just like that, I was back to worrying. Armaeus appeared healthy enough, despite the hovering of his arcane medical team. Had I missed something important? "Meaning?"

"Meaning that if he has charged you with finding his memories, you had best be careful when the pieces of the Magician are once more made whole," Mercault said. "Keep in mind, the Magician you know has never been complete. If you reassemble all his parts, he will, perforce, be a changed man."

I made a face. That sounded far more ominous than I wanted to think about. "I don't suppose you have a cheat sheet on what parts to leave out?"

"Sadly, I do not." Mercault leaned forward. "But you must focus, Madame Wilde. I did not undergo this transaction with you tonight to speak only of the Magician."

"Your secret intel, right," I said, but I remained far too distracted by what Mercault had told me. "Where is this home of the Magician here in Paris? The one he hasn't been to?"

Mercault rattled off the address, and I frowned, not recognizing it. "And it still stands?"

"It still stands. But it is not what is most important here. Please, you must ask me directly for the intelligence I need to share. And stop being so selfless, or we will be here all damned night."

I blinked. "The information is about me?"

Mercault sighed with genuine pleasure. "Yes, Madame Wilde. You. Thank you." He didn't say anything more, and I rolled my eyes.

"And that intel would be..."

"There are those who are following you even now," he said quickly. "Seeking you out. Having clearly learned about my conversation with you, they journeyed to French Guiana but were too late. However, they picked up your trail again the moment you returned to Paris."

My brows lifted. "Because you told them I was coming here. You set me up."

He spread his hands, the soul of innocence. "Only for the most altruistic of reasons."

"Uh-huh." Mercault never had only one reason for doing anything, but I was willing to let this play out. "So, they — whoever this is tracking me — knows I'm with you right now."

To my surprise, Mercault shook his head. "Happily, no. They are only as good as their eyes, and their eyes lost you once you began moving through the city. But they are making a net this night, Madame Wilde. One that is gradually narrowing, with you at its center. They have the resources to do so, and that is distressing to me as well."

"Why is that?"

"Because for all the intel about them that I've received, I do not know who these people are. No one does, but I *should*. Someone with this much power, in my own city? I should know who they are. But I do not. I only know that the Magician has decided to re-find his memories, and there are those who probably do not want that to happen who are on the move. And you are the only person who has a chance of standing in their way."

Mercault lifted the gold artifact from the tray by its leather strand and tossed it to me. I caught it midair, shivering as its undeniable power rippled across its golden surface.

"What are you doing?" I asked. "I just swallowed half my body weight in Atlantic Ocean stealing this thing for you."

"Then consider it a gift, Madame Wilde," Mercault said, regarding me with an expression of unexpected concern. "May Guabancex protect you from the coming storm."

Chapter Four

My audience with Mercault had left me in a decidedly foul mood for a lot of different reasons. For all the information he'd provided, I knew without a doubt he was still holding out on me. He'd given me just enough intel to put me on notice, but not enough to truly help.

Had that been on purpose? And if so, who else was paying for his information?

And what would I find at the Magician's Parisian hideaway?

The answers to all these questions preyed on my mind as I moved across the seventh arrondissement of Paris and into the sixth, leaving behind Mercault's tony Paris apartment and angling toward the Jardin du Luxembourg, which lay between me and the address Mercault had given me for Armaeus's secret home. It was night, and the wind had picked up in fits and starts, cooling off the humid evening, but the garden was still alive with people. Judging from the lights playing ahead of me near the palace area, there was some sort of boating festival going on in the octagonal basin in front of the palace. Hopefully there weren't kids out at this hour, but then again, this was Paris.

I shoved my hands into the pockets of my jacket. Lightweight enough not to smother me in the warm summer evening, it paired well enough with the designer jeans and T-shirt that were about as far as I was willing to go for fashion, even if I was in the City of Light. My boots cost more than the whole ensemble, but I could run, kick, and stomp in them. That was money well spent. The Guabancex totem bounced against my sternum as I walked, safe on its leather thong. I had no idea why Mercault had given it to me, but I supposed I should be...touched?

A woman's delighted laughter caught my attention as I moved into the long walkway surrounding the park, unconsciously falling into step with the occasional couples murmuring and talking. In another few hours, the garden would be completely deserted, but it was a warm night in Paris, and, with the help of the gusting breeze, the heat of the day was abating. I didn't mind the crowds. I could disappear into a crowd like this, mulling over this mysterious home of Armaeus's. I'd texted the address back to the Council immediately after leaving Mercault's, and the results hadn't surprised me. Apparently, Armaeus didn't remember it either. Hopefully, it wasn't currently being used as an Airbnb.

A flicker to my left caught my attention, and I squinted toward it, but there was nothing moving in the shadows. Still, I picked up my pace slightly. I'd felt out of sorts since leaving French Guiana, and my visit with Mercault now explained why. Someone was following me, for reasons nobody fully understood. Who had I pissed off? The possibilities were endless.

And that wasn't the only question I had. What memories had Armaeus jettisoned in 1478 and again in 1571, and what had happened in the mid-1800s? Finally and, for me, most importantly, what about this most recent memory wipe several days ago? He'd shoved me out of his mind for sure, but was that it? Or had he secreted away something else?

Almost undoubtedly, he had. But what? What could the Magician as I knew him fear so much that he had to forget it completely...along with me?

And why had he forgotten *me*, of all people? There had to be a reason.

The chatter of the crowd collected around the octagonal basin in front of the palace finally reached me, the lights growing brighter. Again, while I didn't mind crowds tonight, that didn't mean I wanted to be trapped in one when what I really needed was to get through the park and across another several blocks to the tight collection of museums where Armaeus's town house could be found. I'd never been there, so I couldn't simply poof my way to it, but walking through the city was never a hardship. There were always people on the move.

Except tonight, there was also a net being drawn around me.

I shot a glance across the interior of the garden, where the wide swaths of grass lay between the tree-lined walkways. Predictably, the space was empty at this hour. Cutting across would be simple enough, especially with my boots to counteract any dew already accumulating on the grass. I hesitated, though, and saw it again.

A shuffle, a redirection, a movement in the crowd indicating a person who'd been moving forward, now dodging slightly to the side as my gaze moved across him. Was I imagining this?

Scowling, I kept to my original trajectory, the basin. If I was being followed — or worse, herded — I wanted to know by whom. I had no shortage of enemies, but in my role as Justice, I also had no shortage of supplicants. I didn't want to blast someone out of hand.

No, I didn't want to blast anyone *at all,* I corrected myself. I was in a crowd of people, the vast majority of whom were probably not Connected. I didn't need to disrupt their perfectly pleasant weeknight—

The movement to my side happened so quickly, if I hadn't already been hyperaware, I might have missed it entirely. A body stepped close, too close for ordinary movement, and the hand that came up and toward me was thick, heavy, and gloved. I didn't wait for it to descend to my face but ducked and swung away into a pair of elderly Parisians, startling the white-haired woman and knocking the cap off her husband as both of them spluttered in surprise.

And then there wasn't one man, but three, and the two flanking the first thug were far leaner and right on top of me. *Crap.*

I turned toward the grass and took off, leaping the low chairs and hurtling onto the soft, springy lawn. I'd gotten about halfway across the open space when I realized my mistake—another set of runners, both of them looking equally fit, was approaching from the other side. At this point, I'd be caught in the middle of a bad-guy sandwich, and I didn't even know what toppings we had!

Fortunately, footraces were sort of my specialty, and I wasn't too proud to use the skills I had at hand— particularly when they would be far less noticeable than hurling fireballs from my fingertips. Kicking my speed up a notch, I turned right and ran hell for leather toward the Palace of Luxembourg and the shallow basin in front of it.

I'd guessed correctly. The basin was the focal point of the evening's festivities, with light-strewn miniature sailboats winking in gorgeous splendor as they jetted around the pool. Some of the boats seemed to be making their way with the help of long sticks poked at them from the side, while others were being guided with little handheld remote controls clutched in the hands of wide-eyed children. All this I took in in a blur as I quickly surveyed the basin. I'd left my pursuers far behind me, I had no doubt, but I was running too fast to burst directly into this crowd of people. With a simple course correction—

The impact of two large male bodies crashing into me from behind at the same time was immediate and impressive. I catapulted over the low wall of the octagonal basin of water and splashed directly into the pool of the Luxembourg Gardens. Even before my feet touched down in the shallow water, I was launching forward again, dashing across the choked pool, still subconsciously trying to miss the tiny works of art that Hurricane Sara was devastating, but that was a lost cause. And I got no farther than a couple of steps when once again my assailants were directly behind me, creating their own mini tsunami. What the hell was going on? I didn't have time to figure out why my unnatural speed was being unnaturally matched before another of my attackers clipped my shoulders and sent me sprawling face-first into the water.

Naturally, I came up swinging, but though I was fitter than the average twenty-something, supernatural strength required more than a dice roll for me, and, given the screaming of the crowd around me, this was not the time to light up like a Christmas tree just to get these asshats off my back. As if they could read my thoughts, one of said asshats reared back and unloaded a roundhouse punch to my jaw, once more sending me back into the pond. Fetid Parisian muck shot up my nose and mouth, finally kindling my anger.

My entire body crackled with Connected awareness. I might not have the strength this dude certainly did even without supernatural powers, but there was no way they should be able to keep up with me. If they were going to play with magic, so was I. I just had to keep it on the down low — the very down low. I leveled my gaze across the water. The only boats still in play were the ones that were remote controlled, most of them hightailing their asses out of the imminent danger of a fight in the center of the pool around the fountain.

Not so fast, Sparky.

My hands extended underwater, my third eye flipping open. Just like that, the motorboats wheeled around. In a heartbeat, I traced the currents of electricity both magical and man-made that were bouncing around the basin like date night at laser tag. I co-opted all of them and followed them into the boats, which picked up speed as they raced toward my attackers. To make things a little more interesting, I also sent a little charge to their forward hulls. Because what would be the point of these boats running into anything if they immediately broke? All this took place in the course of the three seconds it took me to stagger to my feet while the men lunged for me — actually, two men and one woman, I realized now. My commandeered fleet of toy boats triumphantly surged forward, some of them coming up out of the water to crack into my attackers en masse, the combination of water and electricity helped along by yours truly creating an entirely new light show that would've been far more satisfying if I had the chance to enjoy it.

Instead, I turned and ran.

It took me only a few long strides, this time moving so fast, I barely grazed the surface of the water, to get the hell out of the pool and onto dry land. A chorus of shouts and screams went up around me, but I didn't have time to deal with that as I heard the unmistakable crunch of very dry boots racing toward me from one direction while whistles and shouts signified that the police were heading my way from the other side. I blasted another quick jolt of energy behind me to keep the water electric, satisfied by the screams of my assailants in the center of the pool, then took off again.

The moment I cleared the public space and dove back into the tree-lined walkways of the gardens, I gave up all pretense of playing fair. While it was true I hadn't done anywhere near enough work on developing the psychic abilities I'd so quickly and haphazardly assembled over the past several months, there was a time when minds wiser than mine had tried desperately to get me to accept some level of training. I flashed on the placid expression of Sensei Chichiro, a Japanese trainer who'd taken a pound of flesh out of me en route to getting me to embrace my skills. One of those skills was the ability to manifest whatever I needed, in whatever quantities, and while I tended to forget that one in the heat of battle, what I really needed right now was a diversion.

There were so many possibilities. A park full of Pikachus, a swirl of stilettos, a tidal wave of toy trains, but I needed something that would disappear in the midst of a sweltering Parisian night almost as quickly as it appeared, and I needed it fast. I focused on Mercault, the refreshing sparkle of his gin as it splashed over the ice…the ice.

Really, what could be more refreshing?

As I focused on the ice in Mercault's glass, I thought of it doubled, and doubled again, and doubled a third time, over and over again until there was a virtual wall of ice cubes in my mind, large enough for me to vault over. In my mind's eye, I did vault over it, whirling around to shove it backward.

The effect was so gratifying that this time, I did turn to watch as my four pursuers took a face full of frozen water with ice cubes the size of boulders. I'd been caught in a few hailstorms before, none of them of my own making, but this was worse. Far worse.

I twisted back around with only enough time to throw up my arms to fend off yet another assault.

A woman the size of a nine-year-old sprang out of the trees like a gymnast ninja assassin, her hands flicking out and releasing a half-dozen throwing stars in the space of a couple of breaths. I missed getting struck only by dropping flat to the ground; then she was on me.

Once again, I recognized how feeble my physical training regimen had become. Well, too bad. I'd gotten used to relying on magic to solve my problems, and now wasn't the time to improve my push-up count.

My hands burst into flames that swept over the woman, wrenching a scream from her. I thrust her away from me, the spurt of fire so quick that only the most careful observer would've even noticed I'd used it. And there were no observers here, *thank God*. Not with all the excitement back at the pool. I staggered to my feet, whirling around, but the pursuers in the middle of the park were still on their backs groaning, surrounded by a deeply wet patch of grass. Worked for me. But I wasn't finished yet.

I stumbled across the park to where my petite attacker with the throwing stars still writhed from my personal Taser hit. I rolled her over. Her face was caught in a paroxysm of impotent rage, and I didn't waste my time asking her who she was. I whipped out my phone and took her picture even as she struggled to scoot away, her neck turning and craning away from me. Which give me the opportunity to take another picture of a tattoo barely visible above her high collar. I'd never seen anything like it, and surely that was helpful.

"You bitch!" she hissed in French, and as I flipped open my third eye, I realized that she packed her own Connected punch. Frankly, that made things a little easier. So I decked her with another burst of fire and hauled myself up to my feet, keying a text to my right-hand everything, Nikki Dawes.

Nikki would get the photo of the woman to the Council, and I could trust her to tell me not only their response, but their reaction. If the Council was aware of who these people were who were gunning for me, and hadn't warned me…I needed to know that. At this point, I needed all the information I could get.

I burst out onto the street and immediately saw my next problem.

A man stood leaning against a Ducati motorcycle, staring at something on his phone. The moment I broke through the edge of the Luxembourg Gardens, he glanced up across two lanes of busy Parisian traffic, and there was no avoiding his gaze. He saw me and I saw him. I got the faint impression of surprise across his face, but he was nobody I'd ever met before, I was sure of it. Tall, slender, and dark-haired, he could've hailed from any country, anywhere, but I didn't think he was American, for some reason. We stood there staring at each other for the briefest seconds, and I knew that this was the man behind the people following me, tonight. This was the caster of the net.

The truth was, though, I was tired of being chased. I might not know where Armaeus's fashionable walk-up was located in the city, but there were other parts of the city that I knew like the back of my hand. One of them would do. Any of them would do.

Even as the man across the street straightened, I yanked out my phone and snapped his photo too. Then I stepped back into the shadows and was gone.

CHAPTER FIVE

I expected the church of Saint-Germain-des-Prés to be empty at this hour. Once again, I was wrong.

The ancient church, built and rebuilt over the centuries, had proven a haven to me more than any other place in the world when I'd first gotten started as an artifact hunter. When my treasure hunting had resulted in me crossing paths with a retired Catholic priest who worked at the church, I'd expected that I'd use the man only for information and guidance and then be on my way. Instead, he'd gradually opened my eyes to the harrowing truth about the lives of Connected children, particularly in Europe, where superstitions about magic and psychic ability ran deep and long.

It was Father Jerome who'd set me on the path to helping protect those children, a path that had gradually led me to pitching my services to bigger and bigger clients (and reaping larger and larger payouts), all in the service of paying for the care and protection of the most vulnerable members of the Connected community. Along the way, Father Jerome and I had become fast friends.

Right up until he'd been killed because of me.

I pursed my lips tightly, steeling myself against the unwanted tears that always threatened when I thought of the priest. Since his death months earlier, I'd done my level best not to think about him at all, which was both unfair and cowardly of me. The upside of all that cowardice, however, was that I was able to focus on my job. People who got too close to me inevitably got hurt. It was all too easy to fall into a deep well of guilt if I thought about that list too long, so I elected not to. Far better to push everyone away than put them at risk of illness, injury or even death—and for what? For nothing, other than their eventual bad luck in knowing me.

I grimaced, my mood turning fouler. Still, it was hard not to remember the priest when I was standing in the church he'd spent his life serving. A knot of people up near the altar were apparently receiving a special midnight tour from a young nun, a few hardy parishioners were praying in the pews, and I—I could see Father Jerome everywhere. Bustling up and down the aisles, his heavy robes always proving to be the perfect hiding place to secret away either artifacts I'd stolen or piles of cash I'd handed over to help fund his safe houses throughout France.

His eyes had generally remained merry even as his shoulders had grown more stooped, his face gaining lines and his hair thinning and going to gray. He'd still seemed invincible to me, unendingly earnest as he'd told me of yet another family targeted for their children's hands, eyes, or heart, or describing in harrowing detail a new brutal cabal that had encroached upon his territory, seeking to exploit the youngest members of the Connected community as psychic slaves. Every story had been worse than the last, and I'd bent myself to the task of making as much money as possible to help him, until it'd become clear that money alone wouldn't solve the problem.

But how far in my pursuit to protect Connecteds had I really come?

Suddenly restless, I moved down the long corridor of the shadowy cathedral, closer to the nun and her charges. They were younger, I realized as I approached. Not little kids, but mostly in their late teens and early twenties. Dressed in street clothes, they looked like any ordinary group of tourists, but there was something a little…off about them. I paused in the shadow of a wide column and flicked my third eye open.

I sagged against the cool stone bricks, my mouth going dry.

The young adults who stood with the nun weren't ordinary mortals, or even ordinary Connecteds. Even with the briefest scan of their energy, I could tell that these were some of the most powerful twenty-somethings I'd ever seen, and I'd seen my share of young Connecteds over the years. As I looked closer, another anomaly struck me. The energy that surrounded them leaped and swirled, but as I drilled in to focus on the Connecteds one by one, I realized their individual readings were far more normal. It was as if singly they were impressive, but together, they completely soared off the charts. I'd never seen anything like this before, had never even heard of it.

During the time I'd worked with Father Jerome I'd learned that most of the children had come to him in ones and twos, sometimes with their families, but far more often alone, either abandoned by their parents or given up willingly in the hopes that the children would be more secure in one of Jerome's safe houses than with their own families. It had proved a heartbreaking decision for some parents, one fueled by both fear and love. But most of those children, even as they came together, were quintessentially loners.

Not this group.

"Where is he now?" The question was high and clear, and I glanced sharply at the young woman who'd asked it. Her hair was dark, her eyes large and luminous, and her skin pale. Her accent was Russian, though she asked her question in perfect French.

At the head of the group, the woman in nun's attire smiled. "He's passed into the hands of the Father, his tireless devotion at an end," she said, her words gentle but firm. "Father Jerome understood that his role on this earth was to shepherd the children of God, particularly those with gifts beyond normal mortal understanding. He didn't seek personal acclaim for his work, only to share the love of God with those who needed it most. It is in his name that we continue our work today, but he didn't want anyone to cry by his grave. We can honor him most by doing the work he loved so much."

By now, I was grinding my teeth. I hadn't been with Father Jerome when he'd died, but I'd watched it happen on-screen. The man responsible for that death was also dead. That didn't make any of this any easier. Father Jerome had been my lighthouse in the storm, one of the few people I'd trusted, especially in my early days as an artifact hunter.

I should have kept him safe. I hadn't.

"So who's in charge, you?" another boy asked, a tawny-haired young man of no more than eighteen. He was thin—far too thin—but his clothes were new and he looked freshly scrubbed. Had he just arrived at Saint-Germain-des-Prés, another of Father Jerome's rescues? "I left behind an entire extended family of people like me. I may have been the strongest, but they're all at risk."

The nun folded her hands over her stomach, her face remaining serene. "I'm here to help you get your feet under you again, and we are here to help each other. You—all of you—will go back out into your communities when you're ready, keeping vigilant watch. If there's a child or family in need, you'll know where to call."

"We should fight," the boy insisted. "It's not enough to herd our people from camp to camp, protecting the most Connected until they're strong enough to hide on their own. We have skills. We should band together and fight."

A wave of dizziness made me take a step back, and I reached for the nearest pew, catching my balance before sliding onto the polished wooden bench. The church seemed darker now as the nun continued leading the group of young men and women closer to the altar. I couldn't hear her words anymore, but I didn't want to hear them.

Fight.

That's what the boy wanted, and none of the others had gainsaid him or objected in any way. Even the nun hadn't reacted with much more than patient understanding. But these kids—these vulnerable Connecteds—didn't understand what they were asking. The battle they wanted so desperately to join couldn't be won. Out of the seven billion people in the world, there was a little more than a few million Connecteds. Out of those, only several hundred thousand had abilities strong enough to do much more than bend a spoon. Most of the most highly skilled Connecteds were old enough to keep themselves well hidden from the world, but the children…

Only there were more young Connecteds now than ever, it seemed. And they were stronger too. Significant numbers of Connecteds had leveled up recently, most especially the children and young adult Connecteds. Who was teaching them, guiding them, now that they were turning out in numbers that could make a difference? Who was keeping them safe? I'd taken on the role of Justice to help police those Connecteds who had decided to use their influx of power to harm others, and there was no shortage of work in that regard, but was it enough?

Would it ever be enough?

I don't know how long I sat there in the shadowy embrace of the great church, staring at the dimly lit altar. I was surprised the church was open at all, but then again, I hadn't come in through the front door. It was simply sanctuary, a place for me to catch my breath before I went back out into Paris and made my way to the Magician's Parisian property. Hopefully without my merry band of pursuers following me either.

And who *were* those guys, anyway? Mercault didn't know, obviously, and I'd gotten nothing back so far from the Council on either picture I'd sent. I hadn't been in Paris long enough to piss anyone off, and my most recent work since I'd become Justice had been confined to narrow groups—a cabal of magicians, a coven of witches, and a band of souls yearning for the return of the ancient gods of Ireland. The threats posed by these groups would have had a major impact if I hadn't nipped them in the bud in time…but I had. Who had I upset by stepping in?

A movement at the front of the church caught my eye, and I blinked in confusion as I recognized the figure of the young nun from the tour—only now, she wasn't wearing her habit. Ordinarily, I wouldn't have a problem with this. I wasn't a big fan of even the modified penguin look, though it absolutely served its purpose. But it was the look she was now rocking that made me sit up and take notice: A beat-up pleather jacket and jersey hoodie combination on top, scuffed jeans and boots on the bottom, her brown hair pulled back in a nondescript ponytail.

She looked like me. Or the me of a few years ago, anyway, roaming the streets of Paris with little more than my instincts and a deck of Tarot cards to guide me. I flicked open my third eye and narrowed my other two. The young nun—or whoever she was—*did* have some Connected ability, but scarcely enough to get her a good run at the lotto counter. I didn't know how her abilities would manifest, but they'd likely be little more than sparkles and fairy dust, nothing she could use as a weapon. And she didn't seem like the aggressive type, exactly. She seemed like exactly the kind of woman who'd become a nun. Sweet, generous, gentle.

As I watched, she pulled a gun from a holster I hadn't seen snugged up beneath her jacket and checked the chamber.

Okay, so maybe not so sweet and gentle.

Part of me wanted to stop the woman where she was and ask her what the hell she was doing...and maybe where had she scored the sweet hoodie combo. But I wanted—needed—to know more about why she was dressed like me. So I followed her instead.

I stepped out into the breezy Parisian night, and impulsively reached out to Armaeus with my mind. *Knock, knock...*

No response.

Stuffing down my disappointment, I picked up my pace behind the nun-turned-Sara Wilde cosplayer. As it turned out, we didn't have to go far.

The Metro trains in Paris don't run all night to all stations, but the station nearest to Saint-Germain-des-

Prés was in operation, and there was enough of a crowd that I could slip in behind the woman and not be noticed. She talked to no one, keeping her head down and her body compact. While the train rattled along, she pulled out a small notebook and paged through it, glancing at notes and pictures I couldn't make out. I had to say, she looked as badass as me. In fact, as weird as it seemed, every time I glanced her way, she looked more and *more* like me, until by the time she exited the metro at Gare du Nord, I began to get a sinking feeling about what was going on here.

That suspicion was borne out a few minutes later when she met her party at Gare du Nord.

Once again, I hung back in the shadows and watched the young woman move forward with what seemed like a newfound self-assurance, rocking my clothing, my hair, and now, without question, my face. I watched her eye the incoming train terminal with intense focus, then turned to see what she was looking at. It took me only a second to see the man looking up from the crowd disgorging from the train. His face registered recognition, and his smile stretched wide. He moved forward with a woman beside him, a child huddled against her in turn, but the energy of this small family was weirdly chaotic. He was excited; they were terrified.

Too terrified.

As the nun moved forward with her bold, confident stride, the man's excitement hiked another few levels, his hand shifting to his side as he shoved away the woman cowering beside him. That was all the warning I got, but fortunately, it was enough.

Moving quickly, I leapt away from the wall. I came up behind my doppelgänger and pushed her out of the way even as the man freed his gun. He brought it up to shoot, but I was still running fast, and fortunately, running didn't look all that impressive even at the speeds I was able to pull off on short notice. I barreled directly into the guy, sending his gun flying as the mother and child spun off in the other direction.

"Get them out of here!" I shouted back to the nun, who'd started running after me, while I knelt on the guy's chest. With all the experience I'd just scored at the Luxembourg Gardens, I knew exactly what to do to keep anyone from realizing that I was using magic. My hands flat on the man's chest, I blasted him with enough electrical current to set his whole body quivering.

"Who are you?" I demanded. He looked up at me, his eyes wide with confusion. "Where's the man you took those people from?"

"There are — two of you?" he managed in a guttural Eastern European accent, his gaze pinging back to the now wailing woman and her child, both of them pointing urgently at the train and ignoring the young nun who was pulling at their arms.

"Where's the father?" I asked again, tightening my hold. At this point, I was so mad, I could probably choke the man to death with no special skills required. That thought seemed oddly appealing, but I restrained myself. "I don't know how much you got paid or who paid you, but trust me when I tell you, it's not enough for what's about to happen to you."

He looked at me and grinned as the police whistles started blowing shrilly around me, and his eyes turned bright white.

"Welcome to Paris, Sara Wilde," he said, only this time, his voice was rich, cultured, simmering with wealth and arrogance —

I decked him cold.

CHAPTER SIX

I peeled away long enough to watch from a distance while the Gare du Nord police came, collected the unconscious Connected bogeyman, and found the missing family member. My doppelgänger, still in her Sara disguise, handled it all as if it was another day's work. Herding the traumatized family onto the metro, she got them to Saint-Germain-des-Prés without further incident, bustling them into the church while I waited outside. The young nun emerged twenty minutes later, looking decidedly less like me as she smoothed down her habit and adjusted the hood. Her quick, efficient steps brought her close to me, though. She knew I was waiting for her.

"I can explain," she said, speaking to no one in particular as she approached. I stepped away from the wall, and she turned.

"You don't have to," I said. "Just tell me who you are and how long you've been using your psychic abilities to mimic me. Because, frankly, you were better at being Sara Wilde than I am, at least for those people on the train."

"If I could mimic your powers, then that would be even more impressive, but my skills only go so far." She smiled and gestured to a bench on the sidewalk, and we sat. "My name is Emma Fearon, and I'm not actually a nun either. But I was one of the children Father Jerome rescued from the arcane black market. That was eight years ago."

My brows lifted. "Before my time."

"At first, yes. I grew up at one of the smaller safe houses, and was already working in the field by the time you joined ranks with him. But I saw you from a distance often enough, and of course, Father Jerome talked about you anytime he got the chance. He was so very proud of all you did."

My heart knocked sideways, and I grimaced. "I didn't do all that much. I found things and got money for them, then handed that money to Father Jerome. He did the heavy lifting."

She smiled. "That's what he always said you would say when he tried to thank you. But that's not really true. Father Jerome had been fighting long before he ran into you, and you didn't need to help him. But you did. Without any questions. You simply started funneling cash to him, cash you could otherwise have kept for yourself."

I didn't have much to say to that. Of course, she was right, but it hadn't seemed like a difficult decision at the time, especially once he'd shown me some of the children he'd rescued from slavers—one who'd had her eyes removed, another little boy with his hands cut off. It hadn't been a hard choice. "Those kids…"

Emma chuckled softly. "Oh, I know." Something in the tone of her voice made me glance back at her, and I barely stopped my recoil. Her face was no longer the serene, pale-skinned visage of a young Frenchwoman, but a mass of scars that swept down from the right side of her hairline to her chin. One eye socket was completely covered over with scar tissue, while the other, though still bright with focus, was deeply set in her damaged face.

A second later, her face appeared to me again, normal.

"My God," I murmured. "You couldn't..."

"Get plastic surgery? Yes, of course. Father Jerome wanted me to, had the money for it and everything, but..." She waved a tired hand. "There were always better things to purchase, always more children to save. And with my skills, it was not so much of a hardship. I've been effecting the glamour for so long, it's no different from keeping good posture at this point. Even when I sleep, it rarely slips."

"But how — ?"

She glanced away briefly, then met my gaze again, her own eyes clear and frank in her adopted features. "When I was young, I was an aspiring actress. I didn't realize that I was taking on the faces of the people I was mimicking, and my family didn't so much notice it. When something is right in front of you all the time, it's remarkable what can seem normal to you. But others noticed. Rumors started, and one day, two men walked into town and grabbed me and knocked me out with some foul-smelling drugs. They proclaimed me a witch and wanted to see my real face — by skinning the 'mask' off me. They got as far as they did before the pain broke through my delirium and I showed them the face they most wanted to see."

She gave me a grim smile. "Apparently, I make a convincing demon. I got away, but by then, even with my glamour, I couldn't see out of one eye, and my family was terrified it would happen again, and further afraid I would get attacked because of my demonic manifestation. A week later, Father Jerome arrived in our village and brought me to Paris."

By this time, I was staring at her, though her face had long since returned to its placid good looks. "And the men?"

"Gone. I didn't search for them—they were only two of a thousand who would have done the same thing. It's the world we live in, a world mired in fear, despite all our advancements and education." She shook her head. "But my pain has its benefits. Some of the children who come through this church are scarred worse than I am, and far more wear their scars inside. When I can show them that I *do* understand to some extent what they are enduring…it helps."

"Of course it does." I blew out a long breath. "How long have you been impersonating me?"

"Since a few weeks after Father Jerome died," she admitted. Her chin tilted up with self-assurance, but not defensiveness. "No one knew what to do. Father Jerome had always been the one to greet the newcomers. His was the face they expected, the only face they knew from the church. We lost several newcomers to the streets of Paris before we could get to them, simply because they got confused and then were lured away. The streets are not kind to those who've never been in a large city."

"You needed a new welcome ambassador."

"Anyone in the Connected pipeline that led to Father Jerome knew who Sara Wilde was. Some even knew what your face looked like, but most merely your general description. For me to show up as you, provided these refugees with the visual link they needed to get them off the train and into the system quickly and quietly before anyone noticed they'd arrived. When Sara disappears and I reappear in my habit, they don't blink. They merely assume she's done her job to make them safe and has moved on."

"And it works every time?"

"Enough that I've continued doing it. Enough that I'll keep doing it. We don't have very much time when they arrive, and if they're coming to our door, they're very attractive to the arcane black market hunters. There are always vultures waiting to strike."

"Like the man at the train station."

"I knew something was wrong when he didn't rush over immediately upon seeing me. By the time he went for his gun, you were already in motion. Thank you for that."

"Do you always carry?"

She hesitated. "As of recently, yes."

That answer didn't make me happy. "That man knew you were coming. Or that I was coming, either way. And he had a gun. He was prepared."

"I don't think so." Emma held her ground, surprising me. "He had the look of an opportunist, not necessarily sure of who would be getting off that train, but knowing someone would, someone he could sell for a profit. The police won't be able to hold him, but I suspect he won't stick around either. There's always more game to catch. And Paris is a target-rich environment."

I frowned. I would have accepted her answer, except for how the man spoke to me. The aristocratic vocal style he'd begun using was vaguely familiar to me…that couldn't be coincidence. Emma might be right that he'd been an opportunist, but someone had used him to let me know I was being watched, tracked. Which meant my adversary remained one step ahead of me, even when I thought I was safe. But those were my problems, not Emma's. Emma's were challenging enough.

"So the situation for Connecteds has gotten worse, not better," I said.

"It's gotten different from the battles you fought alongside Father Jerome, certainly. The promises being made by unscrupulous black-market harvesters to Connected families are different. Now these families are being asked to let their children join research studies and fancy educational institutions. They know in their hearts they should resist, but when you've lived your life on the edge of poverty, the chance to make things better for your child can be overwhelming. And some of them simply don't know how to say no to that much hope and money all at once."

"Even if it's all lies."

Emma shrugged. "Especially if it's all lies. That's all some of these people have ever known."

"Do you know anything about the man who intercepted your runners tonight? He seemed a little...special. Maybe not so much your usual opportunist."

"Oh, no." Now she did sigh, as if recognizing a greater gravity to the situation. "His eyes went white on you, didn't they?"

I shot her a look. "They did. Is that relevant?"

"Only in that it's been happening more and more, particularly with high-value runners. Which we didn't know about this family, but it'll come out in their intake process. Ghosts—that's what we call them—are getting deployed all over Europe in increasing numbers and have since the start of the new year. They are the worst to fight because they don't hesitate to use their weapons in public. They don't care who dies, even themselves."

"Skills?" I asked, thinking about the group of asshats in the Luxembourg Gardens. But Emma's response surprised me.

"None, other than being bounty hunters. We've never had one of them attempt any use of psychic ability to restrain their prey, just basic intimidation and brute force. We don't actually believe they're Connected, just being used by Connecteds, which is frightening enough."

She wasn't kidding. "No special strength or speed at all?"

"Beyond probably being drugged with technoceuticals, no. Actually, we suspect those who are using these ghosts to do their hunting have plenty of abilities, but are trying to keep a low profile. We've got people trying to track down who might be behind it, but so far — nothing."

"Got it." My phone buzzed in my pocket, but I ignored it for the moment. Hopefully, it was Nikki with information on the chick with the tattoo in the Luxembourg Gardens or her motorcycle-riding partner in crime, but I couldn't walk away from Emma yet. "So exactly how is this working now? You're in charge of the Saint-Germain-des-Prés drop site, but who's taking over for Father Jerome in general? Because you can't be running the whole operation from here."

She bristled, as I expected her to, but the truth was only the truth.

"I can't?" she challenged.

"No. It has nothing to do with your age or your strength — you've got skills. But you're not connected enough in the nonpsychic sense of the word to pull off what Father Jerome was able to do. Father Jerome had to know that. He would have left someone else in place." And, great friend that I was, I should have known who that "someone" was. *Alas.*

She grimaced. "He knew you would come after he died, whenever that happened. Not right away, but eventually. And that you'd be asking these questions. But he didn't tell me who he wanted to be in charge — I still don't know. I get my information about new drops by either phone or email, but it's an untraceable sender in both cases."

Oh, *fantastic*. "You're kidding me."

"I'm not. I don't bother questioning it, because without fail, a day or two later, someone shows up needing my help. Fortunately, we have enough security measures in place to make sure that no one enters our facilities without legitimately needing to be here. And they have to go through a long process before they end up in one of the secret safe houses we've set up."

"What is this, Charlie's Angels? You seriously don't know who's running the show?" I could hear my own voice rise defensively, but of all the crazy answers I expected Emma to give me, "I don't know" wasn't one of them. I passed a hand over my brow, trying to focus. "Father Jerome had friends in high places in the church and in government, but I don't think in Interpol. Otherwise, I would've been cut a little more slack. He worked alone except for…"

I lifted my face from my hand, focusing on the young woman again. "Max Bertrand," I blurted, pulling a name out of my memory banks — a laughing, happy-go-lucky great-great-something-great nephew of my very own Armaeus Bertrand, who I'd run into on jobs a couple of times before, and who'd also worked with Father Jerome on occasion. "Do you know that name? He was with Father Jerome for a while, but — not anymore. What happened to him?"

"I know Max, of course." Emma smiled. "But he's no longer with us. He had all the fire you could want in a crusader, but Father Jerome was convinced that a role within our organization is not what he was brought here to do. He believed that God had loftier plans for Max."

"So where is he now?"

"The last I knew, he was renting out a series of condos in southern Spain."

"Really? That's what God intended for him?"

She chuckled. "He's safe, which mattered more. I think Father Jerome worried about Max, but more what your reaction would be if anything happened to him. He often told me that you didn't believe you were worth the sacrifices of those around you, even when those sacrifices were gladly made."

Her words struck a hollow spot in my chest I hadn't realized was there. Father Jerome had been right about that, anyway. I stood abruptly and pulled out my phone again, pointing it at her.

"Well, if Max isn't in charge here, someone clearly is. There's a financial component we can track down, if nothing else. I don't like that you don't know who's pulling the strings at the top of this operation, and I don't like that they seem to know exactly when the next runner will be coming. Father Jerome was entitled to his secrets when he was alive, and I'm not going to lie, I had my own problems to solve. But now that we've had our little chat, I'm officially making myself involved again."

"You don't need to do that," she murmured, glancing away. But her fingers were knitting together, almost in prayer.

I smiled gently. "Yeah, I kind of do. Because you're using my face, and that face can get you in trouble with the wrong people."

Her gaze snapped back to me. "But the people who come here *need*—" she started, and I held up a hand.

"I know. I understand. Really, I do. But that's all the more reason for you to have more protection than a pistol tucked into your jeans. You'll be contacted by Ma-Singh, the general of the House of Swords within the next couple of days. Did Father Jerome ever talk about him?"

"He was your head general when you were Mistress of the House of Swords," Emma said, nodding. "Father Jerome liked him. He felt that if anyone could keep you safe, Ma-Singh could."

Me safe. I tightened my lips. I wasn't the problem, here.

"Well, he's also got the resources of an entire network of Connecteds at his disposal, and more money than he knows what to do with. He also owes me. If you have a way of contacting whoever it is who's checking in with you, you can let them know he's coming. The unknown successor can either choose to work with Ma-Singh or he can step out of the way."

Emma hesitated. "But this unknown successor, as you call him, has been helping us. We've been financially supported, and our work has continued uninterrupted."

"Sure, but he hasn't once told you who he is — or she is, for that matter — or why he's being so generous. I don't like it. It may be completely on the up-and-up, and if so, great. But until we know for sure, I'm calling for a little oversight."

"On what grounds?" Emma challenged right back, understandably irritated that I was throwing my weight around when I'd been MIA here in Paris for months. She wasn't belligerent, but she had backbone, and I appreciated that. But she was missing one critical point.

"On the grounds that it's my face you're using to convince these people they're coming to safety, security, and a better way of life. I have no problem with you using my face either. I just want to make sure that we're delivering on the promises that face is making.

"We?" she asked, looking up at me. I now stared back into the eyes of a young woman with half her face scraped away, the remaining eye glistening with something that looked too much like hope. Once again, my heart gave a hard, sideways knock of guilt.

"We," I agreed. Keeping the Connected children of the world safe was no longer my only fight. At the same time, it would always be my fight. "We. I'll be back as soon as I can."

And with that, I stalked away from the ancient church so beloved by the first man I'd ever trusted in this world, the man whose death I'd caused. The man I'd missed more fiercely than I ever imagined I'd miss anyone…until Armaeus Bertrand had vanished before my very eyes.

My phone buzzed again, and I glared down at it. It was a text from Nikki, but I couldn't quite read the screen. I blinked hard enough to clear the unexpected moisture from my eyes, but still couldn't make the words make sense.

Armaeus has split. Call ASAP.

CHAPTER SEVEN

I didn't call right away.

Call it a perversion of the spirit, call it fear, call it an excess of caution, I didn't want confirmation of Nikki's words. I knew what she was going to tell me, and I was out on the street—alone, exposed. I didn't want that either. I half walked, half jogged a few blocks in the rough direction of the address Mercault had given me. My side jaunt to the church had taken me farther from my destination, not closer, but I wasn't heading to Armaeus's house tonight anymore, anyway. I needed someplace quiet and anonymous where I could regroup. Preferably with free Wi-Fi and coffee.

Bending against an unusually stiff breeze, I turned onto rue Chomel and took in the Hôtel Signature Saint Germain with a sweeping glance. It was midnight, but they'd left a light on for me, because after all, this was Paris. Or at least I assumed that was the reason. I stalked in and immediately felt a warmth that far exceeded a Parisian hotelier's typical hospitality. My third eye flicked open.

Rolling circuits of energy stretched out to greet me, enveloping me in comfort and relaxation—not enough to trip my psychic triggers, but enough to know that more was going on in this building than turndown service. Was that good for me, or bad? And exactly what would it be like staying in a hotel run by Connecteds?

By the time I reached the counter, an older, competent-looking man had taken up his position behind the counter. "Bonsoir, madame. How long will you be staying with us?"

"Just one night." I felt the urge to use English as the man had, but I suppressed the perversion to contrariness. One of my abilities was language, and I'd be a fool not to use it. A French-speaking woman was less noticeable roaming the streets of Paris at night than an American, and my accent was flawless.

"Of course, of course." The man switched back to French without batting an eye, then proceeded to tell me of the amenities of the room and the details of checkout. I paid little attention as I handed over my card. I didn't know which ID it was attached to, but it scarcely mattered. It would go through. The Arcana Council might have its share of issues, but it had good credit.

My focus shifted to the problem at hand as I eschewed the ancient-looking elevator and mounted the five flights of stairs to my floor — about two flights more than necessary, I decided, but the exercise cleared more of the emotion from my mind and allowed me to center. I entered the room and gave the chic, elegantly spare furnishings a quick glance, then pulled out my phone again and stabbed it on, propping it on the desktop while I settled behind it. I could never remember the time difference when I was traveling, but I thought it was more or less afternoon in Las Vegas. Nikki might not be prepped for a video call, but she was the one who told me to check in.

I should have known better.

"Dollface!" Nikki crowed, her eyes bright and her smile wide beneath an enormous pile of red hair. "Tell me everything. Especially about the food."

I cracked my first genuine smile of the night. When I'd first met Nikki Dawes, she'd been serving as the occasional chauffeur and even more occasional assistant to the Arcana Council, for reasons that had more to do with her own entertainment than her needing the job. That, and the endless supply of clothing the position seemed to afford her. This afternoon, she was wearing a deep-cut sea-green sequined minidress that left no room for a gun or even a particularly deep breath, while acres of red hair cascaded over her shoulders in Princess Ariel ringlets. She stood back from the table to reach for something I couldn't see, and I caught sight of the tips of white leather go-go boots—no doubt platform boots, taking Nikki's already impressive height and boosting it well over six feet tall. Her makeup was flawless—giving her arched eyebrows, glittering lids, contoured cheeks, and dazzlingly dewy lips—and she looked unreasonably energized for someone not on a dance club floor.

"Are you pregaming?" I asked, and she rolled her eyes.

"Vegas hops round the clock, dollface, and so do I. You, however, look like shit. You really should eat something."

"I'm fine." I resisted the urge to run my hand over my brow. I was sure I looked only marginally worse than I felt. "Where's Armaeus? What happened?"

"Two things. First, we briefed him on your talk with Mercault. He seemed way more interested in the gold you scooped out of that cave pool than anything Mercault had to say, by the way, especially the storm goddess totem. You left that with Mercault?"

"Negative. Mercault insisted I take it with me. It's…uh, somewhere on me." I glanced down to my jacket with a frown, patting my pockets absently before I realized it was still looped around my neck. "But what did Armaeus say about the dates? Did they trigger him? Is that why he took off, because he remembered something?"

Nikki shook her head. "We don't think so, because we didn't give him that part of the briefing."

That made me sit up. "What do you mean? Kreios is keeping that intel quiet? Why?"

The Devil of the Arcana Council was Armaeus's best friend in the world, and one of the most strategic members of the Council after the Magician. He was also currently in charge of the Council, along with the Emperor, which was a cakery of crazy I had no intention of slicing into. But the Magician, I was sure, had his reasons. Just as the Devil had his.

"He isn't thrilled with Armaeus's progress, and he didn't want him haring off before he'd fully recovered. So much for that idea. Worse, we've been getting a lot of intel on some new activity on the arcane black market, and we don't know if there's a link to what's going on with the Magician."

"What kind of intel?"

"Apparently, there's been an uptick in the technoceutical transactions that have been taking place of late across Europe, with newer and more devastating varieties of psychic-enhancing drugs hitting the market way faster than they should. It's basically like they're getting created and packaged and then poofed into existence at key points along the supply chain, but nobody knows who's doing the poofing or how they're pulling it off. Because that kind of magic is top-shelf stuff. The Council would know about anyone able to wield that kind of power and—they don't."

"Great." I rubbed my hand over my brow, thinking about Mercault's comments regarding the unnamed group after me. He'd suspected they had very deep pockets. Did they also have very deep magic? Were they tied to this surge in technoceutical traffic? "We need to get Armaeus's memories back."

"Roger that. We're working on narrowing down some places for you to get started, either Spain or England, given Mercault's mention of Queen Elizabeth, which puts you in a very tight little nexus of influence, by the way. Kreios didn't like that either. He said Armaeus would have stored his forgotten memories a bit more broadly if he'd had any amount of time to work with. He thinks we're missing something."

I shrugged. I thought the same thing, but it made a certain sort of sense. "England and Spain—and France, for that matter—were doing their level best to declare ownership of everywhere back then. Nothing that says we don't start in the Old Country but end up in the New. But if you didn't tell Armaeus what I'd learned, where'd he go?"

She pulled a face. "I wasn't here for that part. When I got your text, I was out on the Strip with Detective Delish."

"Dressed like that?" Brody Rooks was another long-time friend of the Council, and an even longer-time friend of mine. He was also a detective with the Las Vegas Metropolitan Police Department, with a habit of drawing the short stick of crazy when it came to psychic complaints or crimes. Of which there were more and more in Vegas of late.

"He knows how to roll well enough. I needed the backup of Las Vegas's finest, and of course, that meant him. After the Beltane crazy a few weeks ago, the local Connected community is amped to the max. And there's another festival going on this week, so he asked me to help him handle it. On the down low, he said, drawing no attention to ourselves."

I snorted. That explained her dress. Nikki didn't do anything on the down low.

"So anyway, I showed him the text you sent of the woman who attacked you, and he had me send it to his phone. He didn't think much of her tat, even questioned that's what it was, but I could see it plainly. After I told him he was clearly blind, he zoomed in on just that part, taking everything else out of the frame, and sent it off to some friends of his. Good enough. He didn't recognize the motorcyclist either. Then I shipped both images over to Kreios, who happened to be with Armaeus, and he showed them to Armaeus. They talked for another few minutes, and the Magician claimed he was tired, wanted to see Dr. Sells, all that. Kreios went off for her. When they came back, Armaeus was out of his bed—vanished."

"Cameras?"

"Everything we had on him shorted out with a spike of electricity, from the looks of it. It's back online now, but what we've got is the Magician lying in his bed, looking about as lousy as you do, staring at the tablet where he's got an image of Chick Vicious. Kreios is out of the room at this point and something shifts in the Magician's face, like he's put something together. He lays down the tablet, he lifts his chin, he closes his eyes, and he goes poof. We've got no electrical signature on him, but we don't think he's in Vegas anymore. We think he's with you."

I made a show of checking the room around me. "Pretty sure I would've noticed that."

She grinned. "I'm pretty sure you would've too. Simon's watching all his regular residences, but we think he's gotta be focused on the house Mercault sent you to. It was bugging the shit out of him that he couldn't remember the significance of that home, even though records check out that it's been in his family since at least the French Revolution, and probably long before. At first, he said he didn't want to go see it himself. He understood he's operating with less than a full deck, and everything was comfy cozy in his little hospital fort. All that changed when he saw the picture you sent."

Great. Just what I needed, a half-baked Magician trying to find his way home. "You guys figure out anything about that tattooed symbol?"

"That would be negative. According to Simon, it's probably important but not *too* important given where the girl chose to emblazon it on her skin. Most super-secret symbols are a little more hidden away than that."

I thought about the woman who'd attacked me, all fierce energy and rage. "Unless she didn't give a crap."

Nikki finger-gunned me. "There is that. But if that was the case, why would you use her on an important op? Sloppy."

"She didn't come in until the end," I mused aloud. "I'd taken out two rounds of asshats before that. She was a high-level Connected, but she was running on something more than her love of life. It's possible she wasn't supposed to take an active part in the capture, just the aftermath, at which point no one was expecting me to be in a position to take selfies."

"I can buy that," Nikki said, nodding. "Detective Dreamboat seemed to think the symbol could represent a major high-end gang, though he's never seen it before.

And he should have, given all the paper he's read on international drug syndicates. So he's not happy."

"And you think Armaeus is here, in Paris, after seeing that tattoo? Why?"

"No clue," Nikki admitted. "The original plan was for us to pore over data while Dr. Sells continued to monitor the Magician's cell regeneration. Apparently, he's got off-the-charts growth happening with his neural circuits, and there are some other physiological changes that have her all atwitter. Vascular expansion, higher oxidation of his blood, the whole nine yards. It's like he's getting pumped up for *American Gladiators*."

"And his neural circuits?"

"A total cluster. Some areas of his brain are lit up like Christmas, some are completely dormant. There's absolutely no correlation between his brain activity and typical neurological activity of sample subjects, and he sleeps like it's his job."

"Well, maybe he's having a growth spurt."

She snorted. "He's definitely doing that. But even he recognized he's nowhere near one hundred percent. If he joined us in the search, he almost certainly wouldn't improve our chances of finding his missing memories."

"Yet he took off anyway."

"He did. And you should know, he didn't ask about you once. Kreios worked up the full report on your injuries, your enemies, any information we could get to figure out who the assholes were who jumped you in the park, because he figured the Magician would want to know. But Armaeus never asked. Which is definitely not normal."

It was a testament to how used to the new reality I'd become that Nikki's words didn't faze me. Much. Over the past few weeks since Armaeus had suffered a trauma in Ireland, in large part to protect me, he hadn't seemed merely walled off from me, he'd been completely absent. Almost aggressively so, as if he was deliberately pushing me away and not focusing on me or anything I did or said. At first, my feelings had been hurt... Okay, my feelings were still hurt. But I knew enough about the Magician to know he had a plan in what he was doing. I just didn't know what our relationship would look like when he came out on the other side.

Was I truly a threat to Armaeus, like I'd been to Father Jerome? *Was* he better off not knowing me?

I pushed those thoughts away. "What's Doctor Sells's assessment of his physical capabilities at this point? And how much of his magic does he still have? Did he undertake any tests along those lines?"

"Kreios says no, that he was focused entirely on his internal healing, but I call bullshit. Since he left Dr. Sells's care and returned to Prime Luxe, Armaeus has been squirrelly. I pulled the cameras for the last few days since you were running around the jungle. He stayed in his actual bed the bare minimum, but I have no idea where he went. The moment I get a chance, I'm going to pin Simon to the ground and figure out where Mr. Magus was spending his time. That said, I think we'll find he stayed pretty damn close. He's got everything he needs for full-on conjuring in that fortress of his. He's prepared like that."

"So why come to Paris still broken, without all his toys?"

"Maybe he has different toys in Paris?"

"Maybe..." I drummed my fingers on the hotel desk. "Do you have eyes on his Paris house or apartment or whatever it is? The one Mercault pointed me toward?"

"Simon's tapped into the security system there. It's pretty basic. Home itself doesn't look used other than to be kept clean by staff, who don't live on-site. Conventional security in the main, but it hasn't registered another person in the house. Since Armaeus blew town here, there've been no alarms or even a stray heartbeat picked up on any of the monitors. What that means, though, I don't know. Either Armaeus is there but neutralizing his presence, or we're wrong and that's not where he went. But we don't think he would've gone after the operative whose photo you snapped directly. Especially not knowing where she was, unless he knew far more than he let on to Kreios."

"He wouldn't have done that." My certainty about the Magician's behavior had less to do with his friendship with the Devil and more to do with his sense of practicality. With the Magician under the weather, leadership of the Council had been split between Kreios and the Emperor, Viktor Dal. It was a deliberate delaying tactic, and it made for an unreasonable number of meetings, part of the reason I was glad not to be in Vegas. But Armaeus was letting Kreios take the lead, and he wouldn't throw the Devil under the bus deliberately. "Something simply must've clicked, and the shock of his discovery sent him flying."

"I'm afraid so."

Still, I suspected I was missing something. "Armaeus knows there are two chunks of memories that he's lost, maybe three if he dropped other pieces besides his memory of me. But he has zero knowledge of this group that's following me or these rumors of threats to the Council. What's going on?"

Nikki blew out a long breath. "Based on their conversations, Kreios suspects that the Magician now believes that the Council is going to be straight up overthrown as a result of current events unless they follow a distinctly specific course."

"Overthrown?" I blinked. Nobody had said anything about the Council being overthrown. Attacked, yes, damaged, sure. But how could you overthrow the most powerful group of Connecteds in the world?

"Sells doesn't concur. She believes that Armaeus implanted that particular belief in his mind at some earlier point, to come to the surface at the necessary time to create a sense of urgency. But, now he's gone. And we've got no record of him in Paris or anywhere else in the world. He's in the wind."

"I'll find his little Parisian bungalow as soon as I've caught some sleep," I said. "I'm just short of hallucinating, and that won't do anyone any good."

"Agreed." Nikki nodded. "Because you look like—"

I stabbed the phone off before she could finish, then sat back in my chair. On any other mission, I would reach out to the Magician with my mind, seeking the connection between us that was equal parts galvanizing and healing. But I'd locked down my mental barriers against Armaeus the moment he'd stopped recognizing me. Part of that was for his benefit, not wanting him to see how distressed I was and have it distract him from his own healing. Part of it was self-preservation, not wanting him to see how distressed I was out of simple pride.

But the time was rapidly coming that I'd need to put aside my fears and open myself up to him whether I liked it or not. Because he wasn't healing on his own. I wasn't sure I could heal him either, but it was theoretically possible, even if he no longer remembered I had that capability. In healing him, and giving over such a personal part of me, would I lose myself in the complex construct of the Magician's altered mind? Was

I strong enough to heal him and preserve myself as well?

I slumped further, my mind racing through everything I'd learned since coming to Paris. First, someone was targeting me — me and, apparently, the Council at large. That somebody had a well-equipped army of Connecteds large enough to deploy in the streets of Paris on the off chance they might pick up my trail. That army, combined with the whispers Mercault had picked up, spelled money and influence.

Second, the arcane black market attacks on the most vulnerable of the Connecteds hadn't gone away simply because I'd stopped paying attention to them. If anything, they'd gotten worse. And someone was now deploying low-level Connecteds as their eyes, ears, and hands in grabbing these children off the street. The same somebody who was targeting the Council? Odds were good.

Third, Armaeus was in worse shape than I'd realized, worse shape than he should be. The image I'd messaged him of the motorcyclist bad guy and the fierce young female warrior and her tattoo had sent him running...straight to Paris, I was sure of it. Yet he still hadn't tried reaching out to me.

Which meant he wanted me to come to him.

Right?

"All right, Armaeus," I whispered to the empty room. "We'll do this your way."

The room gave no response. Or if it did, I couldn't hear it, as sleep finally took me down.

CHAPTER EIGHT

Morning dawned way too soon, and I awoke with the first beam of light through the opened curtains. If anything, I felt more drained than I had when I'd gone to sleep, but a scalding-hot shower helped. The coffee and croissants cheerfully offered in the hotel's lobby also went a long way toward restoring my will to live. The morning was cool and clear. Jacked on espresso and buttery goodness, I made good time walking through the streets of Paris, finally consulting my phone map to narrow in on the appropriate street.

The address corresponded with a largeish patch of green that had no name or title indicating it was a public park. My curiosity grew the closer I moved to my destination. Rue du Chambourg was impossibly charming, with trees and green space not entirely common in this section of Paris anymore. The mansion rising behind an elegant wrought-iron gate was equally unusual. Especially because it looked like it was resting at the front of a multiacre secret garden.

How could Armaeus have forgotten a house that looked like this?

The three-story structure most resembled a baby Palais de Justice, with its creamy marble front, gilded doors, and curved roof. The grass surrounding it was manicured and stretched luxuriously to either side of the building before flowing back to a stand of heavily pruned trees. I itched to see the extent of the secret park, but there was the problem of the wrought-iron-and-stone fence that surrounded the property, fronted by an imposingly ornate gate. There was absolutely no sign of life in the building, but this was Paris, not the American South. Armaeus wouldn't likely be sitting out on the front porch sipping sweet tea, waiting for me to come calling.

That said, who locked their gates against friends? Even friends they couldn't remember anymore?

I blew out a long breath as I curled my hands around the gate, eyeing the lock. But no sooner had I touched the cool metal than the clasp snicked and the gate popped open. Not due to any of my own effort or electrical pulse either. Which meant someone had been waiting for me, no rocking chairs required.

The speaker crackled beside me. "Please come in, Miss Wilde."

I couldn't stop the full-body shiver that Armaeus's words, spoken in his rich European accent, caused me. I was so used to hearing the luxurious roll of syllables inside my mind, elegant and articulate, that hearing him speak out loud was always a visceral pleasure. But while he'd known I was leaving Vegas for French Guiana and a trophy hunt for Mercault, the Magician hadn't spoken to me about the trip. He hadn't said two words to me alone since he realized he didn't know me.

So this...this was different. This almost felt like we were meeting for the first time. I wasn't good with meeting anyone for the first time, let alone a man who had, up until very recently, been my lover. There really needed to be a self-help book for that.

I couldn't stop the weird hitch to my pulse as I moved down the smooth stone walkway, which was hedged by overflowing pots of flowers that looked generously tended. The thick stone walls of the mansion, trimmed with more stone in mellow white, gave the impression of money—lots of money—and age. I could easily believe this home had originally been built for French aristocracy, and I wondered idly when Armaeus had picked it up. Had he needed to guard it behind its sturdy fence from the bloodthirsty rebels of the French Revolution? Had he watched Napoleon's armies assemble from the upper windows? The park space behind the building alone must be worth a fortune, but the Bertrands had never lacked for funds.

I jolted as the door swung open, and Armaeus stood in the shadowed lee of the shallow front porch. "Were you planning to spend the morning staring at the house?" he asked.

My cheeks flushed at the wry comment, but it was his smile that nearly undid me. Armaeus looked at me with curiosity and interest—but for the first time since his collapse, it was an interest that was edged with sensuality. It was as if he'd finally recalled that there *had* been something between us, even if he wasn't sure what, and that there might again be something between us, along with an appreciation of the delicious state of uncertainty in the present.

I had less of an appreciation for the present, frankly. Especially since I was still wearing yesterday's clothes.

I said nothing but moved forward, mounting the few steps and entering the fortress as Armaeus stepped back. The interior was exactly what I would have expected in any house that had its walls cordoned off by little velvet ropes and a discreet placard suggesting an optional donation at the front door in exchange for a colorful map.

"When in the world did you live here?" I blurted, my gaze immediately going to the paintings that lined the walls floor to ceiling, the gilded balustrade of the staircase that started deep in the foyer and wound sumptuously upward, and the shadowed hints of polished floor chasing deeper into the house.

"It would appear I maintained an active residence in the late 1500s, during the portion of time I have conveniently forgotten. I quit the house abruptly in 1571, though I no longer know why, and didn't return to Paris for any reason until the Revolution. At that point, I remained long enough to secure the interests of myself and my family, as well as offer what protection I could to those who were caught on the wrong side of history."

"Protection," I echoed. "Or, in other words, you were willing to tip the scales in your favor to keep your family and friends safe."

"I never made any assertion to the contrary," Armaeus responded smoothly. "The balance of magic must be maintained at all times, yes. But as long as that is assured, I'd be a fool not to use the benefit of my position to protect those who should be protected."

The comment wasn't untrue, but it still made me blink. I was used to the other members of the Arcana Council being mercenary, and I certainly made no excuses for my own avarice. But Armaeus had always seemed above that fray, separate and apart from righting the petty wrongs of ordinary men.

What was going on here?

"We can speak more comfortably elsewhere in the house, I think," Armaeus said, watching me closely. "If you'll follow me?"

I didn't meet his gaze, fixing my attention instead on a richly textured oil painting of Venus, clearly an original. "Sure."

He turned and moved silently through the house, his expensive Italian loafers making barely any noise on the polished floor. In comparison, I clomped behind him in my scuffed boots, driving my hands farther into my jacket pockets. I found myself thinking thoughts I hadn't dredged up since the very early days with Armaeus—mostly about how someone like him would be interested in someone like me…and why.

Those doubts had been answered early on, of course. The Magician had never had any compunction about explaining to me that his interest in me had started on an entirely professional note. He wanted to understand my unusual psychic abilities and how deep they went, particularly because I was one of the few human beings whose mind he could not immediately read. He was more than willing to use his own psychic skills to help with the discernment of mine—with the somewhat awkward caveat that his aptitudes were intensified and driven by sex. And once he'd realized that I'd reacted very strongly to the spark of attraction he was naturally inclined to fan between us—and that this spark had ignited a very different fire within me, one that expanded my abilities—he'd continued to push me to push my limits, break through my blocks, and achieve my potential.

After that…well, here we were. Quite the raggedy pair.

We reached the back of the mansion what seemed like fifteen minutes later, though I'm sure was only five, the sound of my boots thudding in my ears. I stepped out onto a gracious back porch where a low table was set with coffee service and more pastries, the delicious smell of freshly baked bread wafting up.

"You have a staff here?" I asked, recalling Nikki's insistence that nobody was moving inside the house.

"I do," Armaeus allowed. "And I have a highly sophisticated security system which, as of a few short hours ago, thwarts the abilities of even the Fool to circumvent at short notice. Fortunately, I won't have to deceive Simon for long, but I wanted at least a few hours to get to know the place again. Do you have anything else you would like to ask me about my home?"

Armaeus's voice retained its edge of humor, enough that I had to force myself not to become irritated on general principles. He was fully aware I was offering filler conversation, questions, and thoughts to crowd the space between us, creating a buffer. Well, too bad. I needed that buffer.

"I'm good." I moved forward and took a seat nearest to the coffee. I'd rather be jacked to the nines than stuffed senseless, and I was definitely going to need something to distract me. Armaeus swept up beside me and settled into the next chair, but instead of leaning back, he moved forward, his hands on his knees, studying me.

I had to laugh. "I know that look," I sighed. "Even if you don't remember it anymore."

His brows arched. "Oh?"

"It used to make me feel like you were studying a bug."

"And now?"

"It still feels like you're studying a bug, but it bothers me less. When we first met, I never quite knew if I was a distraction, a curiosity, or a genuine puzzle to you. Probably a little of all three." There. I'd done it. I'd broached the idea of me and him, together. Of us. My heart had started thudding nervously, my hands were sweating, and my breath didn't seem to be filling my lungs, but I'd done it. I totally deserved a parade. With trombones.

"At the beginning, I suspect it was all three," Armaeus agreed. He sat back and crossed his legs, still eyeing me curiously. "I have talked to Kreios about you, and I know the timeline of our relationship, if that helps."

I took a sip of the killer rich espresso, my last barrier to the morass of crazy I was about to fall into. "And what did Kreios have to say?"

"The bare minimum. Though he worried excessively that he wouldn't be present when we finally had the opportunity to become reacquainted. The truths that might come out intentionally or unintentionally and all that."

"Right." I snorted. Leave it to the Devil to put things into perspective. I was making this a bigger deal than it needed to be. "So let's get to it. Why did you forget me?"

The words were out in the air between us before I could stop them. That wasn't how I wanted to ask this question, that wasn't even really the most important question I needed to ask. But once spoken, I couldn't recall the words, and as I stared resolutely at Armaeus, I was at least glad to note that my voice hadn't wavered. Much.

"I don't know," he said evenly, meeting my gaze. The sensual flicker in his eyes was gone, and his expression was both neutral and mildly fascinated, neither of which I found at all reassuring. I clenched my fists in my lap, willing myself not to be an idiot, but it was tough going.

Armaeus continued. "The options are certainly intriguing. Did I remove you from my awareness because of your role as Justice? Because of some shared memory that was clouding my understanding of our current dilemma? Or did I plan it at all?"

"You had to have planned it in part," I replied, striving to keep my voice even and rational. "There was a letter written to Justice the first time you pulled this stunt in 1478, which said if I was receiving it, then I was also the key to the solution. But that's all it said: if you're getting this note, you're a critical part of the solution. Which, for the record, that wasn't super helpful."

"Noted."

"And then there's the history of the Mercault family and their assertion that you've done this at least twice that they know of." I didn't even hesitate to share this additional information. Armaeus was already out in the field, regardless of whether or not he should be. He needed to know what I knew about his lost memories. "In 1478, as we already determined, and in 1571. Any chance either of those lapses makes sense now? And have you any idea what you forgot besides me this time around?"

"First, let's address the present," he said, lifting an elegant finger. "From what I have determined based on accounts of the incident in Dublin, I was pumped full of energy from the ancients in a bid to short out my circuits, to overwhelm me, you could say. That didn't work. I kept taking more and more energy, but not dispelling it. From everything we've charted, my brain activated and replicated cells to manage the influx of energy, creating new compartments. But that energy was unformed, unfocused. It wasn't a learning, it was only a potentiality. When I understood I had forgotten you, I assumed it was simply an overflow issue. That I had to remove something in my mind in order to make room for something else. But I could find no other incidence of a forgotten set of information besides all memories attached to you—yet I sensed incontrovertibly that I *had* forgotten something else. Then I realized, as you say, that I had done this before. Twice before, in fact. With that, the situation became a little…murkier."

"But how would you know whether you've forgotten something new or not this time?" I asked. "You wouldn't know you couldn't tie your shoes anymore until you attempted to tie your shoes."

He smiled. "True. But it appears that after the second excision of my memories in 1571, I undertook a rigorously detailed inventory of everything I could remember, everything I'd ever studied or written down. So that I would know if it ever happened to me again, especially if it had been done to me unawares."

I squinted at him. "Unawares? Were you worried about that?"

He spread his hands, his eyes glittering. "I worry about very little. I consider everything."

"Okay, fine. So, let me guess. When this happened again, you created an SAT test for yourself, and you passed with flying colors. Except for anything categorized under Wilde, Sara."

"Exactly," Armaeus said. "Or that is what I thought. Until I saw the first picture you texted."

"The woman who attacked me, the one with the partial tattoo."

"Yes."

"And you realized that you didn't know the symbol, but should have?"

"No," he said, surprising me. "I realized I *did* know the symbol, but that I shouldn't."

"Whoa, whoa, whoa." I held up my coffee mug, not willing to release its velvety goodness just because my head was exploding. "Explain."

Armaeus leaned forward, consumed with an energy that seemed strange for him — too intense, too excited. I'd always considered him the soul of restraint, but how well did I really know the true Armaeus? Would I ever know him fully?

Or, for that matter…ever again?

The Magician's eyes flashed as he began. "Simply stated, I instantly recognized the symbol. Once I did, I understood the true nature of the problem we now face. A problem that I had not recognized as it was building virtually in front of me for centuries."

"You know what, I don't think I have enough caffeine for this," I said, slumping back in my chair. "So this has nothing to do with you forgetting me."

"It has a great deal to do with it, in fact. I believe that it was only because I forced myself to forget you that I was able to see the truth."

I squinted at him. "But I haven't been around for centuries. I've only been in your life for a couple years. How could that help?"

"You have not been around for centuries, no. But you are Justice of the Arcana Council, the first Justice since the mid-1800s, a position vacated by Abigail Strand and not refilled until you took up the role."

"And…"

"And having forgotten you, I find that I now remember a great deal more about Madame Abigail Strand than I did previously."

My eyes shot wide. The former Justice had remained a mystery to me in many ways, but I hadn't considered there'd been any nefarious reason for that. "I just assumed you were holding out on me."

"Not at all. My memories of Abigail Strand were hazy — she died well over a hundred years ago. But they were intact, or so I believed. I knew the bare minimum about her — her tenure with our organization was brief and troubled, and I brought her into the Council during a tumultuous time. I couldn't exactly remember the nature of that tumult, but it was the Victorian era, the Industrial Revolution was in full swing, and there was significant global unrest. The entire world was in a state of extraordinary transition, including those of the Connected community. Then Justice Strand died, and I felt in part to blame, so you could argue that I repressed my memories of her further to somewhat absolve myself of the damage I'd caused to an innocent."

"Okayyy…" I watched the Magician carefully. He was right that Justice Strand, my immediate predecessor for all that she'd ended her tenure in 1853, had died far too young. Abigail had endured myriad mental challenges that had made it difficult to cope with her work as Justice, and the role had proven too much for her. Of course, I'd learned this well after it had become too late for me to leave said role, but details.

Armaeus clearly knew something I didn't, however. He was practically vibrating with energy, the energy of a mad scientist on the cusp of a major revelation, and one I wasn't sure I wanted to know.

"And that means…" I prompted him.

"The symbol that you saw inked on the neck of your adversary is something that jogged my memory, but I was shocked to learn that I had no record of it in my files. Not one. But I did find examples of it here. In this house. A house I'd quit rather suddenly in 1853 for no discernible reason, and to which I'd never returned. Never truly thought of, in fact, until earlier today, with the revelation of that symbol."

93

"And it's a symbol of what, exactly?" I pulled my phone out and scanned the photos. The tattoo was there, of course, but now that I saw it again, I had to frown. "Um, how did we even get a tattoo out of that? It barely looks like more than a bad rash."

"Detective Rooks thought the same thing, but he cannot see the way you and I can see, when we make the attempt. In the exigency of the moment, you utilized the sight of your third eye."

"Oh." Obligingly, I flicked open that lens, and I saw the tattoo much more clearly. But that also explained why the woman had felt comfortable displaying it—most people couldn't see it, even the bit that showed above the woman's high collar, so she was effectively hidden in plain sight. Fortunately, my sight wasn't exactly plain.

"So it's a crown of some sort, super stylized. I remember now," I murmured. "What's the connection? You said you know it."

"I *knew* it would be a truer statement. This symbol was employed by a rival council. An ancient adversary of the Arcana Council that we had destroyed in…let me see. The Bronze Age, originally, well before my time. Then again in the 1300s, just after my ascension. Then again in the mid-1400s."

I shot him a glance. "I think you're misunderstanding the word destroyed."

He continued without acknowledging that. "After the blow we leveled in the 1400s, there was no rebuilding of the organization. You could say we salted the earth they stood upon, utilizing every tool at our disposal, as they had used similar tools against us."

"Kind of intense for an Arcana throwdown, wouldn't you say?"

"They more than deserved it. The Shadow Court supported some of the most perverse Connected criminals of the Middle Ages, and it became clear they weren't going to stop unless we made them. At that time, Justice Hall overflowed with complaints of their actions against Connecteds—enslavement, torture, death, mutilation—and they sat on piles of gold, which made them far too influential with both governments and the Church."

"Hmmm," I muttered. The library of Justice Hall would have qualified as one of the Seven Wonders of the World, if anyone had known it existed outside the Arcana Council. In addition to being the repository for all crimes against Connecteds perpetrated by other Connecteds since the dawn of time, the library had also become home to certain arcane texts and treatises, the more dangerous, the better. "The Shadow Court. I haven't heard of them."

"You wouldn't. That's the point. They were old news." The Magician shook his head wonderingly. "I'd forgotten all this, but there was no reason for me to remember it, specifically, as something to be concerned about. The Shadow Court was gone. They remained gone, an artifact of the past that was well and truly vanquished. Until the mid-1800s, it would seem, when they reached out to Abigail Strand, and she helped them by removing any current awareness of the Shadow Court from my memory. I knew they had existed and that they were destroyed, but I had no idea they had resurfaced. Or, I should say, I apparently had become aware they had resurfaced, and then I had that awareness removed. By Justice Strand."

"What?" I blinked. Justice Abigail Strand was a bit of a cipher, admittedly, but she'd never impressed me as being incredibly strong. "She could do that?"

"With the right amount of help, she could. She must have done so, in fact. When I removed my memories in 1478 and 1571, I must have directed Justice Hall to expunge any files regarding that which I no longer wanted anyone to know. When she ascended to the role of Justice, Abigail, in turn, must have somehow realized the break in the historical records, learned how it happened, and shared that knowledge with people who knew what to do with it. When new complaints surfaced and I refocused on the Shadow Court, she was given the tools to expunge my memory. And so it was done— done so expertly, I never even noticed what I'd forgotten. Our enemies have had more than a hundred and fifty years to operate under our very noses without any checks or balances. They could be our friends, our colleagues, and all the while working assiduously to take the Council apart, brick by brick. And now, with me at my weakest, they are choosing to strike."

"That...doesn't sound good," I allowed.

He looked at me. "It is not, Miss Wilde. The Shadow Court is about to destroy everything we have built—and send the world into chaos—and we're almost too late to stop them."

CHAPTER NINE

I stared at the Magician, both unwilling and unable to process so much crazy in one sentence. "They've got enough power to destroy the Council, and you didn't *realize* this was going on right in front of you? All these years?"

His mouth twitched with irritation. "Miss Wilde."

"Don't you Miss Wilde me. You *knew* there were gaps in your mental history. Two big gaps at critical points during world history — not that there's arguably any point during world history that isn't critical, except for maybe the Dark Ages. Those were kind of a long stretch of simply trying not to die from the Plague."

"Miss *Wilde*."

"But it never occurred to you that a similar memory gap existed around the mid-1800s? With as much" — I floundered for a second, wanting to come up with a better term than navel-gazing, no matter how much it applied — "*introspection* as you subject yourself to, I think you would have stumbled over it."

"And you would be correct, in the main." His gaze shifted to the wall again. "But even the pieces I knew were missing, I couldn't entirely identify in terms of scope. That took decades — centuries of careful teasing out, often starting with the end in mind. Some aspect of the world that was there, and then, quite suddenly, not. A problem that was building toward an irrevocable conclusion that was never heard of again, that sort of thing. I didn't conclude those efforts until this last, quite forceful period of, as you call it, introspection."

"And you think you've cracked that code."

"I have cracked that code in part for the first two memory lapses. Thanks to your help, I have cracked the beginning of the third, but I am in no way certain of what this knowledge nets us. You can rest assured, however, that either acting rashly or ignoring this knowledge entirely will be to our detriment. Right now, the Shadow Court isn't aware of my evolution of understanding."

"Well, after last night, they're certainly aware of *my* evolution of understanding, and they have to know we're besties."

Something in my tone finally seemed to snap through Armaeus's mental absorption. He slid his gaze back to me. "I can understand your impatience."

"Oh, I'm pretty sure you can't." I wanted to say more, I did. I wanted to unburden the pain that was once again cresting in my traitorous heart. But as soon as I drew another breath, Armaeus continued.

"I've summoned those who can most help us navigate this maze I've set for us. There's no point in reviewing the information relevant to that strategy until they arrive. Your anger is, unfortunately, of no use without resolutions in hand to resolve it. That will not be possible until the team assembles. You're not strong enough."

I blinked at him, my angst dissolving in this shower of unexpected wtfery. "Wait, what?"

"In addition, discussing this without the other members of the Arcana Council present is not efficient."

Slowly and carefully, I sat back in my chair, shoving my hands into my pockets. The Armaeus of a few weeks ago would have quirked a smile at the move—it was something I did, too often, when I was annoyed. The Armaeus sitting in front of me, however, had no idea about my little habits or mannerisms. Which, of course, did nothing to improve my mood.

"Actually, I think I need to get some of this out of my system before they arrive, if we're going to be all about efficiency here," I said. "Nobody has explained to me exactly *how* you can excise a section of your memories and why that was ever a good idea and what it means. Do you just rip a page out of a notebook, ball it up, and throw it in the corner?"

Armaeus's gaze rested on me, but I knew he no longer saw me. His gaze was fixed on a far-off point through me, his mind working through a thousand and one calculations. In that moment, he looked so achingly like the Magician of old, it made my heart hurt. Fortunately, my head was pissed off enough it superseded my heart, because nobody had time for that.

"Your anger is unwarranted, Miss Wilde," he said again, far too mildly. "I fail to understand how it contributes to our current—"

"I'm *not* angry," I countered, bottling up all my anger and shoving it far to the back of my brain for later fermentation. "I'm in a full-on panic attack. I am a member of the Arcana Council, and over the past year and change, with your careful guidance, I've been a science fair project of epic proportions. I've learned skills I didn't know were possible. I've developed abilities that literally set my hair on fire."

He scowled. "I should not have allowed that. It was too dangerous for an ordinary mortal to undertake."

I gaped at him. Since when had I become an ordinary mortal? At every turn, Armaeus had told me there was no limit to my potential. That was okay, because he was installed as the head of the Council and, worst case, he could help me work through any issues should I end up exploding a beaker in the chemistry lab. What was going on here?

Only the obvious, I suddenly realized. Armaeus had *forgotten who I was*. Who I was, what I could do, and even what I might be able to do once my super-secret decoder ring came in the mail. And now he was staring at me with absolute curiosity, wondering what I would say next. Because he *didn't know*.

I clenched my hands into fists against the deep pool of sorrow this insight opened up within me, catching me off guard. I would not cry, I would not react, I would not anything, I resolved. I. Would. *Not*.

"Okay, let's set all that aside for the moment," I finally managed, my voice sounding only slightly strangled. "The bottom line is, you've forgotten me. Everything about me. And from what I'm picking up, you didn't plan on doing any of this after all. Maybe you don't remember this part either, but that's not like you. You plan for everything."

He quirked a smile. "I prefer to."

"But you didn't here. Why not?"

Armaeus blew out a long breath. "I simply don't know, Miss Wilde. From what I've been able to gather from Kreios, you and I were quite close."

I looked at him in horror. "You asked the *Devil* to give you dirt on our relationship?" Aleksander Kreios had many foibles, but one of his most enduring was a long and unremitting desire to tell someone exactly the truth they most sought to hear. Very, very rarely was that truth as reassuring as the person hoped it would be. "What did he tell you?"

"Only one thing," Armaeus said levelly. "That you had allowed me to read your mind before, and that if I wanted to understand our past, it would be fastest if you allowed me to read it again."

My mental barriers, already locked down tight, suddenly bulged out about six times thicker, like a blowfish in a flop sweat. The panic that shot through me at the very thought of Armaeus rifling through my brain left me quivering, and I forced myself to stay in my chair, staring at him, instead of fleeing the building as I so desperately wanted to do.

"No," I said flatly.

He tilted his head. "He also said there was likely no way you would allow me access to your mind. I find this curious."

"And I find the Devil to be a pain in the ass. That's more relevant." The panic wasn't going away, unfortunately. I felt my hands begin to tingle in my pockets, the shard of Nul Magis throbbing in my right palm. I'd caught that curious enchanted splinter from a sorcerer bent on destroying the magic ability in a rival, and it tended to react whenever there was too much magic being flung in my direction. Like now.

"You're afraid of me," Armaeus said quietly, his tone edged with dismay and what sounded like genuine concern. "I've hurt you, haven't I?"

"Oh, for the love…" I cast my gaze away from him, taking my turn at staring at the wall. "I don't want to have this conversation."

"I think you can see, for the benefit of the mission that we're about to undertake, it's a conversation that needs to happen."

He'd caught me quite neatly in the trap, and I knew it. Opening my mind to him *would* be the fastest way for Armaeus to remember the events of what had happened between us, but there was a very distinct flaw to that plan, which he clearly was discounting, but I couldn't quite.

I swung my gaze back to him. "You read minds all the time, right? It's a thing with you."

Whatever he'd expected me to say, it wasn't that. "It's certainly a skill I've derived great benefit from over the years, of course," he demurred.

"And the information you get, how do you know that it's accurate? Eyewitness accounts are notoriously flaky."

"Not all of them," he countered. "There are some accounts that are cool and rational and accurate as far as they can be. When there is a great deal of emotion or energy around information I seek, I take the consensus among several parties."

"Okay, well, then you've laid out the problem. Thing one, no one has ever accused me of being cool and rational. And my eyewitness account of our *association*, as you call it, is definitely not cool and rational. It's colored by all sorts of emotions that have fogged the past, confused my memories, created willful denials and equally willful manipulations of our shared history so that what I remember may or may not even be accurate, let alone useful."

"I assure you, I am well accustomed to sorting through the vagaries of human emotion."

His nonchalance made my stomach clench. "Thing two," I continued on, feeling the sweat trickle down my back. "There's nobody who can give you a consensus of our relationship because the most important bits didn't have an audience."

Perhaps not surprisingly, his gaze lit with interest. "We had an emotional relationship, and a physical one. That was...reckless of me. You would not have been prepared for that."

I made a face. "See, this is exactly the kind of thing I'm talking about. I've had *plenty* of experience with you, enough to note that it isn't unreasonable for you to have thought at one time that our relationship was reckless. But we still *had* that relationship. It wasn't something you undertook without careful consideration either, though you certainly pushed the physical barriers between us early and often."

He frowned. "I would not have done that unless there was an urgent need to advance your abilities. And even then, I would have told you why I was doing what I was doing."

"Yeah, well, let's just say that I was focused a little too much on what you were doing and not so much on what you were saying. Regardless, the beginning of our relationship was extremely fraught. Obviously, there was a sexual attraction, but when we started acting on it..." I broke off, a sudden wave of embarrassment overtaking me. I could feel my cheeks flush, and now my hands were no longer sparking, they were cold and clammy. "I can't even believe I'm telling you this. I can't believe I *have* to tell you this."

"If you would simply let me read your mind, I could spare you the embarrassment. It would take a matter of seconds."

Perversely, that upset me too. "I know you've been the Magician for an awfully long time, Armaeus, but just as a point of reference, not too many women would like to hear that you can hoover up your entire multi-year relationship with them in a matter of seconds. But moving on from that, my initial issue still holds. My perspective of what happened between us is flawed. I am flawed. I'm a basket case of neuroses and anxieties which have done a good job keeping me alive, but which are not necessarily useful in getting a clear-eyed perspective on what has happened between us. And there's nobody to tell you otherwise until you remember our relationship on your own."

"But—"

"Why did you *forget* me?" The question was out again before I could restrain it, and it carried a level of raw emotion that finally broke through the Magician's façade. He looked at me sharply, as if seeing me for the first time, and true remorse clouded his expression in a way I'd never seen before.

"Miss Wilde, I assure you, it was not something I did lightly."

"But you don't *know* that," I countered. "You don't know who I am. At all. Wiping me so cleanly from your memory banks was a deliberate act on your part. You don't know if you did it lightly or not."

"That…that's not true." His earnestness caught me up short, piercing the shroud of self-pity I was currently draping around myself.

"I am experiencing pain at this moment," the Magician continued, the wonder in his voice somewhat mitigating the impact of his statement. His eyes widened as he looked at me. "I'm enduring physical reactions consistent with great loss and great sadness. That has never happened before when I've tried to recall the memories I've released. I don't know its significance."

I passed a hand over my forehead, feeling as limp as a rag doll. "Well, it's not like I can help you out with that."

He watched me even more keenly. "You don't want to share your memories with me for another reason. Can you tell me what that reason is?"

"Oh, will you stop," I sighed. He was right, of course. I was being completely truthful when I told him that my filter of our relationship would probably not be the most accurate assessment of what really went on. I made no apologies for that. But there was also the very nature of our personal relationship to consider, which had been forged under a set of unique circumstances. The memories that I would share with him would not create a reinstatement of the Armaeus I'd known before. It would create a new and different Magician, working off a set of premises that originated outside himself. I didn't want that. It'd be like programming a computer instead of knowing somebody chose to feel the way he did because it was how he felt.

All this was *way* too much emo for me to actually explain, of course. "There's got to be another way. What else can give you the information you need without you spelunking through my mind that way?"

His brows went up. "There *are* other events I cannot recall that you might," he acknowledged. "At the moment I lost my memories, Kreios advised me you were there. He gave me a partial accounting of what he saw, but he was not focused on me at the time. Were you?"

I grimaced. "I was. You were in the middle of a city park in Dublin, Ireland, helping us take down the ancient gods of the Irish. You don't remember any of that?"

"Actually, I do," he said, surprising me. "Up until I moved to the center of the green. There was a bright light, and then I woke up in Dr. Sells's care."

"Oh," I said. "I...well, I can help you there. I can show you that—only that." I could, right? I could compartmentalize, keep everything safe that needed to stay safe, while sharing information that the Magician legitimately needed.

Without saying anything more, he reached out and placed a hand on mine, and I let my mental barriers slip before I could reconsider. It took a second, no more. I felt Armaeus's touch as a fleeting presence in my mind, retreating almost as soon as it took hold. He looked at me in horror.

"My dear Miss Wilde," he whispered, his eyes tortured. "I am so sorry."

CHAPTER TEN

O h, will you *stop*," I protested, kicking myself for whatever errant emotions and memories had slipped past my control. "It wasn't that bad."

The words had barely had time to coalesce between us when a tinkle of bells sounded throughout the house. I stiffened, pulling back. "What's that?"

Armaeus didn't move for a long moment, then seemed to shake himself back to reality. "That would be the team I summoned. They landed at Charles de Gaulle forty-five minutes ago. I'm surprised they got here so quickly."

"Who—"

"We're not finished with this discussion, Miss Wilde," Armaeus said quietly. "Please know I will work to make right all that I have done to wrong you."

That seemed a little more ominous than necessary, but Armaeus was already standing and turning toward the front of the house. I took an extra second to rub my hands over my face, surprised at how wrung out I felt. I didn't remember much about the moments leading up to the Magician's collapse at St. Stephen's Green. He'd been attacked by the ancient gods we'd assembled to push back beyond the veil, back into the In Between and beyond. His assailants had attempted to turn back the Magician with a powerful electric current, but Armaeus was made of energy. Most of their assault, he'd absorbed. The rest, he'd endured. He'd been hurt, but how badly, I hadn't known. I'd only known I needed to get to him, get to him above all other things, that he was the most important part of my universe.

Was that what he'd seen when he'd read my mind? Was that even useful?

I shoved myself back from the table and set off after him. I could hear raised voices in the foyer, but it wasn't until I neared the front of the house that I truly focused on who Armaeus had assembled to help vanquish the Shadow Court. Then I stepped into the room, caught sight of the four newcomers, and was nearly bowled over by six foot seven inches of pure sartorial perfection.

"Dollface!"

Nikki Dawes would be impressive no matter where she showed up, but for Paris, she brought her A game. Her hair was now styled into a close-cropped, gamine black bob, which paired perfectly with her black-and-white minidress, the top cut into a halter style that showed off her powerful arms. Her legs were bare and gleaming with some sort of glittery lotion visible above the tops of her jet-black thigh-high fabric boots. I had no clue how she kept those up on her legs unless the secondary ingredient of her lotion was glue, but as always, she pulled it off.

She hugged me longer than was technically necessary, but as I instinctively shifted back, she hissed, "We gotta talk." Then she leaned away from me with a broad smile, giving my shoulders a squeeze. The smile didn't reach her eyes. I knew why, and it didn't have anything to do with the information she had to share with me.

Like most midlevel Connecteds, Nikki's psychic abilities tended to focus on a very narrow set of skills. In her case, she could read the memories of anyone she touched. The memories, not the minds, which was an important distinction, and one that had been particularly helpful in her former life as a Chicago cop, well before her years as a Vegas-based psychic. With her embrace, I knew she had access to any memories I wanted to share with her, and the ones she swept up from the surface of my mind apparently knocked her back a step. I wasn't feeling very forthcoming today, so that was all I wanted to share. She knew me well enough not to pry until I was ready. Nikki always knew what to do and when to do it. And apparently, she had intel I needed to hear.

But not yet. As I emerged from her embrace, I was surprised to see the other team members Armaeus had assembled, which included the Devil, the Fool…and a completely unexpected man hovering at the front door, looking at the foyer like it was going to bite him. "Uh, Brody?"

"Before you ask, no. I don't know why I'm here," Detective Brody Rooks said gruffly, shifting his gaze to glower at the Magician. "I've already got a job. A job I love. A job I'm *good* at."

The Magician merely smiled. "The Las Vegas Metropolitan Police Department has very graciously allowed you to be on loan for the foreseeable future. I'm surprised they didn't share that with you."

"They did share it with me." As usual, Brody wore a rumpled gray suit over a clean white button-down and a tie of undetermined provenance. His sandy-brown hair was as tousled as his jacket, and his blue eyes were electric with annoyance. "They were practically jumping up and down to share it with me. But you don't just get randomly assigned as a special liaison to *Interpol*, Armaeus. That shit takes time and paperwork, and none of it was in play before yesterday, I know for the God's honest truth. Yet now, suddenly, I'm here."

"I'm sorry you don't approve of my methods."

"What I don't approve of is you playing fast and loose with institutions you don't plan on taking care of when shit goes south." Brody looked around the room, his gaze resting worriedly on me. He clearly knew the same thing Nikki did, whatever it was, but he jabbed his finger at the Fool. "And this guy is a federal investigation waiting to happen, and wayyyy too lax with his security protocols, you ask me. Which means you guys *want* people to know what you're up to."

"Okay, time out," I said. I didn't say it particularly loudly, but there was a weird shimmy to the walls, and everyone looked at me, none more sharply than the Magician. I was beginning to have a weird "outside" voice crop up when I got angry, and I really hoped I wouldn't start spewing demons from my mouth by the time this was done. "What do you all know that I don't—and don't start," I said warningly to Nikki, who snapped her mouth shut and winked at me, clearly deciding whatever quip she had loaded in response to that question wasn't worth it given the tension in the room.

No one else stepped into the sudden silence, so I fixed my gaze on Kreios. "Spill."

The Devil was perhaps one of the Arcana Council's most striking members, both in his appearance and the sheer joy he took in his job. Unlike Nikki, he hadn't modified his usual appearance to acknowledge his arrival in one of the fashion capitals of the world. Then again, it would be difficult to improve upon his everyday appearance. Tall, tawny, and sleekly muscular, Aleksander Kreios looked like a Mediterranean surf god just in from the beach. He wore his usual long linen shirt, worn khakis, and heavy sandals, but somehow still managed to look like he should be on the cover of *Forbes Magazine*. Or at least *GQ*.

"It's been a busy twenty-four hours, you could say," he allowed. "When you sent across the image of the young woman's tattoo, it set off a cascade of events that grew ever more intriguing with each new development. Armaeus, as he's no doubt shared with you, recognized the symbol immediately and, with the opening of that doorway, gained the awareness of a certain lapse in his memory that he had heretofore not recognized."

"Yeah, we covered that part."

Kreios nodded. "Further investigation of said symbol took us quite quickly and unexpectedly to the arcane black market, and a rich—yet exclusively oral—tradition of an organization so powerful that it left no record of its transactions, yea, though they were many, since its incarnation in 1850—or reincarnation, I should say. The Shadow Court."

"The Shadow Court." I narrowed my eyes. "I played in the arcane black market for a very long time, Kreios, and I didn't recognize that name when Armaeus mentioned it to me. You want to explain that?"

"You're not alone," Simon put in. The newest member of the Arcana Council before me, he had ascended to his position in the 1980s, and his attire matched it. A close-fitting skullcap topped his messy dark hair, and his pale skin practically glowed with the blue computer light that comprised most of the radiation he got on any given day. He was the Arcana Council's resident computer geek, hacker, tech guru, and infrastructure whiz, and he had his fingers in every network that spanned the globe—the internet, dark web, and arcane web included. "I found nothing online or in any kind of archive, and the organization has assiduously worked its collective ass off to keep people from naming it. From what we were able to glean from the oral record, though, the heretofore unnamed Shadow Court has most recently been in operation since the mid eighteen hundreds and presents a credible threat."

"Threat to whom?" I asked.

"Everyone who crosses their path," Kreios said, taking up the story. "But the spell that quite literally took them out of circulation—important wording there, if I do say so—was powerful. Those members of the Arcana Council who should have recalled them because they were present during their early development, the High Priestess, the Hierophant, Death—have no recollection, much like Armaeus. There's only one way that's possible."

"Someone was working from the inside," I said. "But someone stronger than all of you combined? There's no way." My head was spinning. "Abigail Strand wasn't powerful enough to generate that kind of spell."

"Nevertheless, Abigail Strand was Justice of the Arcana Council from 1850 to 1853. There is no mention of the Shadow Court even among the dead after that time," Kreios said.

"Among the dead," I echoed.

"I'm telling you, we tapped every network out there," Simon offered helpfully. "Whoever said dead men tell no tales was, you know, wrong."

"Jesus, Mary, and Joseph," Brody groaned. "I don't even know how you people can live with half the shit you do."

Armaeus took up the story. "But the accounts of the deceased prior to 1852 were fairly uniform in their description of the organization. Much like any of the dozens of syndicates that sprang up during the Middle Ages or well before, the Shadow Court had its own assassins' guild, deep financial pockets, and dark machinations, rites, and protocols. From what we have been able to infer, the Arcana Council, including myself, were aware but not particularly bothered by the Shadow Court, except when they became too powerful for their own good and attempted to meddle in our affairs."

"Oh, just then," I said drily.

"It was less often than you might think," countered Armaeus. "For most of their existence in this newest incarnation, the Shadow Court had no specific agenda against the Arcana Council, but merely wanted to advance the interests of the Connected, particularly the wealthiest Connected. This was not an especially distinguishing feature."

"So why go to the trouble of erasing themselves from everybody's memory banks?"

"A very intriguing question." Armaeus nodded. "And one that proves even more interesting given they have only just come to light now. I can't imagine it was part of their plan to be discovered."

I scowled. "Gotta say, I kind of disagree with you on that. Not too many people knew I was in Paris. Nobody outside the Council, I'm thinking, and you guys had only the most basic information. Checking out Armaeus's digs here was a side trip for me, not the goal."

"And what did you learn in Paris?" Armaeus asked. "Specifically."

I eyed him. I'd managed to escape any deeper inquiry regarding Mercault only because the Magician was obsessing so heavily with his own lost memories. But while I could keep him from reading my personal memories, there was nothing to stop him from systematically blowing through the city of Paris and identifying anyone with a recollection of me. Mercault wasn't a strong Connected either. It would take Armaeus about twenty seconds to discover the truth. So I went ahead and gave him the rest of the story. "I told you that Mercault's family has records of two of your memory lapses. Apparently, you were a changed man afterward. When you removed your memories, your personality received an upgrade as well."

"An...upgrade," Armaeus said thoughtfully.

I didn't elaborate. "Mercault also knew someone was following me, but not who, exactly. He needed the guise of a financial transaction between us in order to share all this intel with me, by the way—it apparently was the kind of honesty that only money could buy."

Kreios smiled widely, leaning forward. "My favorite kind."

"Wait a minute," Brody said. "Why'd you need to bribe Mercault for the truth? I thought he was on your team."

"Ah, there are teams, and then there are teams, Detective Brody," Kreios answered for me. "Mercault is at heart a dealer of rare antiquities and artifacts, and there is nothing worth more than information for which he's been paid to keep quiet. It would take a very impressive lever to pry it away from him."

"Or you could have blasted it out of him," Brody countered.

"Not without consequences." The Magician was now eyeing me again, and I could almost hear the well-developed gears in his mind turning. Either that or he was once again going to tell me I was too weak to blast anything more than a bottle cap. "You wanted to provide him with a legitimate higher bid. What was it?"

"What it always is," I said dismissively, though the hurricane goddess icon now hanging around my neck felt impossibly heavy. "An artifact and some gold. And in return, he gave me the information I was seeking, which corroborated what I feared. Someone's hunting me down. And by me, I mean us."

"The Shadow Court?" Nikki asked.

"It's the only new player we've discovered out there, and I know all the usual players," I said. "But they moved quickly after I left Mercault's. I hadn't gotten halfway across the arrondissement before I picked up a tail, and there were more of them waiting for me in the Jardin du Luxembourg. They would have needed time to get set up there, time and information."

Brody grunted. "Mercault sold you out ahead of time."

"Probably." I nodded. "But he also probably needed to do so, to keep his own reputation intact. And his betrayal was pretty minor. Most likely he let it be known I was asking questions and that he would do what was needed to get me to Paris. He did that, but while he was up, he tipped me off to what would be waiting for me."

"Both ends against the middle," Nikki said.

I nodded. "He's been playing this game for a long time."

"We've got extra eyes on him now," Simon put in. "So far there's been no trouble, but we're looking inside and out. Mercault wakes up dead tomorrow, we'll know about it before he does."

"Which takes us to the next step in this plan," Kreios said. "It appears that our good friends at Interpol are not quite so helpless as they would lead us to believe. There is a splinter group within the organization now tracking the activities of the Connected technoceutical trade more assiduously than we anticipated. This group is gearing up for a more active role in pursuing those Connecteds on whom they can hang a drug charge. As it so happens, they stumbled on just the man they were looking for to join their team: the illustrious Detective Rooks."

I blinked, swiveling my head to stare at Brody. "You joined Interpol?"

He grimaced. "I did not join Interpol."

The doorbell rang. "Who the hell is that?" Brody asked, exasperated.

"Interpol," Armaeus said succinctly. "Your new team."

Chapter Eleven

That's our cue to bounce," Nikki announced, linking her arm in mine and steering me toward the rear of the house. "Sara's track record with Interpol isn't great, and I'll just distract the poor dears. This place have a back door?"

"You're not just going to leave me here to deal with these—" Brody began, then broke off, sputtering. "I hate it when you do that."

I turned to see what distracted him, only to find a very officious-looking man in a crisp dark suit straightening his cuff links where the Devil had been standing not ten seconds before.

"You'll find it can work to your advantage more often than not," Kreios advised Brody, still speaking in his indolent Mediterranean drawl. "In case you're wondering, I am the special assistant of the US ambassador to France. All the proper notifications have been made to put you into your advisory position for the agency. I must tell you that the pay is less than adequate, but the perks can be well worth it."

"How is this even happening?" Brody groaned. "There simply have to be processes for this kind of thing."

"Oh, there are, Detective Rooks," Kreios assured him as Nikki and I stepped out of the foyer and into the cool confines of the long, art-lined hallway. "We've merely sidestepped them."

"Poor Detective Delish," Nikki chortled in a low voice beside me, sounding completely unrepentant. "He doesn't know what's about to hit him."

I eyed her. "And you do?"

"That's part of what I needed to talk about, but only part. How far back does this house go, anyway? We need to get outside and stat, and I don't want you utilizing Crispy Express to get us there."

"Why?"

"Because we don't know who's watching us anymore. If these Shadow Court people are as big-time as we fear, Simon says they'll notice spikes of magic anywhere that's unwarded. Here we go." Nikki and I had reached the back porch where Armaeus and I had resolutely not eaten breakfast only a few minutes before. She released my arm long enough to grab a couple of napkin-wrapped croissants and eyed the coffee service longingly. "Who in the world uses real china anymore? He seriously needs a to-go cup service."

Almost before she finished speaking, two large recyclable cups with lids appeared next to the complicated-looking coffeepot. Despite myself, I felt a little thrill of pleasure at the gesture, minor as it was. No matter what was going on at the front of the house, Armaeus had been listening into our conversation. That felt right. That felt normal.

"Now that's what I call a smart house," Nikki quipped, handing the croissants to me while she scooped up the coffee cups. Gesturing me down the gracious stairs into the manicured garden, she kept up a steady clip even as she swapped the topmost croissant for one of the cups. The coffee was hot, rich, and laden with cream. Not how I usually took it, but delicious all the same.

"So since we're doing this the hard way, lay it on me," Nikki said. "I take it there's no breakthrough in Armaeus's memory regarding you?"

"That would be negative. He doesn't know anything except for what I'm willing to show him."

Her eyes widened. "You let him read your mind?"

"Only for an account of what happened in Dublin — and believe me, that was enough. Best I can tell, the moment I let my guard down, he sponged up enough of my memories and the emotions I'd attached to them to make some educated guesses about our relationship. But he doesn't know anything on his own." Which broke my heart a little, frankly, to know that Armaeus's first thought was to try to grasp something — anything — that he could from me, to try to understand the emotions he was feeling for a woman he couldn't remember. In some ways, that almost meant more than him remembering outright.

Sighing, I glanced around the park. "This is still part of his property, isn't it? How do we know he's not listening in right now?"

"Technically, we don't. He could have the trees bugged. But I believe he'll have his hands full with the Interpol agents."

"Since when?"

"Since we discovered the little tattoo you found, or the edge of the tattoo, whatever it is, and I drew it freehand for Brody to see clearly. Apparently, that design has shown up in an unnerving number of places. Specifically, on the personal belongings of agents, executives, government heads, multinational organization flunkies, cops, doctors, spies, hairdressers, you name it."

"You're kidding me."

"I am not. Once we knew what we were looking for, it was everywhere—and still nowhere, because nobody was looking but us. We got the information we did because of Simon's technology and the Magician's super laser vision, but no one would have been able to see it ordinarily. No one would be looking for it."

"I saw it." I shook my head. "I still don't know how I caught it on my phone, though. There's no third-eye filter on my camera, and she works for the Shadow Court. I mean, shouldn't she have wards?"

"She probably did." She waved her croissant. "But you decked her."

She took a large bite, chewing enthusiastically as I frowned. "Well, yes, I decked her. What does that have to do with anything?"

"Right hand or left? It was right, amiright?"

I had to think about that. "Yes. My left hand was pinned. I'm also right-handed, so it would almost certainly be my right hand."

"Well, there you go." She finished her croissant and took a long swig of her coffee. "That Nul Magis shard you have in your right hand dropped the woman's cover long enough for you to get that snap. She was rocking a kind of glamour that ordinarily would not have been displaced, except your Tinker Toys are better than hers. As they should be."

"I...I guess that makes sense." I munched on my own pastry. "The symbol's there, but no one sees it. I wouldn't have seen it except that I temporarily displaced her glamour, and even then, the pic itself looks like no big deal except to a high-level Connected. But after I catch sight of it, Armaeus recognizes it and then he goes looking and we find it's everywhere, all over the world. Even in Interpol."

"Especially in Interpol. It's like they have a mini cabal inside an agency that most people treat as an afterthought, to put it kindly. But their anonymity is part of the problem."

"Interpol agents have access wherever they want…"

"They do, and they're everywhere and nowhere. Always on the fringes, never in the action. There's been some noise about upping their relevance, but that never comes to anything. They're ghosts."

I grimaced. There seemed to be all sorts of ghosts in the world these days. "So Armaeus wants someone on the inside."

"Armaeus wants more than that. The double whammy of you being out of the country and Armaeus not operating at full speed has given me a lot more one-on-one time with Kreios. Since Armaeus's memory lapse, he's been looking at everyone and everything with a fresh eye, including Officer Hotness."

"Why? Brody isn't Connected. Much." It was true, and no one should know more than me. I'd known the man since I was fourteen years old. He'd been a rookie in the Memphis police department, and I'd been a kid with a deck of cards who wanted to help find a string of missing children who'd made the local news. He'd been stuck with me — and we found the kids. Most of them. Now, nearly fourteen years later, he was still working with the local psychics. Which was awesome of him, but…

"Wait a minute," I said, looking at her. "Armaeus thinks Brody's some kind of psychic whisperer? That's why he wants him in Interpol?"

"Bingo." She saluted me with her coffee cup. "Nobody will suspect Officer Ogleworthy of doing anything but his job, which is counseling a group that supposedly knows nothing about psychics or how to handle the loony people."

"But they know him. He's been involved in several cases — cases where I also was involved."

"Tragedy of circumstance, my friend. The fact remains that Brody isn't Connected. Much. He's been amped a little due to his association with you and the Council, but what's a guy going to do? He happens to be based in Vegas. He's never betrayed a word of the Council's existence, or yours beyond you being a psychic who actually makes money at the game and who also occasionally provides the LVMPD with intel. He's shown up in some interesting places, sure, but he's mostly been at home tending the hearth fires. He's not on anyone's radar."

"Interpol agents know him."

"Those agents are out in the field, not in the mother ship." Nikki's brow furrowed. "What are you worried about?"

"I don't know," I confessed. And I didn't. Brody didn't need me to protect him, certainly. He was a cop, and a long-standing one. He had worked in worse situations than this. In all our shared challenges, he hadn't been put in danger either. Not much, anyway.

"He doesn't seem happy about it," I finally offered lamely.

"Oh, give me a break. His buns wouldn't know what to do with themselves if they weren't hot and crossed." Nikki grinned and waved me off. "He's just mad because he's got cases to clear back home, and he doesn't want them handed off to some numbwit, which, for the record, they probably won't be because no one wants to handle his cases. Psychics may have hit the mainstream to us, but not to the common people, and certainly not to the bureaucracy of government or law enforcement."

"It's coming, though."

"That may be." Nikki shrugged. "But not today."

We stopped at the edge of the park, having finally reached what seemed to be the edge of Armaeus's property. Nikki looked around, apparently satisfied, then eyed me again. "There's more."

"I figured."

"Well, you should also figure you're not going to like it, because you won't. Armaeus tried to enter the library at Justice Hall and damned near set himself on fire in the process. He incinerated the front office as well."

"The front..." I stared at her. "When was this? He didn't say anything."

"Yeah, I didn't figure he would. It was yesterday, right before he split. I didn't know about it when we talked. He got the mess cleaned up, but there was a hell of a noise, by all accounts, and he didn't bother to wipe that from the memory of the hotel guests staying on the floors beneath Justice Hall. So they all heard a big boom with nothing to show for it."

I grimaced. "Airplane maneuvers?"

"That's what the Palazzo's management decided, yup, and shared as an official announcement," Nikki said. "Just a little broken sound barrier, nothing more. But the important part of this story is that Armaeus didn't get in."

"Was anyone hurt?" I had a librarian on staff at Justice Hall at all times, and she had young assistants. If Mrs. French or any of the boys had been there when the Magician had detonated his Open Sesame bomb...

"Okay, that's an important part too," Nikki allowed. "But the answer is no. Mrs. French told him he wouldn't be able to enter the inner sanctum of the stacks, told him she couldn't let him in physically without you being there. Abigail's wards were that strong."

"Yeah." This being the same Abigail who'd apparently managed to cut away the existence of an entire organization from Armaeus's mind, she clearly was more than the Magician thought she was. "What was he looking for?"

"Mrs. French asked him the same thing, which made him...laugh."

Nikki's emphasis on the last word made me glance at her. "The Magician doesn't laugh. He smiles sardonically and lifts an eyebrow. That's about it."

"Honestly, I think his reaction startled Mrs. French more than the explosion, and the explosion did a number on her. But when she asked the Magician what he was looking for, he replied that he didn't know. And that struck him as so funny, he doubled over, nearly choking with laughter."

"Choking with laughter? Or simply choking?"

"To hear Mrs. French tell the tale, he was thoroughly amused. And not terribly concerned either, more intrigued by the fact that he couldn't get inside the library. To him, it's proof positive that there's something important in there that he needs to get his hands on. But it's a big place, and if he doesn't know what he's looking for..."

"It's the perfect hiding place," I agreed. "But for what? Justice Hall has some books and manuscripts deemed too dangerous for public consumption, but those are all accounted for, I thought. Other than that, it's filled with information related to crimes against fellow Connecteds. The complaints, criticisms, accusations, wails and lamentations of the victims, that sort of thing. All the cases I haven't gotten to yet, in short. How can that help Armaeus?"

"Miss Wilde. Miss Dawes."

We turned to see Armaeus standing at the edge of the clearing, Kreios and Simon beside him, but only Kreios and Simon. "Where's Brody?" I asked.

"Off to his onboarding interview, I suspect," Kreios said. He had returned to his usual appearance, looking far more comfortable for it.

"Wired to the gills with the latest tech too," Simon interjected excitedly, clearly unable to contain himself. "If all goes right, we'll be able to find this interior cell pretty quickly. The ground agents know nothing about it, the cops know nothing about it, governments know nothing about it. Except for those who were in on the game. But we will. Soon."

"And we don't have any intel so far on what the goals of the Shadow Court are?"

Armaeus interjected, "There are two likely options. One is that they're looking to suppress those who make magic, similar to organizations that have existed for thousands of years. The other option is more intriguing."

I rolled my eyes. "If by intriguing you mean more of a pain in the ass, fantastic. We already solved the problem of a bunch of Connecteds wanting to fly their freak flag too soon. We can't be doing this every time we turn around."

"That's why I find it intriguing," the Magician countered. "If this group has been in existence for hundreds of years, then even if we don't understand how it's happening, why haven't we already seen them manifest in the form of more Connecteds reaching their pinnacle of ability or acting out in a more aggressive way? Why are they suddenly acting now? What's changed?"

"In the last few months? Try just about everything," Nikki deadpanned. "We have new members on the Council, waterspouts of unrest among the Connecteds, an uptick in activity on the arcane black market, and a surge of megalomaniacs who are making their bid for power. Take your pick."

"Wait...that's it," I said, turning to Nikki. "That last one. That's important."

"Megalomaniacs?"

"Exactly. What's the job of Justice? To answer the call of the oppressed. Since I've come on board, that's what I've done. I've stopped individuals who were taking it upon themselves to change the destiny of other Connecteds against their will. I mean, granted, this is a little different. This is a faceless organization, not a person."

"Behind every organization, you'll eventually find a face," Kreios said.

"Then there you go." Unexpectedly, I found myself thinking of Emma Fearon walking through the streets of Paris, wearing my face and body to reassure those coming to the city seeking help. *My* help. Help I wasn't giving.

"There's only one way to figure out who that face is," Simon put in. When we all turned to him, he grinned. "I mean, it's a game, man. You gotta play the game. Armaeus has forgotten four things: something in 1478, something in 1571, these Shadow Court people in 1852 or '53 or whatever, and his memory of Sara. Am I right? You haven't forgotten anything else?"

He asked this last question of Armaeus, who grimaced.

"I don't believe so, but you see the issue with relying on me to make that assertion."

"But now that you've got the dates, you've already started making connections," Simon said. "You gotta assume 1478 is important because of the Spanish Inquisition. So we start there. Or *you* start there. The year 1571 could mean anything, but if you do a search on the most important monarch in that year, you get Elizabeth the First. So, we start there."

That tallied with Mercault's comments, but I still eyed Simon, a little aghast. "You're relying on a random Google search to start this investigation?"

"You could as easily flip a coin, I'm telling you," Simon insisted. "All it took was one glance at a symbol and Armaeus was on to the Shadow Court. I'm thinking it won't take much more than that for the other two dates. His memories are gone, but he's the Magician — nothing can stay hidden forever from him."

A low buzz of panic whirred to life in my stomach at Simon's words, but he kept going.

"So, you guys go to Spain, and we'll go to England, and maybe by the time we reconvene, we'll know what the hell is going on. If we do, great. If we don't, we're probably dead anyway and the world is in chaos and game over."

I winced. "Game over doesn't sound really good. How long do we have?"

"Not long," Simon said. "The Shadow Court knows about the other two lapses, I bet. The minute they see Armaeus is tracking those down, they'll start worrying about what else he's remembering, especially now that you've been attacked once."

"Twice," I corrected. "There was a punk at the train station trying to snatch a Connected, and I stopped him. His eyes went white, and he welcomed me to Paris. The young woman at the church who was providing refuge for the Connecteds told me they called these white-eyed kidnappers 'ghosts' and said they're coming out of the woodwork. I don't know if that's relevant."

Simon sighed and tilted his head, his eyes getting the distracted look of a gamer making deep, strategic connections. "I don't either, but I'll check into it. And either way — we've now got less time than I thought. So we better start playing this game to win, and fast."

CHAPTER TWELVE

I t was two a.m. in Barcelona, Spain, so of course, the entire Gothic Quarter was hopping. But even if the people of the city didn't sleep, apparently museum curators did.

"There's no way the synagogue will be open," I murmured as Armaeus and I moved through the tight, winding streets off the Plaça de Sant Jaume. The music and laughter of the busy square faded behind us as we approached the darker, older buildings of El Call, where our destination lay.

"Agreed," Armaeus said, his voice equally quiet but startling me nevertheless. He'd been deep in a meditative trance since we'd arrived in Spain hours earlier, and this was the first he'd spoken in hours.

"Oh, hey, you're back. Welcome to Spain."

He nodded. "Our destination remains the same regardless of the hour, Miss Wilde. Every mental trail I've attempted to follow in this country ends in those two rooms, and until I see them myself, I won't understand where to go next."

I peered down the ominous-looking alley. "Are you sure we're even in the right city?"

He shot a look at me, clearly startled. "Do you always doubt me so openly?"

"I do, actually. It's kind of one of my charms." My gaze shifted to the dark buildings encroaching on our walkway. At this point, we were one of only a few couples walking the quarter, the streets barely wide enough to allow two pedestrians to squeeze past each other. There would be no way any vehicle larger than a roller skate would be able to get back here.

Armaeus's low, rich voice rolled on beside me. "I have determined that the nature of the memories excised by my own hand has been markedly consistent. Arcana. Lore. Knowledge. The repository for such information is almost always a book."

"Or a scroll," I pointed out helpfully. "Or a fortune cookie."

"In fifteenth-century Spain, it would have been a book. The most well-known book of arcane lore that emerged from the country in the preceding centuries would have been the Zohar, the Book of Radiance."

"Ahhh…" I tried to call up my knowledge of the tome, but it was scant. "That's Jewish mysticism, right? The Kabbalah?"

"The Book of Radiance is extreme even for kabbalists. Some consider it pure apocrypha, and still others maintain its greatest teachings have been willfully withheld, a lost chapter secreted away to protect the masses."

That caught my attention. "Well, that's starting to sound more like it."

We stopped in front of a completely nondescript building fronted by our narrow alley. It looked…exactly like nothing at all. "Uhh…this is it?"

Armaeus reached out and laid a hand on the bricks, releasing a long, satisfied breath. "The Sinagoga Mayor is considered one of the oldest synagogues in Europe and was the center for Jewish life in Barcelona up until the purge of the Spanish Inquisition forced so many Jews to leave the city in the 1490s. According to most documentation, the synagogue was used as a storeroom in the intervening centuries."

"Yeah, but a storeroom for the lost chapter of a book that most traditional Jews would consider at a minimum goofy, and at an extreme heretical? That's kind of an interesting leap."

He glanced at me, his eyes somehow managing to gleam in the heavy darkness. "I have been reliably informed that I am kind of an interesting guy."

Once again, the strange, almost lighthearted humor of Armaeus 2.0 caught me off guard. Actually, I needed to amend that moniker. I didn't even know if this was Armaeus 2.0 I was experiencing, or if the Magician's sudden good-naturedness was part of the effect of having forgotten me.

Had I brought the man down somehow simply by existing in his memory? Was he better off without me? Happier?

My mouth tightened as I resolutely turned my gaze from Armaeus and stared at the wall. It was 2:00 a.m. in a snarl of dark, narrow streets that smelled like old stone and anguish. I was allowed to be neurotic.

"The door, Miss Wilde," Armaeus murmured.

I squinted where he pointed, but there was absolutely no lighting on this street. I fumbled in my pocket for my phone and directed the beam onto the heavy sealed door. There was nothing to indicate it was the opening to a famous synagogue.

"They're not all that big on signage, are they?"

"You can see the ancient letters here—and here," Armaeus said, pointing to chiseled indentations that arguably could have been letters at one point. "We're in the right place. Now we'll need to get inside. Which I cannot do, because I specifically warded myself against entering."

The certainty in his voice made me look at him curiously. "And you expect me to get us in? Because let me remind you, I'm no good as a Woober driver if I haven't been someplace before. I can assure you, I've never been here."

"You are Justice of the Arcana Council, and your call is to serve those who have been harmed by Connecteds." He rocked back on his heels and looked at me. "I intensely dislike involving you. I can sense you are not prepared for this challenge. But it must be done."

The rueful apology in Armaeus's tone knocked me off my pedestal of pain and back onto the field of annoyance. I tried to stuff down my impatience at his assessment of my apparently limited skillset, but the problem remained: I couldn't get into this place. Maybe the cards could offer a hint —

"Not the cards, Miss Wilde." Armaeus's voice stopped my hand as I edged it toward my pocket. "You don't need them."

"I do need them," I countered. "Because you're not giving me enough to work with, here. Granted, maybe you haven't seen the Justice process recently, but it hasn't changed so much since the process that Abigail used. You remember Justice Strand, right? The one who caused all this mess?"

His expression hardened, the look in his eyes going flat.

"I thought you did," I continued. "The way it goes, people have a problem, and they send that problem to me in my office at Justice Hall. It appears as a canister of information in a pneumatic tube, lots of whooshing and thumping. Very progressive for its time, and I haven't gotten around to changing it. But that's how it's done. No one whispers the lamentations of the damned to me out of creepy old stones in the middle of the night, giving me the secret door knock."

"That's only because you're not listening."

Armaeus raised his hand, and the world turned suddenly silent. There was no longer the sound of echoing footsteps or of faraway music and laughter. It was as if a shroud had been dropped over the Jewish quarter—or, not exactly that. It was more like the shroud of modern sound had been taken away. The silence was deep, echoing, and more than a little unnerving.

"What are you doing?" I whispered harshly. Every hair on my body was standing at attention, and I could only draw in the shortest of breaths. "This isn't exactly a good time for a teaching moment."

"Justice hears the cries of the people," Armaeus murmured again. "The Magician does not. I'm looking to find a man oppressed by those around him, an acolyte, a man who wants more than anything to share the truth, but who fears that truth might bring the ruination of his people. He's been damned by the very book his master wrote in a fugue of metaphysical passion, convinced it was delivered by God himself. The master rests, unaware of what he has wrought. The servant runs, not knowing what to believe."

As Armaeus spoke in a low, mesmerizing voice, I swayed toward the old stone wall, the heavy door fit into the stones. In my mind's, ah, ear, I could almost hear the mutterings of a man bent over, pale and worn, his arms clutching a sack he held against his body as if it held all the riches in Europe. *He is wrong, he is wrong, he must be wrong. Please save me, Father, he is wrong.*

I frowned as I lifted my hands and pressed them against the wall. Now that I was focusing, there was a rushing hiss of noise around me, the sound of prayers being lifted up in the old quarter—old, new, ancient, modern, in a wild mix of languages and accents, but none so loud as the prayer of the man who was slowly making his way up the dark street. "That's him," I murmured. "He's afraid of the manuscript he's carrying. He stole it. He fears the truth, and he fears the book. He wants it to be made right. Desperately."

The wraithlike man walked right through us, pausing only slightly to shudder, and stepped inside the door.

"Follow him."

Armaeus wasn't usually one to give commands like that, but in the sway of the spell he was wrapping around us, I nodded. I could see what the messenger saw as he stepped into the synagogue, and because I could see it, I could be there as well. But I watched for a moment longer as the man moved through the outer rooms and into a very modest-sized room, a sacred space where candles burned and incense hung heavy in the air. The image was so compelling, I stepped forward. Heat danced over my skin as I crackled Armaeus and me into the old synagogue.

The old synagogue had changed.

Overlaying the images I could still see because I was looking through the eyes of the man I followed was what looked like a tidy, timeworn space, a present-day chapel with pews and an altar and unlit candles. But the flickering shadow of the messenger still hastened forward, and I realized there was another person in that long-ago room. Clad in heavy, simple robes, a rabbi stood next to a burning bowl and watched the man approach with kind and knowing eyes. He reached out his hand, and the messenger thrust the bag at him, pausing only to receive a blessing before dropping to his knees.

"Please—please, you must read it," the messenger implored.

"It will be cleansed in fire," the holy man said, but this wasn't the answer the messenger was looking for.

"No! You must read—!" he insisted, but the holy man turned and, without any fanfare at all, set the manuscript into the burning salver. It immediately caught fire with a bright burst of light, making both men shrink back. Then the fire guttered out, and it was clear from the other flames in the room that the chapter remained in the salver. Charred, but otherwise unharmed.

The messenger groaned. "You must—"

The man slumped to the ground, and only then could I see what his dark cloak had hidden before. He was bleeding through his clothes.

The rabbi erupted into a flurry of movement, but the scene instantly evaporated in front of me. I came to, leaning against the wall, sweat dripping from my face as I coughed. "What the hell was that?"

"The visions you saw were a communication path I am not privy to, as I cannot read your mind, Miss Wilde. I find it fascinating that you were able to keep your barriers tightly in place despite the clear physical distress you were experiencing." He gestured to my damp hair and trembling body, and I hugged my arms around me.

"There was a man carrying a manuscript. The lost chapter, I assume. He was injured. I didn't realize that. In pain."

"He died over five hundred years ago," Armaeus said, not unkindly.

"Yeah, well, it wasn't a good way to go. But why could I hear him? For this to be a problem of Justice's, he had to have been assaulted by another Connected — a powerful one, intent on doing psychic harm. He certainly had enough physical harm done to him. This guy was sliced to shreds."

"There may have been wounds within as well. What happened to the book?"

"I…" I frowned and looked back blindly toward the center of the room, but the images were gone. The messenger had delivered the manuscript to the old rabbi, determined to understand it though he feared it all the same, and the man had promptly thrown the thing into the fire. The fire had not consumed the tome, however. It had made the manuscript glow incandescently bright, then had left it charred but intact. And the fire itself had almost melted away…

"That rabbi was Connected," I said. "Powerfully so."

"One of the most common places for men of magic to hide throughout the centuries was in the ranks of established churches," Armaeus said. "If this rabbi that you saw was a secret kabbalist, a follower of the practices of Jewish mysticism, he would be receptive to a lost section of the Zohar, particularly a manuscript that promised arcane teachings that only he would then know."

"Except he tried to burn it."

"Even in a synagogue only two rooms large, the walls have eyes," Armaeus countered, turning around. "There may have been other reasons too. The book could have been spelled by an outside hand, cursed, or he may have wanted to determine its authenticity. But after…?"

"The vision stops when the man died. He was the one who had been wronged, who was crying out for Justice." I shivered. Would I eventually find his request buried in the shelves of Justice Hall? Had whoever was Justice during the time when this man had lived heard his cry? If so, he or she hadn't come in time to do any good.

But the manuscript…the manuscript had been there. Bound in some sort of leather, thick with inscribed pages. It had been tested by the holy man and survived. What would the rabbi have done with it then?

Armaeus remained off to the side, running his fingers along the walls, as if the stones could speak. I quirked a glance at him. "Are those bricks talking to you?"

"Yes," he said drily. "They're saying the answer still lies within you. So maybe you should move it along."

I blinked in surprise, then realized he was joking again. "You know, I definitely liked you better when you remembered me." Still, I understood what he wanted. I pulled the deck of cards from my pocket and shuffled them as I scanned the rooms. "This place is insanely small for a synagogue."

"You've seen too many cathedrals."

I thought of Saint-Germain-des-Prés and the compact priest I'd met within its soaring walls. Father Jerome would have enjoyed this mission, without question. Though a devout believer himself, he was open to the beliefs of any and all who sought the true path. A lost chapter of the Zohar would have been catnip to him. "That's probably a true statement."

I pulled three cards from the deck, scanning each of them before I handed them over to Armaeus. "I'm not sure how much this helps us. We've got the Hierophant, the Tower, and the Seven of Swords. I was almost certain I was going to pull a card that indicated that the book had been hidden in the stones here, but none of these are leading me to believe that."

"The Hierophant," Armaeus mused. "A reference to the church, certainly. It traditionally represents the pontiff, but it could as easily mean another synagogue."

"Yes—but the Tower isn't a good sign. Was there a synagogue that burned down? Or exploded, somehow? If this is referencing the Jews themselves, they didn't do so well with the coming of the Inquisition. That manuscript could have been spirited out at any time. In fact, that's probably a good explanation for it. If I'd had it in my possession, I would have taken it out of Spain well before the Inquisition got rolling. The fires and death didn't reach Barcelona for a few years, after all. They would've had time."

"They would, but the energy of this city..." Armaeus shook his head. "There must be something more. What are we missing?"

I pulled another card, then frowned down at it. The Ten of Pentacles was generally one of the better cards to pull in the deck, the card of abundance and joy and the kind of enduring wealth that could keep your family rich for generations. But that wasn't helping me here. In fact, standing in this humble synagogue, the act of pulling such a card of obvious wealth felt almost obscene. It was exactly the opposite of what I would have expected to find.

"Miss Wilde?" Armaeus asked.

I flipped the card to him. "Money. A whole lot of money, spilling out around us, only we don't need money right now, we need...what?"

Armaeus was smiling again. While I really wasn't in the mood for another knock-knock joke, I figured I'd appreciate his humor more if I understood it.

He didn't make me wait long. "Where would you hide an artifact of unprecedented worth and unprecedented danger if you wanted to make sure no one would ever look for it?"

"Deep at the bottom of the ocean?"

He laughed. Once again, the sound was absolutely foreign coming from his lips. Foreign, but not bad, exactly. Lighter. Freer. Ever so slightly unnerving.

Was he happier for not knowing me?

Oblivious to the sudden lurch of pain in my chest, Armaeus spoke. "A reasonable choice, but not exactly the answer I was going for. No, I'd say that you'd hide it somewhere directly under the noses of those who feared it most. Not only would that ensure they'd never look for it so close by, it would also ensure that anyone interested in stealing the artifact for their own arcane use would be forced to go through the ranks of their enemies."

I tilted my head, trying to follow his logic. "So, for this missing book of Jewish mysticism, you're thinking the Catholic church?"

"Not any Catholic church," Armaeus said, holding up the Ten of Pentacles. "One that was all about family. La Sagrada Familia, right here in Barcelona.

CHAPTER THIRTEEN

B ack in the relative anonymity of predawn Barcelona, I employed my lesser-known but highly valuable skill of walking without watching where I was going as I searched on my phone, using the Magician to run interference between me and the wave of tourists. There were still way too many people out to be reasonable, but at least they didn't slow me down.

"Well, the Sagrada Familia works great as far as the cards are concerned, and it's a very cute idea to stow a lost ancient book of Jewish mysticism in the middle of a very Catholic basilica, but there's another problem. Gaudi started work on the church in the late 1800s. You banished the manuscript of the missing chapter into Nowheresville in 1478. That's quite a long time where we didn't know where the book was."

As I scrolled, we turned onto the Carrer de la Marina, less than three miles north of the ancient synagogue in El Call. Armaeus didn't look my way. He was too busy looking up—and up farther still. Meanwhile, I kept staring at the phone.

"And it didn't even become a church proper until a few years ago and the darned thing isn't even done—holy crap."

I finally looked up to see what Armaeus was staring at, and the impossible façade of the Sagrada Familia rose above me, illuminated all around by high-tech spotlights.

"I'm fairly certain Gaudi would have been edified by your review," Armaeus said drily as I continued to gawk. The Sagrada Familia looked like a power lifter who'd doubled down on steroids for about five years too long. Huge, sprawling, and top heavy, it sported a massive central nave that exploded up into the sky as if angry at the heavens, and so many thick, soaring spires, I lost count of them almost immediately. It didn't help that most of the spires were surrounded by varying degrees of scaffolding. As I stared, I began to pick out stunning bits of detail: a bunch of bananas perched atop one of the lower pinnacles, a dozen expressive statues built into another wall, a burst of doves flying up the rock face.

"What is this place?" I murmured.

"One of Gaudi's greatest labors of love, a church to honor the Holy Family of Christ." Armaeus pointed to the spires. "Each of those spires represents a member of Jesus's family and closest disciples, with the center spire reserved for the son of God himself."

"But it's enormous. And it's nowhere near *done*, it looks like." Huge cranes as well as draped and fenced construction sites surrounded the church.

"Apparently, Gaudi once told a critic that his client was not in a hurry," Armaeus said, earning another side-eye from me. But the quip was without inflection, so this was clearly not a joke.

"Is it actually in use?"

"It has served as a church since it was consecrated, yes, but it mostly operates as a tourist attraction and spectacle of Gaudi's work. Still, there's no question that he intended it to be used as a house of God and prayer."

I peered at the enormous front doors. "So how is it open this early in the morning? And how are we supposed to find a manuscript in such a big place if it's filled with people?"

Armaeus didn't have an answer to that, electing instead to move me toward the throngs of tourists lining up outside the front door. The spotlights combined with the huge outpouring of light from inside the church made for a fantastic spectacle. It was so bright, my regular eyes flinched away, but something caught my attention as we entered the church, causing my third eye to flicker open.

Crap. "We've got company."

"Who is it?"

The electrical patterns in the Sagrada Familia were unlike anything I'd ever seen before. Although most places of worship featured a stronger electrical signature than regular buildings, whether they were sacred groves, sanctified cathedrals, or the home of a prophet, like everything else about the Sagrada Familia, this church took it to the next level. The enormous treelike columns that served as the foundation of the nave seemed to be generating their own energy source. Electrical currents arced out from those bases, dipping and eddying around every outcropping, leaded glass window, and statue. Those currents of energy served as a canopy for the milling crowd below, but the group of tourists also contributed to the light show. About thirty percent of the audience, roughly speaking, were Connected—and some of them quite powerful, though I almost got the feeling they didn't realize it, the way they were walking around and staring at the magnificent church as if it was the true miracle of this place and not them.

"Um… What's the special event tonight?"

Armaeus closed his eyes briefly, summoning his inner Google, then glanced around. "They are consecrating one of the most recently completed spires, apparently the first in a series of completions scheduled between now and 2026. The guest list is almost entirely Spanish VIPs, but the event is also open to the public. It is just that the elite group will get a special experience once the general public is moved through."

"And they scheduled this for the middle of the night? Even in Barcelona, this is pushing things a little late."

"Apparently, part of the show is a light-based representation of the finished basilica that will gradually dim as the sun comes up. That's not scheduled for another two hours, by the way. More than enough time for us to collect the manuscript."

"You really think it's here?"

Armaeus's sigh was rich with satisfaction. "I absolutely know it's here. This is the first time I've set foot in the basilica since it was roofed over. I admittedly only tried to enter it once, when I was in the city on other business. When it was blocked to me, I assumed it was the nature of my business that caused the problem. I left the city and didn't have any compulsion to return until today. Now I believe I was restrained from entering by my own hand because the missing manuscript was here. And it was not yet time for me to find it. Nor did I possess the key to unlock the gates I had resurrected around myself." He glanced toward me, a soft smile playing at his lips. "For that, I needed you."

"Well, or maybe you simply needed to go for it. Simon said—"

"No, Miss Wilde," the Magician said, his words resolute. "I believe Simon was wrong. The key to me recalling my memories wasn't simply being presented with that which I'd forgotten. It was you. Something about *you* is unraveling even my most carefully crafted spells, now that those spells are detrimental to me. Somehow, some way…you are the key."

We stared at each other a long moment, my mouth going dry at the expression in his eyes. The Armaeus of old had never looked at me quite this way—not only with wonder and curiosity, but with *hope*, I finally decided—and I wasn't sure how I felt about it. Especially since he didn't really know me at all, anymore. How soon until he learned that his hope was completely unfounded?

"Well, keys are good," I finally said, nodding to the collection of goons near the altar. "But what we really need is one that can get us into the cool kids' party in the back room. It doesn't look like those guys are planning a mass anytime soon, but they're ushering small groups to the back, and all of them are Connected. That's…kind of weird."

Armaeus accepted my redirection easily, narrowing his eyes as he took in the small group assembled near the altar. "Interesting. But at least it serves as a distraction to any who might otherwise notice us."

"Yeah, maybe. I'd still like to know what they're doing in there. Can't you just go in and look around, then report back? I don't think the manuscript is going to be stuck inside some closet where they keep the spare Bibles."

"Then where do you think it might be?" Armaeus spoke with the air of someone expecting me to pull a rabbit out of a hat, but I settled for a card from my pocket. Or two, actually. The entire church was lit up like Christmas, so I wasn't going to find the manuscript by its electrical signature. Still, like Armaeus, I did feel it was here.

I handed the cards over to him, glancing around the nave of the basilica. "Two of Wands, Three of Pentacles. Up is the name of the game, I'm thinking. But how far up?"

Armaeus hummed in concentration as he swept his gaze along the church interior's soaring arches. "The book could have been moved well after the foundation for the cathedral was laid, but in thinking back to that year when I first encountered resistance, a lot of the outer ramparts had been completed, but not much of the spires themselves. I would think the book would be contained in this central space."

"That would be handy, except this central space is packed full of people."

"Perhaps near one of the windows?"

I considered the Three of Pentacles. A trinity-style set of windows would ordinarily be a good bet for a location, but once again, logic argued otherwise. "If you had a sacred book, would you really put it someplace where it could get rained on? That doesn't seem super smart."

"Then an interior façade?"

"That would seem most likely. And then too, there's the Two of Wands. Two staffs driven into the ground, a young man between them, looking to a far horizon. So maybe a location that can be seen at a distance…"

We moved along the wall closest to the entryway, our meandering progress unnoticed by the crowds doing much the same thing. It was easy to get swept up in the grandeur of the Sagrada Familia's interior, with each gothic flourish more over the top than the last. There were additional elaborate sculptures of everything from fruit to members of the angelic host, and after a few minutes of searching, my money was on one set of the treelike pillars serving as the key to our Two of Wands. But which set? It was almost impossible to tell one from the other, as large as the space was.

"You said this manuscript contained mystical teachings that were kept out of the original Zohar. But you've read the most recent criticism, and most people think the guy who wrote it was a scammer. Why would he have cut the best section out? That doesn't make sense."

"He didn't," Armaeus countered, his eyes still on the wall. "I doubt he even knew he'd written it. The man you followed into the synagogue took it. He was also deeply wounded, by your account, as if he suffered a great deal to get that sacred text into the right hands, desperate to learn the truth."

I'd experienced this tone from the Magician before, and while in times past, I would have found it deeply irritating, at the moment, it was strangely heartening. "This is a teaching moment for you, isn't it?"

He looked at me sharply. "A what?"

"Never mind." I waved at him. "Carry on."

"We do not know the true motivations of the writer of the Zohar," Armaeus said. "It is possible he was guided by authentic mystical urgency. It is equally possible that he sought to make as much money as he could from an audience eager to find greater mysteries and arcane knowledge in the ancient teachings of Judaism. What we do know now is that there was an additional section of the Zohar that was not included in the final book. That chapter went missing and eventually arrived in the hands of a holy man in one of

Barcelona's—one of all Europe's—most ancient synagogues. There it disappeared. There is also no indication of anyone referencing it, either in mystical practices or as the source of teaching—particularly not the author himself. It essentially vanished. But it clearly existed. Perhaps there were some Jewish mystics who wanted that chapter for themselves, or who wanted to destroy it. And perhaps there were some who wanted to take it from the messenger who carried it so valiantly to the synagogue in Barcelona. That is the man I am more interested in. Was his motivation to secure the text from the kabbalists and preserve it for Jewish leaders, or protect it from a third group?"

"You mean the Arcana Council?"

He frowned. "The Council doesn't dabble in the esoteric teachings of mortals. The kabbalists developed their form of mysticism without our interference."

"But this was something different, wasn't it?" I pressed. "If it was really the be-all and end-all of mysticism, you would have wanted it for yourself, at least to sneak a peek of it. And you can't remember anything about it other than that it was something you forgot."

"Precisely."

I groaned. "I feel like I'm in an Escape Room designed by a four-year-old."

Armaeus apparently didn't think this was very funny, because he moved his attention to the far wall…then stopped.

"Miss Wilde," he murmured, the words barely a breath.

I turned to look at what he saw, and froze as well. In the archway below one of the extraordinary stained-glass windows—a window split into a distinct three-leaf-clover pattern—there was an angel statue with elaborately spread wings perched on a ledge, a book in his hands. At either side of the statue stood two treelike pillars, their leafy stone boughs exactly like the far larger versions that graced the center of the nave. Other than a few electric candles near the statue that could be illuminated with the donation of a euro, no one stood near it.

"We're not going to break into an angel statue," I said, even as we both shifted in that direction.

"The manuscript is within the statue itself, do you think? Or hidden around it?"

"I want to believe around it, not in it. One, because I'm inherently lazy, and looking around the statue for a loose stone is a lot easier than busting it open. And two, because whoever planted that book is presumably religious. It seems like planting it inside a messenger of God would be sacrilegious. Who's the angel?"

Armaeus closed his eyes briefly again, then scowled. "There's no marker. Nothing is written about it."

I grimaced. "Well then, maybe it's just a very pretty angel-shaped box."

As we talked, Armaeus and I moved deeper into the room, where I noticed a third set of individuals as interesting as the tourists and Connecteds, but sporting much more impressive hardware. A private security force.

"Someone's expecting trouble."

"It's a large tourist event at three in the morning," Armaeus said dismissively. "The Sagrada Familia is funded by ticket sales and private donations, so the police won't be called in unless absolutely necessary, most likely in the case of crowd control in the event of a riot. Which we don't want, Miss Wilde. The last thing we need is attention drawn to this location, especially if we're not able to secure the manuscript tonight."

I looked at him oddly. "Why wouldn't we be able to secure the manuscript?"

"There's—a unique energy pattern that's in force that I'm only now becoming aware of, that's beginning to drag on me. I need to understand it, to subject myself to it so that I can study its effects later, but it's draining my energy at a very deep level."

Alarm snaked through me. "Are you doing too much?" I asked him, searching his face. Sure enough, he did look more tired all of a sudden—not a good look on him. "Should you even be out of Dr. Sells's care at this point? Should you sit down? Get a cane?"

Armaeus chuckled, his gaze returning to the angelic statue. "No, no. I assure you, there's no cause for alarm—"

A high, terrified scream shattered the night.

CHAPTER FOURTEEN

The crowd at the Sagrada Familia was comprised of mostly adults in their late forties and older, a few knots of college students, and virtually no children. It was three in the morning, after all, and even Spain had its limits. But the screech in the middle of the crowd was of a decidedly young and female variety.

"No, no, no! You can't, I won't go!" The words were Portuguese, and as the crowd peeled back, I could see they belonged to a young woman of maybe fifteen years who was writhing in the clutches of — no one at all. Both her hands were clapped to her temples, and she whipped her head back and forth violently, as if trying to shake off an unseen attacker. She appeared to be less than successful, but she did create a wide circle of space around her. I started forward to help, then realized Armaeus wasn't moving with me and turned back to him.

He was stone still, his eyes as dark as pitch.

I cleared my throat. "Armaeus?"

He didn't move, didn't blink. All he could apparently do was run his tongue over his lips and gasp one word. "*Angel.*"

Then another scream sounded. And a third.

I grabbed Armaeus and pulled him toward the unmarked statue, but it was slower going the closer we got to it. It was almost as if a force field was emanating from the statue itself, attempting to push the Magician away. Excellent for indicating we were on the right track, but a serious drag, literally, for getting him positioned where he needed to be. By the time we reached the alcove where the angel statue stood, I was sucking wind and Armaeus's skin was the color of cement. For a man with a significant amount of Egyptian blood running through his veins, it wasn't a good look.

I propped him against the far wall and turned, surprised to find the journey that'd seemed to take me the better part of forever had actually taken only a few seconds. The women and men with their hands over their ears were still midscream, while the first girl was only now inspiring ordinary people to rush to her aid. A curious problem with the aid givers, though—they broke into two very distinctive groups. The first set rushed forward and kept going, the second started out strong, then ended up on the ground.

Some sort of force field, for sure. Belatedly, I realized that the shard of Nul Magis in my hand was throbbing like it was its job, and I gritted my teeth and burst forward toward the knot of afflicted Connecteds.

Just as a shout cracked out over the crowd.

"Heretics!"

Exclamations of shock and confusion burst out as the people closest to the sacristy whirled to see a man in priest's robes come striding out. To either side of him were more of the security force, and there was something unnerving about a religious leader of any sort enforcing the will of his church with guns.

Especially when he also had a force field that was dropping everyone around him like flies.

"Help us," a woman begged me from her position at my knees, her face rigid with pain. But other than drag her bodily out of the room, I didn't know what to do. My mind fixed on the Tarot card I'd drawn that hadn't played out yet—the Tower. Armaeus didn't want to attract attention, and blowing up the Sagrada Familia, which was my first inclination, was probably going to get noticed.

"Destroy the heretics in our midst—you see them. They are marked as unbelievers by *God*." The guy in front of the altar spread his hands as if he were the pontiff himself, and I realized he was exhorting the populace in Spanish. Who was this guy? I'd run into a splinter faction of the Catholic church once before with a hate-on for Connecteds, an organization known as SANCTUS who was both well-funded and off its collective nut, but I'd thought it well and truly disbanded.

I grimaced. Much like the Arcana Council had well and truly disbanded the Shadow Court, only to have them keep reappearing.

I scanned the crowd quickly, running out of options as some of the crowd heard the priest's words and turned toward the suffering Connecteds with blood in their eyes. The Connecteds who were back in the sacristy, appeared to be exempt from the attack, or they were already dead, but these poor souls, I didn't know how to help without betraying my existence and putting Armaeus in danger.

Still, these Connecteds were strong—some of them very strong. So, dammit…they could help themselves. They *needed* to help themselves.

My third eye flinched as the energy patterns in the room crackled and hummed, and I recognized I'd made that surge happen just by the urgency of my thoughts. It was as if the currents were uniquely attuned to me. In a blink, I also realized these Connected were, well…*connected*, their energy systems linking up exactly the way the kids in the nave of Saint-Germain-des-Prés had to create a stronger whole than the sum of its parts. I didn't know why that was happening, but I didn't need to know why, right now. I simply had to use it.

I dropped to my knees, acting like any of the other non-Connected helpers who weren't swayed by the priest's cries of heretics. Not a word you wanted to throw around in Barcelona, no matter how many years had passed. The nearest Connecteds on the floor of the Sagrada Familia jolted, their eyes going wide with the realization that something was happening.

I reached for the woman still huddled against me. "*You* help them. Help all of them," I said to her and hugged her close, pulsing all my energy through her body, lifting the pain from her and using her own Connected ability to reinforce the electrical impulse I generated. Her head jerked back, her eyes going wide with surprise and relief. Then she wrenched away from me, leaping to her feet.

"Enough!" She yelled with so much gusto that her energy then reinforced the energy of the people she was nearest. For some, that was all that was needed to break through the pain locking them down.

I scrambled across the floor until I reached a knot of college-aged Connecteds huddled together, their shoulders hunched against their shared agony. I wrapped my arms around them, and one of them looked up at me, meeting my gaze.

"*Help*," she managed, but before she could get the word out fully, I was already focusing all my healing energy, the strength of my arms, my love, my belief in her until she convulsed, gasping. "Yes—I see it now. Yes!"

She and her friends split apart like struck balls on a billiard table, each of them going in separate directions. I whirled around to keep track of where Armaeus was but couldn't find him. He wasn't leaning against the wall next to the angel statue anymore, and he wasn't on the floor in front of it either. Hopefully, he hadn't climbed inside the thing. I moved toward the statue just as another hand snaked out, grabbing on to my leg.

"Heal me," the man whispered, his eyes wide, crazed, and I moved without thinking, pulsing both health and strength into him. His electrical field swelled like a rose in full bloom around him, and he stared at me with something close to adoration in his eyes before turning and diving back into the crowd.

But for every good psychic Samaritan, there were four other non-Connecteds who saw people in full heretical fits on the ground. Some ran for the door, some stood transfixed between their concern for their fellow man and their belief in a religious leader—any religious leader—some pushed through the propaganda and helped their fellow man...and some turned vicious. Rushing across the open nave, they fell upon the afflicted, kicking and screaming like animals kept too long from their food.

I was only one woman, and I couldn't cause a scene, but really, the scene was already well underway. I grabbed a tall candle in a brass base—

And was smashed in the back by a club.

"Unghf!" I went down like a sack of potatoes, only to see a half-dozen black boots surrounding me. I looked up into the barrel of a machine gun. The chaos and screaming roared all around me, but these guys were wholly focused on only one thing. Me.

Um, Armaeus?

Probably not my best idea to retest our psychic connection when I was in relatively dire straits. Predictably, I got no response. Fantastic.

While I'd been knocked to the ground, winded and badly bruised, there was nothing wrong with my third eye. Flicking it open, I got a bead on the electrical currents vibrating through the space. I flung my arms over my head and tucked my knees up to my chest, more to protect myself than anything, then, at the last moment, stretched my arms out wide and sent another crackle of healing, empowering electricity along the floor, between the boots of my attackers. It reached the nearest Connecteds a second later, and they roared to their feet, flinging off their own attackers with cries that were half rage, half exultation.

Absolute power didn't always corrupt absolutely, but you definitely noticed it.

And so it was the Connecteds who turned on my assailants and started battering them from the other side, people who looked enough like ordinary humans that the guys in black had the sense not to gun them down in cold blood. Smart move, since — *finally* — cops started entering the church from the main doors, blowing whistles and shouting through bullhorns. The gunmen surrounding me broke ranks and melted into the crowd of screaming people, and I struggled to my feet, my gaze immediately pinging to the alcove of the unmarked angel. Still no Armaeus — but someone had shot the shit out of the wall around the angel, pockmarking the stone and shattering the top of the statue. Where the angel's head had once gracefully tilted, there was now nothing but a smoking black hole.

I narrowed my eyes. I hadn't heard any gunshots.

Armaeus…

No response.

"Heretic!" I was surprised to hear the screech again, what with the police and all, but then I realized it was coming from an entirely different location. I looked up, and up still farther, and saw the barest glimpse of crimson robe disappearing from a catwalk that rimmed the top of the half-done spire, as if the priest was being dragged away. Since the guy had been in front of the altar not ten seconds earlier, there was only one person who could have collected him and gotten that high up in such a short period of time. The apparently rejuvenated Magician.

With no idea how to reach the top of the spire any other way, I sprinted across the nave to where the scaffolding lay roped off. I vaulted the obstruction and started to climb. I might not possess super strength, but I did have speed on my hands. Speed, and a whole lot of pissed off.

Armaeus!

Still no response.

I reached the top of the scaffolding where I'd seen the priest pulled away, but on diving through the heavy cloth drapes, it was all I could do to stop myself from sliding across the ledge and crashing through the flimsy plywood barrier that was apparently the only block to the predawn sky. Armaeus stood beside that barrier now.

Holding the priest over the edge of the scaffold.

"What are you *doing*?" I screeched as I scrambled to my feet. Luckily, no one on the streets below us had noticed the dangling priest yet, but the place was lit up like the Fourth of July. Eventually, somebody would look up.

Armaeus turned his head toward me as if he was some kind of robot, and I took one look at his eyes and stepped back. They were black—fully black, which meant he was accessing seriously deep, dark magic.

"Help me!" gasped the priest, his voice barely audible as he clawed at Armaeus's fingers. The Magician didn't seem to notice.

I didn't particularly want to help the priest, but he didn't have an ounce of Connected ability in him, probably because he was filled up with a hundred percent asshat. But as a non-Connected, he was off-limits for a revenge drop kick. Which the Magician certainly knew.

"What're you doing, Armaeus?" I asked, more levelly this time. "Why don't you let the guy back down?"

"Speak." The voice that swelled up from the Magician was nothing like the coolly sophisticated accent I'd grown to know and love. This was a croaking hiss, the voice of a demon, and the priest looked to be on the verge of passing out. But Armaeus shook him, making his feet sway like a rag doll's.

"Ah…if you've got something to say, you better say it," I suggested to the priest, edging slightly closer to Armaeus. I didn't think he was going to throw the priest off the ledge, but something the man had done had offended the Magician, clearly. And then there was that voice. "What were you doing down there?"

"It was—ordered," the priest managed, his breathing growing more labored. "By the Vatican itself. Draw the unbelievers to the basilica. M-make an example of them. Cast them down. They gave us—a machine. A machine to break down magic."

I grimaced. That explained the force field. The energy patterns of the Connected were extremely sensitive electrical circuits, and they could be manipulated as such, but only in the right setting. Like in an enclosed nave of gothic proportions.

More importantly, a machine that took out Connecteds was something that SANCTUS would have been all over. "Who in the Vatican?" I demanded, but the man's eyes rolled back in his head.

Armaeus shook him again, his lip curling in disgust. Then he dropped him.

"No!" I burst forward with a speed even I didn't realize I had and caught the man as he fell. I would have been pulled right over the side of the scaffolding with him, except Armaeus reached out at the same time and hauled me back. For the second time in way too short a time, I slammed against the floor, the wind once more getting knocked out of me as my back screamed in protest.

I pushed the deadweight of the passed-out priest off me and hauled myself around to face Armaeus. "What the hell was *that*?"

"He's a flunky of SANCTUS," Armaeus pointed out, his voice still sounding a little too close to Darth Vader for my taste. "He knows nothing other than what they tell him to know."

"So you've become his judge, jury, and executioner now? Because news flash, that's not your job."

"Who are you to know what my job is?"

That took me back a step. The Armaeus I'd known would never have done any of this, but I *had* known him only a few years. In the lifespan of an immortal, that was barely more than a one-night stand. Nevertheless, there'd been absolutely nothing in anything that Armaeus had done up to this point that indicated he would demand retribution from any human, no matter how depraved. If that was the Magician's jam, he would have started with Pol Pot, not this guy.

"Fair enough," I responded levelly. "So let me guess. You found the manuscript."

His smile was dark, almost sinister. "I found the manuscript."

"And you looked up the secret cookie recipe."

"Do not mock…" Once again, the voice sounded more like a croak than anything remotely human. Then he shook himself, and a second later, a new voice broke through, the Armaeus I'd known and still loved, even in his fancy poltergeist form.

"You're not as strong as I am, Miss Wilde," the Magician warned, his eyes still swirling with malevolence as he took a careful step back, ostensibly to protect me. "You never were. Have a care."

"And you nearly threw a man off the side of the church," I challenged, going for exactly the opposite of having a care. "You need to ratchet it down a few notches."

"I…" Armaeus's entire body jerked again, his lungs heaving. "I read the book."

"I gathered. Where is it?"

"Safe."

I considered that. "Did you eat it?"

His eyes flashed again, this time with surprise and confusion. "What?"

"Stay with me. Why'd you grab the priest?"

"Because he'd given his men orders to kill you. Your defeat would have set in motion any of numerous outcomes, precisely zero of which were positive to me." Armaeus continued to speak in a voice closer to normal, but there still was a ragged edge to his psyche, a degradation at the fringes I didn't understand.

I kept pushing. "How much of what happened downstairs was caused by you?"

"None of it," he answered flatly. "You orchestrated your own rescue. Had you not, I would have. Otherwise, the guards would have killed you, despite the arrival of the police. That was their order."

"I guess today is my lucky day."

At that moment, the priest groaned, rolled over, and began retching.

"You choke on your own vomit and there will be hell to pay, buddy," I warned, but the priest was well past responding to that. He did ease up on the dry heaves, though.

I turned my gaze back to Armaeus. "So give it to me. How much do you remember now that you've read the manuscript?"

"Not enough," he said, his voice deepening again. "I still don't recognize you, other than through our interaction of the last two days. I do fully understand what was happening at the time that I first placed the chapter in hiding and stripped it from my memory, however. I also know why I believed that the arcanum found inside that chapter must never reach mortal hands."

"But you didn't destroy it. Then or now."

He shook his head and blew out a long breath. "I didn't have to destroy it. I just had to keep it safe. It is safe now."

"Mind telling me where?"

Armaeus closed his eyes as if he were considering my request, then opened them again and held out his hand, as if to pull me to him. For the first time, I noticed it was shaking. "There's no time," he said. "We have to go to London."

Then he collapsed.

CHAPTER FIFTEEN

I caught Armaeus as he was falling—he was far heavier than I expected. I'd always believed that reading was good for you, but apparently that didn't include chunking down the salient points of the lost chapter of the Zohar. I staggered beneath the Magician's body while the priest beside me groaned.

"Uh, Armaeus, a little help here? Where in London?" I had no idea where Nikki, Kreios, and Simon were lodging, or if they'd made it to London yet. Asking did me no good. Armaeus was out.

"*Heretic.*" This was from the peanut gallery still sprawled on the floor, and I craned my neck to see him better.

"You know, you're going to need to come up with another line."

"You won't succeed. Not anymore. There are too many allied against you now. And your Magician cannot lead from his knees. The abomination of your kind will be ground under the righteousness of the faithful."

I narrowed my eyes. "For someone who I just kept from being a splat on the pavement, a little gratitude might be in order."

"You are *filth*," the priest shot back. "The champions of God will rise up and overtake you. They will defend all that is truth."

"That what they told you?" I asked as I gave Armaeus an experimental nudge. He didn't move. *Aces.* "Because I hate to break it to you, but anyone who can take us out is made of exactly the same stuff we are. Which makes you a hypocrite."

"No," he growled, weakly batting his hands in the air. "You are wrong. In the hands of the faithful, the tools of science may be bent to God's will, ridding us of the scourge of your kind. You are weak, scattered. Broken. They will come at you with poison, they will come at you with fire, they will come at you with the weapons of technology and the might of God. At last, you will pay for your millennia of…sacrilege…" The priest had the grace to pass out again, saving me the trouble of throat-punching him.

Then sirens shattered the night sky, and the wind picked up, sharply flapping the tarps draped over the scaffolding. I refocused on Armaeus. And London.

Without any other guidance, I had to rely on my own memories of the city, but it wasn't as if I'd spent a ton of time there. Worse, the time I had spent was generally at a dead run. Still, I fixed on one of the most prominent landmarks along the Thames and clutched Armaeus's deadweight as I boarded the Crispy Express, as Nikki had called it.

My memory proved to be pretty good. We arrived bare moments later in London, which was not nearly as hopping as Barcelona was at three in the morning. Lightweights.

The relative quiet of the park area in front of the London Eye Ferris wheel gave me time to regroup. I hauled Armaeus's meat sack of a body over to one of the

162

park benches and dumped him on it, sucking in a deep breath.

"Was that really necessary?" I asked his inert form as I sagged back on the bench beside him. "Could you not simply have waited to pass out until we were in our hotel room?"

I patted my pockets for my phone, but while my ten-dollar deck of cards and ancient storm goddess totem were still onboard, my thousand-dollar phone had apparently not been up to the task of staying on my body. I didn't know if Armaeus even had a phone, and I eyed his tailored suit. What were the odds that he'd incinerate me in his sleep if I tried to pick his pocket? Probably pretty good. Which meant I needed to wait for him to wake up, or drag him to a hotel. I scanned the area. There were several options, but all of them tourist grade, and I wasn't in the mood to draw any more attention to myself than I already had tonight.

"C'mon, buddy," I muttered, risking Armaeus's reaction to take his hand. It was warm and dry, so that seemed promising, and the heat only grew as I touched him. Grew and seemed to radiate out, taking the deep-night chill from the air and replacing it with a mild baking sensation. Not unpleasant, but definitely weird.

"Uh, Armaeus?"

The Magician didn't respond, and my third eye flipped open. Sure enough, the heat that was emanating from Armaeus had a very distinctive signature and a head full of steam. In a few short seconds, it extended out from the Magician in brilliant arcs, gorgeous tendrils of light diving into the earth and skating up trees, shrubs, even dipping into the fountains and swirling around. Another tracery of magic flowed out among the man-made obstacles in its place, benches in concrete and cars and buildings. Separate from and weaker than the strands of energy that were tied to living things, but still connected to them.

It was pretty, but I didn't understand it. I'd never spent too much time analyzing the electrical connections the Magician used to tether himself to this world, so I didn't know if this was new, the results of the arcane lore that he had just assimilated, or if this was just Tuesday night in the park for him.

Then I heard the sound of running feet, and I stiffened.

"Armaeus," I said, more urgently this time. He groaned, the kind of groan that gave no indication of him being actually conscious, and seemed to sink further into himself. Not helpful. I'd settled on trying some sort of invisibility spell when the running feet suddenly came into view, attached to a person. A person in priest's ropes.

Oh, geez. Not this again. I was full up on annoying men of the cloth right now. Still, the short, stout, older man reminded me so much of Father Jerome that I could only stare as he bustled up to us and abruptly stopped.

"They said you would be coming," the old man said breathlessly, surprising me. "They said you would be coming and to take you in."

"They, who?" I challenged, holding up a hand to keep the man from getting any closer.

"It was all around me, voices of angels," the man insisted, flapping his hands. "But you must come! There are too many shadows in this place seeking to banish the light. You will be safe with me, but only if you come now."

With the benefit of my third eye, I could read the man's energy signature, and there was nothing in it that raised a red flag. And the truth was, I needed to get Armaeus off the streets. He was the most powerful

Magician in the world, but not right now. Right now, we were both sitting ducks.

I waved the priest to come closer, and he burst into motion again, his long robes flying. I didn't think priests wore robes this fancy outside their hallowed sanctuary, so that meant there was a church nearby. To my surprise, however, the priest helped Armaeus to his feet while muttering a raft of low prayers, then somehow managed to get the Magician to semicoherence enough for both of us to support him through the park and across the street. The breeze kicked up and seemed to propel us along until we turned the corner, where the priest left me to hold Armaeus and approached an old but decidedly not church-like building. He waved his hand in front of a sensor, and the wrought iron gates that blocked the front door popped open. We pushed inside.

"I'm afraid you've caught me at my studies," the old man said. "If I hadn't been in the atrium, I don't know that I would have heard the call. I'll take you there."

There turned out to be an inner courtyard that'd been transformed into a kind of Japanese Zen garden, with flowing water, ornamental trees that rustled and whispered in the breeze, and long tables with clusters of electric illuminated candles. The man helped me get Armaeus to one of the tables, where the Magician promptly slumped over, his arms cradling his head.

I sighed. "Sorry, I'm not sure exactly what's gotten into him. I've never seen this before."

"It's as may be," the priest said, and I realized that his brogue was less English than Irish—and that his robes betrayed no hint of a Catholic collar at the neckline. "I'm Brother McCullough, and I've seen this before. It happens to every mystic who drinks too deeply of the cup of knowledge. Who is this man you've brought to me? He's very powerful and very broken. It makes for a difficult combination."

I took in the rush of words, more confused than ever. "If you don't know who he is, why are you helping us? And brother of what, exactly?"

McCullough spread his hands. "You're right in asking those questions. I'm no longer a priest, though I can't seem to keep from dressing like one. Force of habit, if you'll pardon the pun. But when I say brother, I mean it most sincerely. I belong to an order of like-minded men and women who believe there is more to this world than meets the eye. We have felt the surge of power, and we have watched the demonstrations, the news stories that quickly get squelched. We've felt the unrest, and we've seen the shadows. We have merely been waiting for a guide."

"A guide to what?" I didn't want to break it to him that despite his many talents, the Magician would make a questionable guide. He didn't care as much about humans as he did about maintaining the balance of magic, and he now seemed to care less about balance than learning. That could be…dangerous.

At that moment, Armaeus stirred. With what seemed like a tremendous amount of concentration, he flattened his fingers on the surface of the table and pushed himself back. Our transcontinental journey didn't seem to have improved his mood any. His eyes were still jet black, now tinged with red, and his face seemed even more haggard.

"Armaeus?" I offered, and he swung his gaze toward me, staring through me without seeing. Then he shook his head slowly.

"I remember," he murmured, and my heart gave a little flip, but he gave no other indication of recognizing me. My hopes were more thoroughly dashed as he continued speaking.

"The reason for the removal of the last section of the Book of Radiance was that it was one delivered directly by angels to the scribe. And the purpose of this last chapter was wholly different from what came before it. It offered not just the motivation to see, it offered to tear the veils from the eyes of anyone who read it."

"I don't understand."

"Master."

Showing a remarkable lack of care for his own personal safety, Brother McCullough rushed forward and put both hands on either side of Armaeus's bent head. And instantly turned into a human lightbulb.

"What the hell!" I wrenched the man away from Armaeus, and then it was my turn to cradle him as he collapsed against the bench. The spectral light went out almost as soon as it had consumed him, but it *had* consumed him. Though he didn't appear to have suffered any physical harm, he'd completely lit up from within, to the point where I could count all his bones. If only I knew how many bones he was supposed to have, I would've given him an update.

"Ohhhhhh," McCullough moaned.

"What happened?" I demanded. "Are you all right?"

In response, the not-a-priest opened his mouth— and started speaking quickly and emphatically in a language I'd never heard before and couldn't translate. Which brought me up short. One of my skills was language translation, so for me not to recognize this...

"English," I interjected, and McCullough jerked himself to attention, his gaze swinging toward me again, his eyes bright and fevered.

"All things are Connected, all things true. All things are Connected, all things true. It is love. It is love. It is always and ever, your love. You can, you do, you are. All things are Connected, all things true. All things are Connected, all things true," he babbled, the words sounding far more deranged now that I could understand them—which was saying something, because they'd sounded seriously messed up before.

"All things are Connected. That's great. What happened to you?" I tried, inserting the brief phrases every time the man drew a breath. But it was no use. He kept muttering the same words over and over again, rocking now, and while he didn't seem to be in any distress—seemed exultantly happy, in fact—I knew this wasn't right.

"All things—"

"Stop," I ordered at last, placing a hand on his shoulder. He shut up, contenting himself with merely shivering.

Another quiet voice broke over us. "You begin to see the problem, yes?"

I turned to look at Armaeus and barely kept myself from flinching away. He now glowed with the same spectral light that'd taken over the priest, rendering his face skeletal, his black eyes ferocious and hungry within.

"There's no end to the problems I'm seeing right now. You mind telling me what the hell is happening to you?"

The sharpness of my question made Armaeus blink, and he glanced down at himself as if surprised by his own radiance. A second later, the light winked out, and he'd returned to his normal Magician-looking self. Even his eyes had dropped their feral hunger, though they remained black as coal.

"Brother McCullough," Armaeus murmured, and beside me, the former priest and present whatever he was suddenly went boneless, the strictures of whatever was possessing him leaving his body. He collapsed so abruptly, I leaned forward and checked him for a pulse, but his heart was beating in a heavy, reassuring rhythm. He was well and truly passed out, but he was no longer in distress.

Armaeus smiled grimly as I turned back to him. "My apologies, Miss Wilde. I had not thought the treasure of the lost chapter of the Book of Radiance would have affected me so extensively. I won't make that mistake again."

The words sounded almost too smooth, the words of a recovering addict who assures you he's kicked the habit for good, but I let them pass.

"But again, you see the problem," Armaeus continued, gesturing to McCullough. "This man is a stranger to us, yet he threw open his doors and came running in response to the radiant energy I put out."

"He's an advanced Connected," I reasoned. "And — uh, he said he'd been told to watch for you."

"Ah, but told by whom?"

I looked down at the collapsed Connected and shook my head. "No clue. The language he was speaking, what was it? I didn't recognize it, and that doesn't happen anymore. I know every language spoken on this earth."

"And therein lies the mystery." Armaeus nodded. "The missing chapter of the Zohar that the Spanish mystic was so certain would lead to the ruination of man was a manual on how to speak to angels. How to open up the channels of connection between one's self and All That Is. The understanding of the deep and awesome power that each of us carries within us and how that power can profoundly affect the world around us, once full connection has been made and the right words are spoken and understood by two souls, three souls, more."

I stared at him. "The missing chapter contains the language of angels?" I wasn't as surprised as I should have been. I'd encountered a nasty cabal of angels in Atlantis not all that long ago, and the Hierophant of the Arcana Council was the freaking Archangel Michael, so I'd met my share of winged warriors. But I'd never stopped to consider that they might have their own language…a language mortals didn't know.

Armaeus continued as if he could read my thoughts, so I tightened up my mental barriers on general principles. "Many would say the angelic language is the birthright of humankind, but the reality is far more complicated than that. Consider it more an operating code of the universe. Once you know the code, once you speak the language, manipulating all that is becomes a ridiculously simple construct. When I first learned of this book's existence, I didn't need to act right away. Man wasn't ready for that information in the thirteenth century, but those who possessed it didn't understand what they had, so there was no harm in allowing it to remain in the hands of humans."

"Until…" I prompted.

"With the advent of the Spanish Inquisition, an effort born of the monarchy, not of the church, the danger grew too great. The sacred tome had to be hidden, and hidden again." He twisted his lips. "Unfortunately, I was still new enough in my position that I believed it was not my place to cast it entirely from this world, and so I entrusted it to human hands. And they kept their pact. They found hiding places that lasted for centuries. One that even I didn't know to look for, as I had excised the book from my memory when I gave it over to them."

"So you trusted them. That's good, right?"

He shook his head. "It was a mistake I realized I couldn't make again. I ran across mention of some dire action in my journals, but nothing at all to clarify that action, and spent much of the next hundred years trying to remember what I had forgotten, to no avail. When the next opportunity presented itself to remove arcane lore from human hands, however, I suspect I was not nearly so foolhardy. Which brings us here to London, where we must find something that is so deeply hidden that no human might ever lay eyes on it again."

"And Brother McCullough?"

Armaeus sighed. "For one brief shining moment, he knew the language of the angels. But now, and evermore, it will be lost to him. It's too much for mortal minds to bear."

I opened my mouth, then shut it again. Armaeus knew the language now, had used it unconsciously, summoning Brother McCullough to us to get us off the streets. Yet he'd also dangled a mortal over the side of a precipice in the wake of learning that language, merely because the man had pissed him off. So how well could *im*mortal minds handle the language of the angels?

I tried not to think about that too much.

We left before McCullough woke, taking care to leave no indication of our presence. The building didn't seem to have a sophisticated camera system, and there was no watchman. Arguably, that meant McCullough would have no evidence he'd been summoned from his studies to bring in two strangers from the park outside under the influence of angelic communication. But as we made our way through the predawn streets of

London, I found my mind turning to another possible issue.

"The lost chapter contained the language of angels, transcribed—like a dictionary," I said.

Armaeus didn't turn toward me. We were walking at a remarkably slow pace as he swept his gaze ahead of us, as if he was mapping a city he'd never visited before. I didn't know if angelic language had a nav system, but it was possible.

"Like a dictionary, yes, and a guidebook," he finally answered.

"And you'd totally forgotten it existed once you decided it was too scary for mortal kind."

That did earn me a sidelong look. "Your point?"

"Well, we kind of have an angel on the Council. A big one. And he's been around since the beginning. Wouldn't he know that this chapter existed too?" The Hierophant of the Arcana Council, Michael the Archangel, wasn't my favorite person in the world, but there was no doubting the fact he would be uniquely qualified to weigh in on the existence of an angel dictionary and helpful how-to guide and its possible ramifications to humanity.

Armaeus chuckled. "As to whether or not the Hierophant knew about the existence of the book— that's somewhat in doubt, given his location when the book was first written. As to his understanding of the impact of the lost chapter on the masses of humanity, that's an excellent question, and one I fully intend to ask him when we reach the others. Who are staying quite close, as it happens. You've lost your phone."

"Okay. Good. And true." I knew the Magician couldn't read my mind...I was pretty sure of it...but I didn't miss the fact that he knew what I wanted to know and why I wanted to know it, and he'd provided me all the information I needed without me asking for it. Was he merely making connections, or did the lost chapter's teachings give him angel vision too? "Simon can hook me up with another phone when we meet up with them. Where are they?"

"Boutique hotel near Buckingham Palace," Armaeus murmured. He turned his head as if he was following a scent like a dog. "I'm not sure we should be walking."

"Ahh...well, you're in charge of transpo if you know where we're going and I don't."

He shook his head. "Also not an option, as you'd see if you would look at me."

His words weren't delivered with any level of censure, but they stung all the same. It literally hurt to look at Armaeus, but that didn't change the necessity of it. Screwing up my courage, I risked another glance at him with my third eye.

And staggered back a step, sucking in a harsh breath. A similar corona of electricity swirled around Armaeus as it had when he'd been passed out on the park bench, but this one was visibly being held in check, presumably by Armaeus himself. It was like watching a volcano erupt inside a trash can, with the sides about to blow at any second. "Uhhh...does that hurt?"

"Not in any conventional way. But we're being followed by low-level Connecteds, and they've picked up on the increase in my energy output. Anyone with a greater level of sophistication will be able to recognize the signature immediately. I need to get to the hotel. But the chaos of—"

The flash of a vehicle approaching us was coming so quickly, so intently, I acted without hesitation. "Get back," I ordered and pushed Armaeus behind me as a sleek dark gray limousine shot up next to us and stopped, the driver opening the door and sticking out one impressive gam.

"Don't shoot, dollface. I come in peace," Nikki declared.

CHAPTER SIXTEEN

The ride to the boutique hotel was fast and warded — which was good, as Armaeus passed out the moment he folded himself into the sleek limousine.

"What the hell happened to him?" Nikki asked through the in-car system. "He's practically crackling back there."

"What do you see when you look at him?"

"Honestly, my gaze keeps shearing away. I try to get a fix on him but can't hold it. Is he doing that on purpose?"

"I don't think so, especially not while he's passed out. But he leveled up when we were in Spain by a lot, and I don't think he's fully figured out what that means. How'd you know to come find us?"

"I was dispatched by Simon, who somehow managed to wrangle this sweet ride on zero notice." She chortled. "Good thing I remember how to drive on the opposite side of the street. Simon said you guys had a tail, but I haven't seen anyone."

"We were traveling on foot. Presumably, so were they."

"Maybe. But that's not the only problem. We've gotten more company since you guys showed up in London."

"We've only been here a little over an hour."

"Yeah, well, it's been a busy rotation. Death and the Hierophant showed up within seconds of each other, both of them pissed. Any idea what that's about?"

"Death, no. The Hierophant, ah...maybe." I filled her in on what information I knew about the manuscript that Armaeus had recovered. She listened without interruption as I explained the angelic Rosetta-stone nature of the lost section of the Book of Radiance, its locations inside the holy places of Barcelona, and Armaeus's reaction to cracking the spine. But when I got to the part about the Spanish priest, I heard her suck in a quick breath.

"Since when does Armaeus do anything to humans? Especially people at that pay grade?"

"Exactly. I don't like it." I studied Armaeus as she drove, not knowing if he could hear me or not, and not particularly caring. Around us, the wind whistled and sighed, cocooning us with its chatter. "It's not like him, and I don't know what that means. It seems that he's remembered the book and what its purpose was and why it was put where it was, but this, what's happening now, is new. He also picked up on the fact that we were being followed, but he said they were low-level Connecteds and he didn't know who they were affiliated with. Which again..."

Nikki clucked her tongue in concern. "Which again is a problem. There are still gaps. This manuscript didn't seem to fill any of them, except the fact that it existed. He picked up Angel Speak, but he's not able to connect the dots about the Shadow Court."

"Not yet," I agreed. "You guys find anything about the year 1571 that's important?"

"There was a lot about 1571 that was important, but not a hell of a lot that was actually written down," Nikki groused. "We think we found it anyway — but hey, here we are. Simon wanted me to dump the car in the staff area, so if you'll just hold on to that thought for a tick, lemme get us inside."

She quickly drove to the back of the impressive building, where an attendant came rushing out the moment Nikki nosed her vehicle into view. Armaeus roused himself to consciousness as the vehicle stopped. Within moments, we were safely inside the hotel.

I could tell the difference immediately, but Armaeus beat me to the punch.

"This hotel is heavily warded," he murmured, and I could hear the strain in his voice. Instinctively, I took a step closer to him, though he didn't seem at risk of immediate collapse.

"Correctamundo," Nikki said. "Apparently, it's why we're here. It's a property that's partially owned by the Council and maintains the strictest security from any sort of cyber psychic attack. Simon's pretty happy with himself right about now, but I'm not sure if he can cover a host of angels coming down for a chat, if that's what you think is going to happen."

Armaeus looked at me sharply. "You told her?"

The question struck me the wrong way, but I fought to keep my tone light. "We're all on the same team here," I reminded him. "Humans and demigods alike."

My answer didn't seem to mollify him, and Nikki wisely stayed quiet. After another second, Armaeus spoke. "There is a great deal of danger to any mortal wielding words of angels. Even those they overhear by mistake. Especially those."

"Then we'll keep all wielding to a minimum," Nikki said. "Here we are."

She ushered us into a palatial suite that would've seemed enormous except for the outsized egos it already contained. The Devil lounged against the far wall, his sharp eyes on Armaeus, missing nothing. Simon sat hunched over a computer screen, his fingers racing across the keys. And, just as Nikki had promised, another two members of the Council rounded out the group. Death and the Hierophant.

Of the two, Death looked more irritated. Tall and muscular, with one side of her platinum-blonde hair shaved close to her skull, and the other side spiked up, she stood staring stonily at Armaeus as we entered the room. Dressed for a biker rally in a black tank top, beat-up jeans, and shit-kicker boots, she crossed her arms over her chest, and the sleeve of colorful tattoos that decorated one arm stood out in vivid contrast to her pale skin. But her light complexion had nothing on Michael the Archangel.

With his skin so fair it was almost translucent, his white hair, and his virtually nonexistent eyebrows, Michael looked like he hadn't seen the sun in thousands of years. Up until a short while ago, that was actually the case. Stuck inside what most humans would describe as hell, he spent his time away from mortals quite by choice. It was only after the Magician had sent me off to fetch him that Michael agreed to exit into the real world. When he first emerged from his hidey-hole, he'd been swept away like a kid in a candy store by all the people and sounds and colors. That wonder had quickly diminished as the problems of the Council increased. Now he spent most of the time scowling, an expression he was currently perfecting. "Where is the

178

lost chapter?" he asked before Armaeus had taken ten steps into the room.

Armaeus didn't stop, however, until he sank into one of the suite's dining room chairs near Simon. I'd never seen him look so exhausted, but his voice was cool and even as he responded to the Hierophant. "Safe. How much do you know about it?"

"Enough to hope that it had been a rumor, a rumor that was never substantiated by myself as I was otherwise engaged. You certainly never indicated such a thing existed."

"Would I have done so?" the Magician asked. "There was an extended period of time when I apparently knew of the manuscript's existence but did not take steps to remove it from the mortal plane entirely. And when I did intervene, it was not to destroy the book or even to keep it for myself. It was to forget it existed. That seems...foolhardy, though no more foolhardy than the manuscript existing in the first place. How is it possible?"

The archangel spread his hands. "It's not my place to know the will of God, only to wonder at it, and occasionally rail against it. His creations can achieve far more than they realize, despite their best attempts at forgetting this fact. Perhaps he wanted to see how far they could go."

I persisted. "You don't have any idea who could have whispered this language into the ear of the kabbalist scribe?"

Michael's smile was cold. "I have a few ideas, yes. But I doubt I'll get the pleasure of confirmation." He shifted his glance to the Magician. "Just as you, Armaeus, to this day, don't know why, specifically, you allowed the book to remain in the hands of humans."

"Maybe you couldn't destroy it," Simon offered from the other side of the table, swiveling on his chair. "Maybe it was spelled or something to prevent any harm coming to it."

Kreios turned to Armaeus. "If that was the case, why would you need to intervene at all? A book that powerful could take care of itself and clearly did for a couple hundred years. Why did you get involved?"

"I don't…"

"He got involved for the same reason he got involved in 1571," Death interrupted, her tone sharp. "There comes a time in Armaeus's analysis where he decides that, despite all apparent indications to the contrary, the most sensitive and gifted humans cannot be trusted to handle the magic their own skills and abilities have led them to, magic that can change the course of humanity. When that happens, in his hubris, he takes steps."

Armaeus turned to her. "Steps you are aware of, apparently."

"Only insofar as they damage the humans whose memories you've stripped," she said. "In the case of the lost chapter of the Zohar, you were fairly circumspect. You ensured the safety of the manuscript without destroying it, allowing it to live on in arcane lore for a few generations after you spirited it into safe hands and out of your mind entirely. That was well done. You were less circumspect with John Dee."

That caused everyone to stop and turn toward her.

"John Dee," Armaeus echoed reflectively. "Astrologer to Queen Elizabeth the First, in the year 1571. An extraordinary man of science, mathematics, and alchemy. It's reasonable…quite reasonable that he would have drawn my interest. But why do you think my second lapse of memory has anything to do with him?"

"Because that was the year he nearly died, well before his time. That was the year he began going slightly mad as well, though no one would recognize it for years. Within two more decades, he would become impoverished and frail. Once the mightiest magician of the Elizabethan age, withered away to dust."

Armaeus stared at her. "*I* did that to him? Why?"

"I never knew the reason, honestly." Death shook her head. "I certainly didn't lay his decline at your door at the time. When I learned that your second memory lapse was dated to 1571, it was the first time I put two and two together. Dee had attempted to take his own life by consuming the very mixtures he was attempting to combine in his laboratory—a beautiful laboratory filled with books of every description. By all accounts, that year he had everything to live for, having just returned from a strange and secretive mission to France at the queen's request. Nevertheless, one night, he was desolate, and he cried out for Death. I came."

"To kill him?" I asked, aghast.

"To collect him, I thought. Then I realized who he was. I knew his position in the world and what work he still had to do. He didn't die that night, not entirely. But something powerful had been taken from him, and losing it broke him."

She turned to Armaeus. "I think you can guess what it was."

"Alchemy," Armaeus murmured. "He'd finally done it. He'd discovered how to change lead into gold. And with a secret that important, there was only one place I'd put it. Which neatly solves another mystery, one that has vexed me for centuries, only I never realized the connection."

Death nodded. "I think so too. You stole the alchemical formula from John Dee...and then you stashed it somewhere you promptly banned yourself from accessing again. A place of this world, but not in it, where even angels feared to tread."

"The In Between," Armaeus murmured.

CHAPTER SEVENTEEN

W hoa, whoa, whoa." Nikki spoke first, bringing up her hands. "I mean, I get why Dee would be upset about losing the secret to alchemy. The philosopher's stone was the holy grail of every scientist back then. Let alone all the money you could make by selling a recipe for turning lead into gold. But why would *you* care enough about that to bury the knowledge from everyone, even yourself, Armaeus? It's not like you have a yen for walking around in solid-gold kicks."

"Agreed," Simon said, his face alight with interest as he leaned forward, tapping furiously on his laptop. "What I got on 1571 and Dee is next to nothing. He went to France like Death said, to the duchy of Lorraine. Nobody knows why, not even my cross-referenced sources." He shook his head in disgust. "Record keeping in the fifteen hundreds seriously sucked, for the, ah, record."

"Do you know why he went?" Armaeus asked Death, who shook her head.

"I didn't know he'd returned from there until far later. He became quite ill after my visit to him and recovered only after several weeks. That period of rest is probably what saved his mind from cracking completely, but he never returned to Lorraine after that. It's as if he'd forgotten why he'd gone, what he'd learned there, and what was important about it." She narrowed her eyes at Armaeus. "You still don't remember any of this?"

"I don't." Armaeus didn't look stricken, exactly, but he also didn't look happy. "With the snippet of the tattoo that Miss Wilde sent, my memory fired, and the knowledge of the existence of the Shadow Court came shortly after, if not all the details. I still don't have all the details."

"Or any memory of Sara either?" Kreios drawled, the interruption surprising me.

Armaeus glanced at him but didn't respond. "The location of the lost chapter of the Zohar was made partially by deduction, much like Dee's, but the moment I stepped foot in El Call, I felt that memory firing as well. But this…" He shook his head. "I have no recollection at all of wresting Dee's discovery from him."

Once again, the Devil intervened. "But you know why you would."

This comment earned him a sharper look from Armaeus. "Yes, of course. Lead into gold was the shorthand that the common person could understand. A precious metal derived from a common lump of lead? There was immediate and obvious value there. But the true impact of the transmutation of substances was far more powerful than that. Dee, like most alchemists, sought to understand the spirit of things, what made them up, long before the discovery of the building blocks of matter. By identifying what their components were—the energy that made them what they were—he sought to then change that energy to operate at a different, higher vibration. Alchemy. Gold wasn't even the highest level. It merely was the most practical target to shoot for."

"And he did it," I said. "Dee figured it out."

"So it would seem. But for me to intervene so clumsily, shattering the man's mind in the process…" Armaeus let his words trail off, but there was no doubting his concern. And it felt wrong to me too, the same way watching him dangle a priest from the ramparts of the Sagrada Familia felt wrong. Who was this man who was willing to do such things? Was reclaiming these portions of his memories really something that was going to help Armaeus? His eyes were shifting even as I watched, regaining their cast of flat black malevolence, though no one seemed to notice it but me.

He looked to Simon. "As Death so ably indicated, there's only one likely location where I would have put this secret. The In Between. I've been barred entry to it since the fifteen hundreds by my own hand, at least in the British Isles. Are there any entry points in London near Mortlake? I doubt there's anything left of Dee's home there, not the original building, anyway."

"That would be negative, but…" Simon's brows lifted. "Dee was born in the Tower Ward. There's a portal below All Hallows by the Tower church, if that makes any sense as an entry point for you?"

Death tucked her hands into her jeans pockets and rocked up onto her toes, simmering with energy. "It would make sense, yes. It would be very strategic, in fact. Dee would be drawn to wherever you stashed his lost memories, but he wouldn't know why. If you entered the In Between at the site of a church in his home ward, then he would assign his sense of nostalgia and loss to the church, perhaps to his family, but not to any mental lapse he experienced at another's hands."

"So that's where we need to go," the Magician said.

"If I may interject." The Devil made a show of looking at his nails as he spoke, but his voice was uncharacteristically hard. "There was a reason for the forgetting of these arcane bits of history. And the reintroduction of the first has hardly proven ideal. You've changed, Armaeus. You don't even know how much. You are undoubtedly weaker for the experience, for all that you have gained in knowledge."

"Which is why it's a good thing you're in charge of the Council, along with the Emperor." Armaeus smiled, all teeth. "I need time to assimilate this knowledge and understand its importance."

"You do need time. Unfortunately, time is no longer a commodity we have to spare. The Shadow Court has made itself known, and we have very little information on it — by we, I mean you. That is the subject you should concern yourself with, not the transmutation of lead into gold or its allegorical equal, no matter how enticing that may seem."

"You don't understand," Armaeus countered. "The one begets the other."

"I would have thought that, yes, except your acquisition of the lost chapter of the Book of Radiance has yielded knowledge only of a very esoteric nature, knowledge currently constrained to one person…you. What it didn't yield was any additional intelligence about the Shadow Court. And it should have. Arguably, when you set this mechanism in motion in 1478, you believed you were at the start of a long-ranging plan."

"A plan that requires the return of all my memories."

"But not all your memories were eradicated by you. The knowledge of the Shadow Court was wiped clean through the efforts of Justice Strand. That means two things—one, that she knew the mechanism by which your memories *could* be erased, along with the memories of everyone else touched by the Shadow Court—that is powerful knowledge. Two, she knew you'd successfully employed that mechanism before."

"So what's your point?"

"His point is that the answers you're seeking may not only lie in the In Between," Death interjected. "They may lie much closer to home, in the library of Justice Hall. Interestingly enough, no Council member in this room other than Justice herself can enter her own hall, by the hand of no less than Abigail Strand. And not one of us sought to argue this point."

"Well, all you need—" Something on Simon's screen interrupted him, and he squinted down at his laptop. "Yo, that's weird," he muttered, lifting his hand to type.

"Has there been any movement from the Shadow Court or any word from Brody over at Interpol about their actions?" I asked as Simon leaned closer to the table. "If not, I have no problem hitting the library stacks to find…uh, whatever it is you think I should find."

"That's a waste of time," Armaeus said, his voice clipped as he turned to me. "You're the key. You should go with me into the labyrinth of the In Between to locate what I hid in 1571. I have no gaps in my memory other than in 1571 and 1478."

"Not true," Kreios drawled. "You have a very large Shadow Court-sized hole that we have yet to fill. To answer your question, Sara, Brody has seen no indication of increased activity by the Shadow Court. They are as silent as they were before their attack on you two days ago. It is as if they're waiting. But oh, I wonder what they might be waiting for?"

"I'm sure you're going to tell us your supposition on that score," Armaeus commented drily.

Kreios grinned. "It would be my absolute pleasure. My supposition is that they're waiting for you to gain the second of two known memory lapses so that you're both very powerful and very compromised at the same time. Then, if they're smart, they'll attack you and leverage the arcane knowledge you've collected for themselves."

"They're not strong enough to do that."

"Since we know very little about them, it's a bit premature for you to make that assertion," Kreios countered. "My question is, why are you not more concerned about them? Why is the pursuit of the missing pieces of your memory, specifically the pieces not related to the Shadow Court, your primary concern? This isn't about the acquisition of lost knowledge. It's about confronting a very real enemy to the Council and to Connecteds at large."

"What you're not seeing is the fact that the arcane knowledge that I'm collecting might *solve* the Shadow Court problem."

"And I could accept that if we knew what the problem was. Although we suspect we know the nature of what you hid in the In Between, we don't know it for a certainty. Our attention must be diverted to the Shadow Court. You know this to be true."

Watching the two of them argue was one of the more surreal experiences of my recent memory, and my recent memory was chock-full of surreal experiences. Armaeus and Kreios had always been staunch friends and absolute supporters of each other. For Kreios to confront the Magician and essentially shut down his treasure hunt was striking and more than a little alarming. For the Magician to glare at his long-time best friend like he was going to blast his head off his shoulders was downright frightening. I was used to dissension in the Council, but not between these two.

"Uh, guys?" Simon looked up from his laptop. "We've got incoming."

The Hierophant straightened. "Incoming what?"

"That's the thing, I have no idea. If I wasn't looking for it, I probably wouldn't even notice what's happening. But of course, I am looking. And it looks like we're being surrounded by shadows crawling along the city streets."

"Shadows?" Michael asked sharply. "You mean like demons? Or wraiths?"

"No, like legitimate shadows," Simon says. "We've got a ring about a mile wide, but they are closing in too fast to be walking and too slow to be driving. I don't know what we're looking at here unless it's an attack by scooters, and that's not showing up on any of the cameras."

"Let me see that," the Magician said. We all crowded around the laptop. Sure enough, a pattern of incoming energy was making a net around our small hotel, and that net was getting tighter. On the street cams, the energy showed up as almost human. A person would be caught in motion, then sort of wink out. Then the same person would reappear a quarter mile away from his last location with only a blur in between.

I made a face. "We're going to be attacked by Sonic the Hedgehog?"

"We're not going to be attacked at all." To my surprise, it was the Devil who spoke again, his eyes unfocused. "They don't know how many members of the Arcana Council are here, and having so many of us together could turn out very well for us or very poorly, but either way, we're not the only considerations.

Should our assailants reach us, we put the other guests of this hotel at risk. We have to leave. Now."

"Leave?" Armaeus turned on him. "There could be vital information to get if we took one of them."

"Not a problem," Simon said. "I can make this place so sticky with bugs, they won't be able to get out without something of ours on something of theirs. We can track them."

"Works for me." I nodded, stepping up next to Nikki. "Where should we meet? It's got to be somewhere I know."

"Justice Hall," Kreios said. "We need to learn what Abigail knew. Simon, how long do you need to stay to keep them on the scent here?"

"Not long at all," he said, his head close to his laptop again, fingers flying over the keys. "I've got tech I can leave behind that I'm charging with enough of an electrical feed to psychically blow the doors off this place — though no actual doors, I promise. It'll short out about two minutes after we're gone. Right around the time they're scaling the walls."

"Do it." Kreios turned to us. "Go."

"Gone." Nikki saluted and slung her arm around me, the two of us crackling instantly out of the posh sitting area of the hotel and reappearing moments later in the decidedly lower-level reception room of Justice Hall. One by one, the Council members appeared — first the Hierophant, then the Devil, then Death…

And then nothing.

"What's wrong?" I asked sharply, looking at Kreios. "I can understand Simon not wanting to show up in the middle of all of us, since he teleports commando, but where's Armaeus?"

Kreios looked at Death, who rolled her eyes. "He can't enter the In Between," she said. "He knows that.

Not even with Simon to guide the way. The Magician was the one who fashioned the locks that bar him. They're unbreakable."

"That was before he gained the ability to talk to angels, though, isn't it?" Kreios asked. "What if he's already struck up a conversation to ask them to help him gain entry?"

Death stiffened. "By the *light*—"

She winked out, leaving the Hierophant staring after her with a curious look in his eye.

I fixed him with a look of my own. "Were those people possessed by demons? Is that why they moved so quickly?" Michael would know. Of all the Council members, the Archangel had a deep and abiding understanding of the demons of this world. But Michael shook his head.

"No. You were more correct before. They are humans with the capacity for super speed, and as we saw, there was quite a number of them. The amount of culling of the Connected population to find that particular trait would take some time, unless it was a trait that was introduced at a genetic level."

I curled my lip. "You mean like they've been bred for it? Please tell me you're joking."

"With an organization as old as we believe the Shadow Court to be? Breeding for traits such as extreme speed could be done easily enough. But more likely it's a combination of genetic disposition and technoceutical augmentation. A potent combination and one more useful in creating a net such as the one we saw in London—and that you encountered in Paris."

"Technological augmentation…" I shook my head. Technoceuticals kept popping up with this group. That couldn't be a coincidence.

"How did they even know where to find us?" I asked. "Did one of us have a tracker?"

"No," Kreios said. "Simon set up a perimeter veil to keep that from happening. More likely they were able to detect the energy spike of so many high-powered Connecteds in one place, much as we were able to track them."

"Which means their tech is ever so close to our own. That's not a good thing," I said. "How is it they've stayed so far below the radar that we didn't even follow the line of technology—whether they're using it to augment psychic skills, nullify them, or simply track them?"

"A very good question. One that I'm hoping you can discover before it's too late."

My brand-new Council burner phone chirped in my pocket, and I grabbed it. The incoming number was international, so I stabbed the phone to connect the call. "Yes?"

"Sara, thank God," Brody said. "Where are you? Please don't tell me London.

CHAPTER EIGHTEEN

There was the faintest rustle of noise, almost like the sound of wings being unfurled, and I glanced up to see our numbers had dropped again. Now only Kreios, Nikki, and I remained in Justice Hall. The Hierophant had left the building.

"I'm putting you on speaker," I told Brody. "I've got Nikki and Kreios with me, and we're in Vegas. Armaeus and Simon are still in London, though." Ish.

"I figured that," Brody said. "Near the palace, I assume?"

I shot a glance at Nikki, and she nodded, clearly having paid more attention to our surroundings than I had. "Up until a short while ago. What happened?"

"A lot. We just got word of a known mercenary squad hitting the neighborhood hard, and a small, extremely fancy hotel had a suite set on fire. Authorities are on their way. The entire building is in the process of evacuation, casualties still unknown. I assume that was you."

"That was. Tell me about the squad."

"That's where it gets interesting. These guys have been on Interpol's radar for about a year now, but they've never hit to kill. Their game is to infiltrate offices, private residences, hotel rooms if someone is traveling with the goods, make their hit, and take what they want. They're masked, they're fast, and they leave any victims intact with all the usual warnings not to tell anyone or they'll come back and finish the job. Most people agree happily enough, but word still made it to the authorities well after the fact, mostly to validate insurance claims for the products that weren't illegal."

My brows went up. "Illegal as in—"

"Drugs and weapons, mostly, but both with a twist. Technoceutical and psychic firepower in particular. I didn't know there were actual weapons out there that could be enhanced by psychic compounds, even in the hands of non-Connecteds, but apparently, it's the hottest new trend on the arcane black market."

Kreios leaned forward. "Do you have any examples? Guns and stunners, or blades?"

"All of the above is the rumor, but anything that's been confiscated by Interpol has gone down a black hole. I've been on the team for a nanosecond, but I can already tell there's something hinky going on."

I smiled, glad we weren't on a video feed as we all exchanged glances. Brody was not a full-on Connected, but he was a homicide detective and had started his career as a beat cop. Most cops who lasted any length of time in their jobs possessed at least a rudimentary level of psychic ability, content with calling it instinct or intuition. Brody was a few levels above that, but not so advanced that he tripped any psychic wires. I could understand Armaeus wanting to leverage that.

"Hinky how?" I asked.

"Everyone I'm talking to is fully aware of the mental terrorist groups—that's what they're calling them; it makes them sweat less than psychic—that are gearing up. They're laying all sorts of shit at their feet, and much of it we already know. Arcane black market and web activity, psychic coercion, drugs, illusion casting, the whole bit. They don't all agree how they're doing it, and the biggest skeptics think it's nanotechnology deployed to influence an entire group at a time, but even the · skeptics acknowledge that if it looks like magic and plays like magic, they've got to understand that people are going to *call* it magic until they prove anything otherwise. So far, so good. The problem comes with how the agency is handling it. We've got two distinct groups forming: catch and destroy the bastards behind all this, or catch and employ."

"So eradicate the Connecteds or use them for Interpol's own purposes?"

"A-yup. And both groups stretch pretty high up. They want to shape the message for law enforcement from the go, but there's a lot of discord over what that message should be. And while people here are arguing it out, the hits keep escalating. This latest one is the most visible and violent, and we got eyewitness accounts of 'spider people' climbing walls and moving at high speeds, so now the story has to get crafted in a hurry."

"They tapping you yet for anything?"

He snorted. "Gotta tell you, I thought my main role here was to sit on my hands and stay quiet, but Armaeus must've done a number on whoever brought me in. I've become the go-to guy on profiling the mental terrorists and explaining what all they can do. Which is damned near anything they want if you get someone high enough on the food chain. Everyone's trying to figure out scope, and they're not liking the answers they're coming up with, especially since we've got nothing to stop these guys."

"Well, you still have conventional weapons," Nikki pointed out. "So far, we don't have anyone out there who can twist guns into pretzels or stop knockout gas from taking them down, right? And now we've got cells of these terrorists striking in the open, taking out civilian targets. They're not untouchable."

"They're not, but it's kind of difficult to take a shot at someone who can scale walls and cover a city block in the blink of an eye."

Nikki tilted her head, considering that. "Fair enough. And law enforcement is looking for a way to nullify their abilities."

"Bingo," Brody said. "And that tech is out there, just not large scale enough to be weaponized for law enforcement. Yet. Hell, they even call it null-tech."

Almost unconsciously, I found myself clenching my right hand into a fist, where the shard of Nul Magis rested. I'd caught that magic-nullifying bullet—literally—a few jobs back, protecting another magician from taking a blow that probably would have killed him. "That's a really dangerous path," I said, and Brody snorted.

"It sure is. And nobody's making the leap that shutting down psychic abilities will do anything more than keep these guys from pulling rabbits out of their hats. I'm trying to explain that it doesn't work like that, that if you rip the magic from people, you'll be damaging them badly, but things are escalating fast. The word's already gone out to develop this nullifying technology, or null-tech, so that it can be mass-produced. Someone's fronting big money for it. Not Interpol, of course. They're not the ones on the front lines. But we're talking government-level money. From what we can tell, another call has gone out for aug-tech, which is exactly what you think it is, tech that provides a psychic enhancement to users of those weapons. So we've got weapons that can amp up ordinary folks and supercharge psychics, and weapons designed to take out psychics. It's not good."

"When did the call go out? The hit on the London hotel just happened thirty seconds ago. Up to this point, the mental terrorists, or whatever they're calling them, have been low-key."

"Exactly my question. What I'm learning is it happened right around Christmas. Apparently, someone noticed the leveling up of the psychics and was savvy enough to know where the money would be eventually. I don't think they expected to be in production just a few months later, so now there's a gold-rush mentality. If somebody develops that tech, they could make a fortune."

"If someone develops that tech, they're signing their own death warrant."

"I kind of get the feeling that'll get sorted out after all the money's been made." Something chirped on the line, and Brody's voice followed a second later. "Gotta bounce. We got another hit in London, Tower Ward. You got boots on the ground there?"

"Crap." My gaze leapt to Kreios, but he was already gone, leaving Nikki and me alone in the room.

"We do now," Nikki drawled. "What's happening?"

"Some church getting swarmed, that's all I got," Brody said. "Will update when I can."

The line went dead, and Nikki and I stared at each other, then at the door in the corner of the reception room for Justice Hall. It was the door that led to the library.

"You have any idea where to start in there?" I asked.

She sighed. "I do not."

We both jerked upright as another noise sounded from the opposite corner of the room. The door to my private office creaked open, and the familiar whitebunned head of Mrs. French poked out, followed by the rest of her body. As usual, my library caretaker was dressed in impeccably tailored period wear from the mid-nineteenth century, spotlessly proper from the top of her high-necked white blouse to the hem of her sweeping, lightly bustled dark gray muslin skirt. And she was holding three glass canisters to her bosom.

"Justice Wilde," she blurted. "I *am* sorry for interrupting, though I kept mum for as long as I could. But these just arrived, and—"

"You were in there the whole time?" I asked her, cutting her off. "Why didn't you come out?"

"Well, begging your pardon, but you all seemed very focused, and then these canisters, well, I thought I should review them first to ensure you got the information you needed."

I scowled. "We're running a little short on time, Mrs. French."

"And that's as may be, but you're apparently not the only one." She stepped back, holding the door wide, and I sighed and trudged over, bracing myself to peek into my office.

The position of Justice of the Arcana Council was all about responding to Connecteds who had been victimized by, hello, other psychics. In order for me to identify anyone as a victim, they had to send me an alert. A cry for help. Unfortunately, the last Justice, Abigail Strand, had rather abruptly vacated the office in 1853, and she'd not been replaced until I'd taken on the job a few months ago. While Abigail's complaint-intake system was dated, it still worked perfectly well, and I hadn't had time to upgrade. I'd actually come to enjoy the whoosh, whoosh, whoosh, thump, thump, thump of incoming canisters—most days, anyway.

Now I stared at the wall of pneumatic tubes that stretched down from the ceiling and ended in a velvet-lined trough that provided a cushion for the new jobs coming in, and blinked. There were easily a dozen canisters still in the trough, and at least twenty more stacked on my desk. "These have all come in this week?" I asked, unable to keep the dismay out of my voice.

"These have all come in this morning," Mrs. French corrected me. "Each more strident than the last, and from all corners of the world, which does make it seem slightly less terrifying, because it's essentially a series of isolated events that wouldn't even get noticed except we're serving as clearing house for all of them at once. But the issue is Connecteds are getting attacked, Justice Wilde. A quite specific type of Connected too, those who live more in the public eye. Now they're getting attacked in their homes, on the streets, at their workplaces by other Connecteds. People who know their secrets, but who haven't yet come out as psychic, in the main. It's—it's unnerving is what it is."

"Jesus, we're eating our own?" Nikki protested, while I narrowed my eyes at Mrs. French.

"Attacked how?"

"Stunners of some type seems to be the consensus. Some of them rather crudely modified, some quite sophisticated, some simply off-the-shelf tasers." She pointed to my right hand, now clenched into a fist. "They're trying to nullify their magic. And a few of them are succeeding. Which is only inciting their victims to anger and violence of a decidedly nonpsychic type."

"That's going to escalate quickly," Nikki muttered.

"Keep tracking it," I told Mrs. French. "But tell me this first. You know anything about the Shadow Court?"

Her brows lifted, a frown marring her face. "Can't say as I do, Justice, though..." she frowned harder.

"Now no, no, I take that back. There was…there was…something, I think."

Her hand fluttered up to her brow as she winced, and I slid a glance to Nikki. "You have the text I sent you still?" I asked. "This is a new phone."

"On it," she said, sliding her phone out of her décolletage and swiping it on as Mrs. French brought her other hand up, starting to massage her temples with her fingers.

"I could swear I have heard that name before, but it isn't coming to me, and it should—it surely should. Because there is nothing that's occurred in the world that I didn't know since the day I arrived here, and that's only the truth," Mrs. French muttered. She dropped one hand to her voluminous skirts, pulling out a small silver bell. She rang it, then placed it on the side table next to the glass canisters, but her face was drawn now, pale with the exertion of trying to remember.

"Here we go," Nikki said. She turned the phone around to Mrs. French, who drew in a sharp breath, then her legs went out from beneath her. She dropped heavily into the overstuffed chair that was, thankfully, right behind her, and I crouched beside her in alarm as the sound of light, running feet pattered from behind the library door. The door burst open a second later, and a quartet of bright-eyed, tousle-headed boys tumbled out, all of them wearing clothes of the same vintage and craftsmanship as Mrs. French's. Her library assistants.

"Boys," Mrs. French said weakly. "There's something I'd like you to look at. I need your help."

Eagerly, they pressed forward and eyeballed the phone. Then the boys all started chattering at once. "The Court—Shadow Court, right?" "They were a regular pain in the bum, weren't they?" "So much trouble, right up till they weren't."

I stared at them. "Wait, you recognize this?"

"Well, not the tattoo itself, ma'am, but the design of it, certainly," the closest boy said. "We got shelves on shelves on 'em, or we…" He stopped and tilted his head, his eyes moving up and to the right as he tried to recreate the library in his mind's eye. "We did, I should say. We may not so much anymore. Justice Strand was right clear on how she solved those problems right down to the nubbins, had us clear out the lot of the cases."

"We didn't get them all, 'course," a second boy said. "We tried. But there was a regular pile of them."

Nikki and I exchanged a look. "You could find them again?"

"Oh, sure." The boys looked at each other, their grins growing. "Bobby would know. He's buried so deep in the library, he didn't hear the bell. He was talking just the other day how he seemed to be remembering more and more about things he'd not realized we had, or hadn't thought of in a while. I bet he'd know."

"Go," Mrs. French said faintly. "Bring back anything you can find and — well, I do apologize, Justice Wilde, I don't know what's gotten into me. Recalling such a simple thing."

I patted her shoulder. Mrs. French had been Abigail's closest companion and still revered the former Justice. She wouldn't take kindly to knowing she'd been afflicted by the same spell that had stolen the memory of the Shadow Court from the Magician. The boys didn't seem afflicted at the same level, which confused me, but as they disappeared through the library door, I continued.

"When they come back, we'll be looking for where the Shadow Court was based. Hopefully, whatever's left of the information about them will make that clear somehow."

"Oh! Oh, that's an easy one," the smallest of the boys said, his eyes bright with satisfaction that he could speak, since the older boys were off on an assignment. "They had a place in Hamburg, Germany. Pretty as a palace, Justice Strand always said."

My hand pulsed as he spoke, and I stared at it. The boys in Mrs. French's care had been spelled into eternal youth, making them fixtures in the library whether they wanted to be or not. When I'd become Justice and had caught the Nul Magis in my right hand, I'd used the shard of magic to lift the spell that'd been placed on them so long ago, allowing them to age normally again. But when I'd touched the shard to their tousled mop tops, had I done more than I realized? Had I also, without realizing it, lifted Abigail's spell that made them forget the Shadow Court?

I hadn't needed to unspell Mrs. French, which was why she was still fighting the effects of Abigail's influence as she struggled to remember what she'd been forced to forget. But the boys...

"Hamburg," I echoed, and the littlest librarian beamed at me.

"Pretty as a palace!" he agreed.

CHAPTER NINETEEN

In all the time I'd been working as an artifact hunter, I'd been to Hamburg, Germany only a couple of times, both for less than a day. The only thing I'd ever heard about it was that it was a test site for one of Elon Musk's goofier inventions, the hyperloop, which made it no different from LA, San Francisco, Reno, and Austin — as well as a dozen other cities across the world. One of Europe's ancient port cities, with a shoreline that glittered above the Elbe River as it fed in from the North Sea, Hamburg was considered one of the top ten most happening cities in Europe.

Tonight, all that was happening was a torrential downpour.

I stared at the inscrutable horizon, a watercolor blur behind the sheets of rain, as Nikki paced behind me, staring at her tablet. "Got an update from Kreios. We've still got nothing on the location of Death, Simon, and the Magician. But the fires in the hotel and church were contained without anyone dying, and most of the victims who did end up in the hospital aren't seriously injured. London is up in arms, understandably so, over the fact they know so little about the attackers."

"Join the club," I muttered.

"Local law enforcement has brought in more Interpol agents on this, including Detective Delish," Nikki continued. "He's up to his ears now as the resident mental terrorist expert, but according to Kreios, there's a rush of other experts flooding law enforcement agencies throughout Europe. They're all in on the mental-terrorist-connection angle, but they're spinning it to be more mutants and aliens than psychics."

That pulled me away from my vantage point at the window. "Really?"

"Really. Whatever the reason, people are *not* good with their woo being too abstract. Way easier to believe in aliens than ESP, apparently."

"Interesting. And outside of Europe?"

"Surprisingly little reaction. We can thank all the regular straight-up terrorists for that, I think. Places getting blown up isn't big news anymore, especially if nobody dies. The psychic element of the attack is either being ignored entirely by the major outlets or blown up by the clickbait farms as a case of wacky Euros believing in fairies. If there's nothing else to feed it, which I hope to Mother Mary and all the saints there isn't, the story will die off in a day or so. Less if there's a political tweet storm Stateside to distract people."

"Never thought I'd be lobbying for one of those."

"Exactly." She swiped her thumb across the screen. "So what's the plan here? Assuming it ever stops raining?"

"I want to find their home base. Mrs. French is going through the cases the boys have found, but there's not much there. Most of the complaints are from in and around Hamburg, but not in any concentration within the city. It's safe to say that the Shadow Court has been here for a while, though. The earliest complaint came in to Justice Hall around 1400. The Shadow Court's only a minor player in that one, probably why it escaped Abigail's notice."

"Makes sense." Nikki resumed staring at her screen, which I could see was a map of downtown Hamburg. "Lot of ground to cover if all we've got to go on is that the place looks like a palace. Most of the older buildings do, though there was a fire in 1842 that knocked out a good chunk of the earliest architecture. By Abigail's time, there'd been some reconstruction, but not a lot. If there was a residence that was pretty as a palace, it probably was one of the buildings that survived the fire. No way of knowing if it also survived the city getting bombed within an inch of its life in World War II."

I nodded and resumed staring out the window. The rain was letting up enough for me to survey the street around the hotel, though there were only a few souls out, most of them hunched over against the rain or carrying enormous umbrellas. Every once in a while, a few people would meet briefly, then spin apart, often with the flare of two lit cigarettes serving as the filament of connection between them. Shadowed by the rain and late hour, it was almost mesmerizing the way the pedestrians moved, like choreography in a silent movie.

"What's their end game?" I murmured. "Why haven't they come after us?"

"Well, they did. The hotel."

"That wasn't subtle enough. It was the opposite of subtle, actually. They were out in the open, stalking us where anyone could see. They had to know we'd disappear before they got there."

Nikki hummed as she typed. "We could have engaged them."

"We wouldn't have, though. There's no precedent for us to do that. So it was a push, but a push toward what? And who tipped them off that we were there? I'm

205

not completely buying it was just our electrical signature. There has to be more to it than that."

Across the room, Nikki leaned back in her chair. She knew what I was asking. "Mercault let slip that you were in Paris, and thirty minutes later, they were all over you with a team of what, twenty operatives? And not slug operatives either."

"They were definitely not slugs," I said. "I mean, I was able to handle them, but not without working at it, and I'm supposed to be the great and powerful Oz. So these guys were good."

"And fast."

"Very fast. But the attack at the hotel had a different feel to it. I didn't sense that they were coming after us to take us down, while I did in the park. That felt more personal."

"We still don't have anything on the woman who attacked you or the guy on the bike. Simon didn't find either one of them in any database anywhere in the world as operatives. There weren't any arrests assigned to them. Or official papers, for that matter, which means they're off the grid. If they are, the rest of them are too."

"Yeah." I leaned against the window frame, my gaze skipping over the hustling and shuffling crowd below, thinning even as the rain grew less intense, the storm finally showing some signs of breaking.

Then I saw him.

A lone man stood just outside the café that had been bustling all night. Unlike everyone around him, he stood absolutely still in the rain, his hands in his pockets, his face tilted up and away from me so that the reflected light from the café played across his pale skin. He wore a dark fedora and rain slicker over dark pants and shoes, but otherwise seemed to be completely unbothered by the downpour.

Completely unbothered, I realized. In fact, the rain was parting around him, his own personal umbrella force field keeping him dry.

"What is it?" Nikki murmured from her position on the couch.

"We've got a watcher, but he's not watching the right place, and I feel like that's on purpose. How'd you check us into the Hotel Savoy?"

"Straight-up check-in. Same as here. Same as the other three places. They knew you there, though. You'd stayed before."

I glanced at her. "No, I haven't. I've never stayed longer in Hamburg than a few hours. Why do you think so?"

"I checked the room out, and there was Glenmorangie sitting on top of the minibar. That struck me as odd, but the card said compliments of the house. I figured they recognized your name and had it sent up before I got there."

"Negative. I would have remembered any of these hotels. So—"

My voice trailed off as the man on the corner turned to face me. His eyes were the same cold blue that I remembered from the Luxembourg Gardens, his face startlingly clear in the rain. He knew where I'd been this whole time, had only turned as I'd made the realization that I'd been had.

I didn't flinch away from his gaze. I wanted to know who this man was, and I wanted to know how such a powerful Connected could exist without the Council's knowledge. For his part, he stared back at me, cool and confident. "What's his game?" I muttered, settling my feet more firmly.

"Sara…" Nikki warned. "This wouldn't be the time to do anything stupid."

"He knew I'd be here," I countered. "He knew, or they knew, exactly when we arrived in London, and they had a team in place to hit the hotel within a matter of minutes of us showing up. Meanwhile, you guys had been there for two days without issue. How did they know? Who's filling them in? And who is the target, me or Armaeus?"

"I vote for option A, since dude's here now. We don't know where Armaeus is. Presumably, neither do they."

"Unless they took him."

"There's no way that's possible."

But despite Nikki's unshakable faith in the Magician, I wasn't so sure. There'd been absolutely no contact from Armaeus since he'd taken off with Simon, and he'd been physically shaky before that attempt. He wasn't operating with a full bag of magic tricks, and the assimilation of the lost chapter of the Book of Radiance had taken a toll on him in a way I'd never seen before. The more I thought about it, the more I realized how possible it was that Armaeus was in serious danger, danger I couldn't even understand, much less counter. He hadn't wanted to get me involved. He hadn't wanted to risk me.

And that…was a problem. Even if he didn't know who I was, *how could he not know who I am?*

"Sara," Nikki said again. "You're not all that good at transpo when you haven't been somewhere."

"I've been staring at this damned corner the last three hours. I know it better than I know my own bedroom."

"I still think—"

I crackled out of the suite and onto the sidewalk in front of the café, where the man had been standing. I didn't expect him to still be there when I arrived, of course. He'd done a good job of anticipating my every move up to this point. The most likely next step would be for him to move just far enough away that he could watch me without getting tangled up.

I was wrong.

The moment I appeared on the sidewalk, the man wrapped his arms around me and slung me into the street, bouncing me off a passing car with such force, I ricocheted right back into his body. Moving too fast for me to wink out of existence before it landed, his gloved fist came around and caught my jaw, whipping my head back as pain galvanized me into action. When he swung around from the other direction, I ducked, using my own not insignificant speed and piling into his body, the suddenness of my movement catching him by surprise enough to make him sprawl back. That reaction lasted only a moment, however, as he regained his feet and launched at me again. By then, I'd already turned as if I was going to run. I didn't mind taking on this guy, but not with so many people around. Like it or not, the skills I had at my disposal didn't work so well for any hand-to-hand combat that involved an audience.

That said, I had to get close enough to hurt the man discreetly, so I had to get creative. At the last second, as he gathered himself to launch after me, I spun back toward him, angling a little. I was able to wrap my arms around his legs, using the flurry of my movement to mask the twin bolts of fire that I shot into his back. He grunted with pain. A second later, I felt the crack of something low against my skull, which earned a much more robust scream from me. At this point, we had attracted a crowd, but no one was stepping in to break us up. Or maybe everything was simply happening too fast.

I couldn't risk another fire bolt, so I lurched to my feet and made to run in earnest this time. The guy immediately took off after me. I shot across the street and passed the open doors of my hotel just as Nikki crested the doorway in time to collide with my pursuer. There, her years on the force came in handy as she cold-cocked the guy, knocking him flat before she whipped out her phone and took several photos. He came to just as quickly and launched up, one hand slicing at Nikki just below her chin. Blood immediately geysered from her neck and I leapt forward, but the man raced away as Nikki toppled into my arms. I clapped a hand firmly over her neck and probed the tracery of the wound with my fingers, my hands crackling with heat as I cauterized the gash with furious magic.

"Go — go!" Nikki gasped, waving the phone at me, but I wasn't about to leave her. I flashed us both back to our room, where Kreios was now waiting.

"I'll take her," Kreios said, pulling Nikki from me almost protectively as she still waved the phone, less convincingly this time.

"Bugged," she said as her head rolled.

Kreios pulled the device from her and swiped it, then nodded sharply. "She got photos. I'll run these through Simon's system to get an identity. But it looks like the same man you saw in Paris."

"How'd he know we were here?" I demanded as he tapped on the phone, sending the photos off.

Kreios shrugged, then handed the phone back to me. "There's no bug in the room, so if he heard you, it wasn't through electronic means. The phone wasn't bugged, either."

"So, what, he's just got really good hearing?" I snapped, but Kreios's attention was already back on Nikki.

"She'll be fine. You healed her clean. There's blood loss, though. I'll help her with that." He lifted Nikki into his arms. Meanwhile, the map that she'd been staring at on her tablet now stretched in front of me on the phone, with an unmistakable red dot moving up the street. I didn't know Hamburg well enough to know the guy's direct location, so I'd have to do this the hard way. An instant later, I was back on the sidewalk where we'd first tussled, and I started running.

It took me a good mile to catch up with the asshat, and that was me going full tilt. Right around the three-quarter-mile mark, however, I realized he had to be running me toward a trap. He would've circled back by now or ambushed me if he was interested in taking me out. There were plenty of opportunities for that in the rabbit warren of streets that made up downtown Hamburg. As it was, our footrace was leading me into an area heavily under construction, with tarps and plywood covering over buildings in dire need of renovation. I needed to stop, think, and be strategic, but every time I made the attempt, I saw the geyser of blood spurting from Nikki's throat. This jackwit was going to pay for that if it was the last thing —

The boarded-up wall beside me exploded out in a fury of movement and violent force. I pivoted to the side, but not quickly enough to avoid the crush of Connected humanity that burst out toward me, easily a dozen leather-clad assailants, all of them with fists flying. I reacted instinctively, my hands balling into fists as they instantly lit into fire —

And were extinguished just as quickly.

What the...

The crowd of my attackers seemed to realize this fact as soon as I did, and, with a roar of delight, they lurched toward me. I crackled into nothingness — only that didn't work either. I could still work up a modest electrical zing of psychic ability, but it wasn't enough to do any of the things I had come to depend on it for. I'd been shorted out.

"Crap!"

I raced across the street to the line of motorcycles and picked one at random. I might not have enough psychic power to transport myself bodily out of this mess, but I sure as hell wasn't going to stick around to become the base layer of a bad-guy wedding cake. With a last furious burst of electricity, I lit the bike up, and it roared to life. I blasted off down the street and was gone.

CHAPTER TWENTY

Another feature of my sudden lapse of psychic ability made itself immediately obvious as my Connected pursuers didn't give chase on foot with supersonic speed, but instead relied on a barrage of straight-up ordinary bullets that didn't quite reach me. Apparently, they were equally afflicted by the psychic dead zone. Silver lining.

But what the hell was that about? I sucked in a breath, my adrenaline spiking, and yanked Nikki's phone out of my jacket. The red dot was still ahead of me, picking up pace. I leaned into the handlebars of my motorcycle, mostly to avoid getting blinded by the rainwater whipping over the top of the low windscreen and lashing into my face. Manhandling a phone while driving an unfamiliar motorbike at high speeds during a rainstorm wasn't going to earn me any discounts on my insurance, but this dickhead had slashed Nikki. He wasn't long for this world, one way or the other.

I followed him all the way to the Hamburg pier, pulling up sharply as he entered a private shipyard that appeared to have no security. Not being a complete idiot, I recognized a trap when I saw it, and I sat back on the bike. The red dot on the phone stopped in the center of the shipyard, and then, of course, winked out.

Asshat.

"Lovely night in Hamburg, wouldn't you say?"

The voice that broke over me was cultured and older and decidedly Western European. I wasn't willing to get more specific than that, but it was the same voice I'd heard from the ghost kidnapper of the family at Gare du Nord, and I was sure—almost sure—I'd heard it before that. Not in any major way, though, which was interesting. This guy hadn't been a direct client of mine in the past, or an enemy. I was sure of it.

But he certainly had my number now, and this was a call I was going to take.

"Does it usually storm on your best nights in Hamburg, or did I get particularly lucky?"

"Particularly lucky. But then, you've been a very lucky girl in your life, Miss Wilde, haven't you?"

There didn't seem to be any need to respond to this, as the guy clearly had a prepared script. He stood slightly behind me and to the right, and I wasn't about to give him the satisfaction of turning toward him to see him more clearly. Why start with the whole maturity thing now?

Sure enough, he continued. "There are those who believe that we choose the lives we lead before we take our first breath upon this planet. That we are here to learn something specific, and that we choose both the graces and the obstacles we face. But your life—well... It's hard to believe that someone would have chosen the challenges you've endured, Miss Wilde. May I call you Miss Wilde? I know that's the title of choice of your Council's leader, and I'd hate to overstep."

Irritation poked at me, but I knew better than to give in to it. Of course this guy would know about me. I wasn't all that anonymous. I mean, no, I didn't have an Instagram account, but people knew who I was.

I didn't speak, but he obligingly continued. "So let's explore your life, shall we? I've studied it so closely, it would be a pleasure to share it with someone else."

"I'll take a pass. Who are you?"

"Ah! Names. Names are perhaps the best place to start. Your name, or so you believed, was Sariah Pelter. Not a very prepossessing appellation, but then you weren't destined to have it for very long. Your parents had far bigger plans for you, each in their own way. Willem of Galt, the current Hermit of the Arcana Council, and the Atlantean goddess Vigilance, though she's gone by many names since then. An impressive and unusual pairing."

"Yeah, they were a big hit at parent-teacher night." I couldn't stand it anymore, though, and I turned to my right to see the man. I wasn't expecting it to be the dark-haired, dark-eyed assassin, but this guy...I'd seen this guy before. Somewhere.

I narrowed my eyes. "I know you."

"I'm flattered," he acknowledged, nodding as I racked my brain for where I would have run into him. It had to have been on a job. But he *hadn't* been a client. A competitor I'd been told to watch out for? A tail looking to get the drop on me and steal whatever artifact I'd just light-fingered myself? Something...like that. But not quite that. Tall and slender, the man was expensively dressed in a buttoned-up trench coat, dark trousers and shoes. He wore no hat, and his light blond hair and cool blue eyes assessed me with the slightest bit of amusement that did a passable job hiding the brutality that lurked beneath. He looked like the quintessential Aryan, in very human proportions—

215

strong, or at least giving the appearance of being strong, but not heavily built.

And rich. It was a characteristic I'd learned to pick up on early in my career as an artifact hunter, and it was always men who projected it most. This guy was absolutely rolling in money and power, and had been for so long, he didn't even notice it anymore. Which meant he hadn't made his money himself, or at least he hadn't made it all himself. He was simply the latest in a long line of moneyed asshats not afraid to throw their power around.

A new layer of annoyance riffled through me as he resumed his monologue. "But you weren't raised by your parents, of course. That wouldn't have done when no one knew you existed and the two were on opposite sides of a millennia-old war. Instead, you were raised by a cocktail waitress in a squalid little trailer park in Memphis, Tennessee. She also fancied herself psychic. Once she realized what you could do, she whored you out to her friends at the salon, the bar, even the local police department to build up her own sense of self-worth, and told anyone who would listen that she was every bit as gifted as you were. Until her big mouth got her killed."

So, we'd officially moved to insults. I tried to keep my anger in check, because there was something truly intriguing about the eagerness with which the man spoke. He wanted to get a rise out of me, sure, but he wanted something more than that. He wanted me to ask questions.

Fair enough. "Is there a point to this?"

"Ah, Ms. Wilde, you disappoint me," he said, though his lips quirked into the barest approximation of a pout. "It's such a fascinating story. The same day your foster mother died, your house was blown up by an ancient dragon god of Atlantis, nearly with you inside it, and you ran away. Not to the police officer who had been your champion and virtual guardian, but *away*. As far away as you could get, yes?"

"Look—"

"And then you were found at a rest area by a kindhearted woman and taken in by her, no questions asked, her and her RV community of retirees. Such a good-natured group, and what a stroke of luck when so many other options would have led you down far darker paths."

By now my blood had iced over. I glared at the man. "How do you know that?" I asked flatly. Very few people in the world knew how I'd spent the intervening five years between my escape from Memphis and my hesitant and mistake-filled return to the world of the Connected, as an artifact hunter for hire. I was pretty sure this guy hadn't made the short list.

I could tell he felt he'd scored a win by the brightening of his smile, the rustle of energy crackling around him. Without breaking eye contact, I flicked my third eye open and, sure enough, the guy was Connected—or at least he was holding down a fair amount of electrical zippity-do-dah. More to the point, I could feel my own echoing fire kindling along my fingertips as I stared at him, which meant I was no longer trapped in the psychic dead zone of downtown Hamburg. Good to know.

What was also good to know was that this guy wasn't killer strong, as far as Connecteds went. I pegged his psychic energy signature at around five or six out of ten, and I suspected part of that number was due to augmentation, not inborn abilities. While that didn't make much difference at a cocktail party, it spoke to the levels of power this guy could access. A natively strong

Connected had deeper wells to draw upon than one whose abilities had been gifted to them by drugs or nanotechnology. So while I may have betrayed the weakness of my interest, he was now betraying the weakness of his body.

Then again, with the kind of money I suspected this guy had, he could buy all the psychic muscle he needed.

"Once you left your makeshift family some five years later, you entered a far grimmer period of your life, didn't you, Ms. Wilde?" he continued as the breeze kicked up around us. "You'd made your name as a gifted child who helped the police find other children, missing children. Children who'd often been abused. It marked you at a very young age, and your work as an artifact hunter forced you to run across more of these children. Dozens. Hundreds. Locked up in cages to be sold at the arcane black market, or left to rot on the side of some mountain pass, the most valuable parts already ripped from their bodies before their blood cooled. It put a damper on your excitement to get rich by selling the trinkets and potions clients sent you after. You could line your pockets for only so long before you felt compelled to make a difference. To save the lives of those who were not strong enough to fight for themselves."

The man's voice had moved to a sort of unctuous, patronizing tone, and it was all I could do not to blast his mocking expression from his face. But there was a purpose to all this, and by now, I felt compelled to let it play out.

"Fortunately enough, you found an able companion in this effort in the form of Father Jerome, at least until his death. So tragic. I rather thought it would have a deeper impact on you. A deeper, more personal impact. That you would have struggled more. But you didn't struggle as much as I expected. That fascinated me, I must admit."

I didn't even twitch. I wasn't going to give this guy the satisfaction of knowing how much his words were cutting me. Because the truth of the matter was, I hadn't yet begun to truly grieve the death of Father Jerome. A death I'd inadvertently caused for letting him get too close to me, the same way I'd inadvertently caused my foster mother's death years earlier, and had brought so much harm to so many people. *So much harm.* Father Jerome had been my only friend for so long during the dark years I'd first worked as an artifact hunter. More than that, he'd given a shape and function to my need to protect the children. After his death…

"But with his passing, there were new challenges for you to tackle, weren't there?" the man pressed. "The Magician of the Council had finally succeeded in getting you to ascend. How long had he groomed you for the position? How long had he manipulated your emotions, your reactions, your very body to help coerce you to fall in love with him?"

He didn't wait for me to respond to that, but pushed on. "And here we are, together at last. Months into your tenure as the Justice of the Arcana Council, grappling with powers that you had no idea you possessed within you. Some of which you've mastered, some of which you've not, some of which you don't even realize exist, at least not entirely. With the call of the persecuted landing in your office through your gleaming pneumatic tubes. Thump, thump, thump—a siren call for you to give aid. Thump, thump, thump."

"You know, you should take your act on the road. You'd kill it at open mic night."

He tilted his head, considering me with his glittering pale blue eyes. "You're still so sad, Ms. Wilde. With all your great and wonderful powers, with the strength of the Arcana Council at your back, what have you truly accomplished? Are you any closer to saving the most vulnerable members of the Connected community now than you were when you worked with Father Jerome? Does that not gall you, to know there are so many other things you could accomplish if only you were given the guidance you need, the support necessary for you to make true, lasting change?"

And here it was. I lifted my brows, and finally, it was my turn to smile. "Geez, all this for a headhunting position? I could've saved you the time. If you really want to recruit from the Council, hit up Viktor Dal. He's exactly the kind of megalomaniac asshat who'd be perfect for your organization."

The man wasn't fazed by my tone. If anything, his smile grew deeper. "Who's to say I haven't already had that conversation with the Emperor? Or that he hasn't been in my employ for years…decades, even? Definitely long enough to convince him to indulge his predilections for the fearmongering and abduction of poor, innocent children in Memphis, Tennessee, perhaps a dozen years ago. Certainly long enough for him to prick the conscience of a shy, unassuming teenager with a penchant for poetry and drawing and — oh, yes — reading the battered Tarot card deck she nearly bought at a used bookstore for three dollars and fifty cents, until the woman behind the counter stopped that transaction from happening and instead gifted the deck to the young girl. You know there's an old superstition about Tarot cards, don't you, Ms. Wilde? That your first deck should be a — "

The outrage burst out of me so unexpectedly, it wasn't even a conscious decision on my part. Hearing this man, this stranger, share a story that'd been so private and personal I'd told no one in my life—not my foster mother, not Brody, not Nikki, not even my dog-eared journals that'd all been blown up in the fire that destroyed my home—completely undid me. It reached into a part of my soul I didn't know existed and released a firestorm that shot straight from my core along my fingers and out, incinerating the man standing to my right. By the time the wave of fire winked out again, there was nothing but scorched pavement.

While the man was now standing on my left, the stiff breeze barely lifting the edges of his hair.

He chuckled. "If you think I would be so foolish as to toy with the temper of the strongest Connected sorceress on the planet and put myself at personal risk, allow me to disabuse you of that notion. I have nothing but the greatest respect for you, Ms. Wilde. It's why I arranged this virtual conversation, and why I have been such a fan from the first time I learned about you."

"Always a pleasure to meet the public," I gritted out. "Is this where you unveil your evil plan?"

"Not at all," the impressively life-like hologram said. "This is where I give you a choice to consider. A simple choice, and one which should prove, in the end, to be an easy one for you. The Shadow Court has used its long years in seclusion from the vigilant eye of the Arcana Council to its benefit. We are on the verge of destroying your Council, in fact. It is a battle you simply cannot win."

"Well, that's good to know. Anything else?"

"Only that I propose that you do *not* attempt to destroy the Court in turn, but work with us. Collaborate. Let us help you accomplish what has seemed virtually impossible to you—the end of the victimization of Connecteds, particularly Connected children. The advent of a new dawn for Connecteds worldwide, where they can grow and thrive and no longer hide in darkness, afraid of being persecuted or killed. There is no reason for our two organizations to work against each other. And every reason for them to work together. Think about it."

The apparition winked out.

"But don't think too long."

The last words of the disembodied voice had barely died away when it was followed by another voice in the stillness, scarcely more than a strangled, halting whisper.

"Miss...Wilde.

CHAPTER TWENTY-ONE

The smoke that billowed up around me should have generated some alarm given what I'd just experienced, but I recognized it immediately as Armaeus's particular form of teleportation. While I was all crackling fire and scattered embers, he dissolved into mist. And it was that mist that was pulling at me now, which could mean only one thing: Armaeus wanted me to be with him. I was more than willing to go.

Eventually, I'd ask more questions before I got yanked out of one place and into another, but today was not that day.

I landed with less of a clatter and more of a decided "oof" as I crunched into a rock floor in the middle of absolute darkness. I fumbled with Nikki's phone to generate light, but that function seemed to be out of order. Fortunately, my hands didn't rely on such delicate tech, and I lit up my fingertips a second later.

And saw…absolutely nothing. I appeared to be in a concrete or stone passageway, which fortunately had ample oxygen, because the path stretched before and behind me, both options curving into the darkness beyond the glow from my fingertips. There was the faintest sound of rustling behind the stone, but nothing coherent. It sounded more like scurrying animals than human feet, and I knew immediately where I was. Or at least I dreaded immediately where I was. The In Between. The series of arcane highways and byways that stretched between this world and the next plane, mapped only in part, but networked across the globe. I'd been in these passageways a few weeks ago, and I hadn't been in a hurry to return anytime soon. The Magician clearly had other plans.

"Armaeus?" I asked into the darkness, but there was no response. That was weird. He'd summoned me. If he couldn't summon me directly to where he was, what did that mean? Had he simply summoned me to where he *thought* he was? That didn't bode well either. It spoke to either a lapse in memory, of which I'd already had my fill, or to Armaeus having blacked out during his time in the In Between. And where were Simon and Death?

"Miss Wilde." The voice came again, weaker this time, and I immediately set off down the path, not at all sure that I was supposed to go down instead of up. But it felt better to be moving, and as I walked, I swept the walls of the corridor with my light, looking for any indication of where I was.

I was destined to be disappointed. Whoever did the signage down here needed to be fired.

Fortunately, I didn't have far to go. I hadn't walked more than fifty feet when a flash of something bright caught my eye around the next corner, and I instantly doused my own light, letting it gutter out as I moved forward more quickly. As I approached, I could see the glow ahead of me wasn't firelight but a weird radiance spilling out of a body. I fully expected it to be the Magician's body, right up until I saw that the guy on the ground was wearing a skull cap.

"Simon?" Something moved beside him, and my hands came up in immediate defense, only to recognize the pale face staring back at me through a creepy hooded shroud. Death. Looking like, well, *Death.*

"Simon!" I gasped again, rushing forward. Death rocked back on her heels, finally speaking as I knelt beside them.

"Why are you here?" she growled.

I blinked at her. "Armaeus summoned me. I mean, I think he summoned me. There was smoke, and I heard my name and…um, where's Armaeus?"

"I wish I knew," Death said bitterly. "I knew this was a mistake the moment he fixed on All Hallows by the Tower, especially since he now knows the language of the angels. He was too weak to make this attempt, his mind too disorganized from the lore he uncovered in that blasted book. Once he'd gotten a taste of what he'd lost, he was so determined to recapture all his memories that he leapt at the chance to learn more."

"But where is he now?" I asked again. "I thought Simon came down with him. "

"He did. I found Simon in this cocoon when I got here. He's unconscious and appears stable, but I didn't want to take him out of the In Between and leave the Magician here alone. There's too much in these halls that are set against him."

Uh… "That doesn't sound good."

She glanced at me with hard eyes. "The Magician has been in his role for centuries, but the man you know is not the man he always was. I've long suspected that his decisions to strip away pieces of his knowledge also allowed him to strip away elements of his personality that were not conducive to what he perceived his role to be. It takes a very strong man to shut down his own demons on a daily basis, and the Magician's job was difficult enough without him having to constrain himself as well."

"His quest for balance." I didn't always agree with Armaeus's interpretation of balance, but I understood his need to strive for it. I'd experienced a similar push-pull between the flawed, earnest, moderately skilled, and highly resourceful human I'd been and the equally flawed but Great-and-Powerful-Oz-ified Council member I'd become. Some days, I wasn't sure who was better equipped to fight this battle, but I didn't have that choice anymore. I had to use the tools I'd forged.

"His quest for balance," Death agreed. "As you may have already figured out, the Magician is not nearly as balanced as he would like everyone to believe. He was reborn in a cauldron of fire when he ascended to the role, and his magic is deep, primal, and base. None of those things lead naturally to balance."

"So when he found arcane lore that he wanted to keep out of human hands, he wrapped it up in a package of his own bad habits and poofed it out of existence." Mercault had mentioned this too, and Armaeus certainly hadn't denied it.

"Apparently so. And he was at peace with those decisions for centuries. But something changed." Death smoothed a lock of Simon's hair away from his face.

"He saw the design of that tattoo."

"No. No, something else. He wasn't driven to seek out the truth about the Shadow Court until he saw the tattoo and it triggered a recognition that he quite naturally resolved to track down." Death studied me with hollow, haunted eyes. "But his forgetting of *you*, Sara, was tied up with something else. A third piece of information or knowledge that he willfully thrust away from his mind violently, taking you with it. There could only be two reasons for that. One, he sought to forget you. I don't think either one of us believes that for a second. The Magician may have a core of surprising darkness, but his love for you knows no bounds."

"Ahh…yeah. Of course." I couldn't stop my cheeks from flushing at the unexpected comment, but the rest of Death's words only increased my anxiety. "What's the other option?"

"That he learned something during his last trial with the Fae that was both too big for him to handle in the moment and impossible for him to ignore. He needed you to be the one to find this knowledge on his behalf. For you to take on its burden. It's the only thing that makes sense."

I stared at her. No way would the Magician's ego allow for that to be the case. No way. "What could I possibly handle that he couldn't?"

"What was the last thing he said to you?" Death countered. "The last thing you can remember, before he awakened without memory of you?"

I scoured my memories, trying to recall, but it was mostly a blur made worse by the deluge of emotion that followed.

"He — um, he told me he loved me," I finally said. "Only it was prettier than that. Fancier."

"See if you can remember the exact words. It's important."

I tried for only a second longer, then shook my head. "I'm sure it will come to me, but not right now. And it doesn't matter. I'm not here to find whatever mystical magical MacGuffin Armaeus was after. I'm here to find him. He summoned me, and he sounded distraught. He must be in trouble of some sort."

"In trouble, or he's found what he blasted into the In Between for, and he'd like your help to manage it. That's more likely." Death watched me as I rolled to my feet.

"He pulled you to him once. He'll pull you to him again. Just start walking. I get the feeling he's close, in any event. I don't think he intended to leave Simon for long."

"Agreed." With no clear sense of what direction to choose, I peered down the corridor. As I considered my options, Death resumed her muttering over Simon's body. Whatever was wrong with the Fool, I suspected it was more than what she was letting on.

I glanced down at her. "Ah…how long do you think you've been down here?"

She shrugged, looking up at me. "I don't know, about a half hour?"

"Yeah, no. Try a few days. Which is kind of crazy, frankly. In Ireland, it didn't seem so bad."

Death gave me a wry smile, completely unperturbed. "The In Between works differently at different places. Some places are closer to the veil, some places are farther away. We are apparently farther away, which, frankly, I didn't know. But that means the danger here is far greater. Be careful."

"Right." I continued down the corridor with my fingertips set to a muted glow. The pathway twisted, then twisted again, and within only a few minutes, it felt as if I'd been lost in this dark and quiet place for centuries. Even the chittering in the rocks had ceased, and Armaeus had not reached out again. Maybe he couldn't? Maybe he was being cautious? Or maybe…

I sighed, struggling to come to terms with what I suspected was the truth. That perhaps I needed to help the Magician reach me more quickly. Armaeus always seemed to have a sense for being able to know whenever I dropped the barriers on my mind, given how intrigued he was at the idea of anyone being able to bar their thoughts from him. So here, so close to where I knew he must be, if I only eased the barriers open the slightest bit…

Light exploded all around me, a radiance I was completely unprepared for. Instead of being surrounded by cold gray stone, waterfalls tumbled down on either side of me. Through their sheer cascading walls, I could see an absolute wonderland of beauty in the space beyond. Emerald grass rustling in a gentle breeze, trees bursting with blossoms, clear blue sky.

"What the hell is *this*?" I was so startled, I didn't shore up my mind quickly enough. With a shock, I could sense Armaeus's touch racing through my brain for the barest second before I shut off access again. Because by that point, I didn't need him to find me. I had found him.

The Magician of the Arcana Council knelt before a pool of water, which was fed by a babbling brook, then spilled out into another waterway. It was such an incongruous place for him to be kneeling in his tailored suit, I blinked in surprise. Then I realized what it was he was mixing into the water and what was spilling forth to the stream that meandered off amid the grass and flowers, and I gaped.

"Is that liquid *gold*?"

Armaeus smiled and turned to me, his expression nearly making my heart stop in my chest.

I'd never seen him look so happy.

"It is," he said simply. "I have transmuted water into rubies, mist into starlight, and now lead into gold." He lifted his hand out of the water and held forth what was left of a dull gray cup. "It's the full formula of transformation that John Dee, Queen Elizabeth's astrologer and head alchemist, had sought for so long, and it's all here, perfectly crystallized."

He sighed with deep and abiding peace. "The angels answered me when I sought entry to the In Between, answered me and opened its doors, though they wouldn't—couldn't—venture inside with me. But this… It's everything I sought."

"Everything?" I repeated, the word quiet and cautious, completely at odds with our rich, exuberant surroundings. I didn't want to think too much about the fact that angels, with all their might and fire, considered the In Between a No Trespassing zone. "What else have you found?"

He lifted his brows, genuinely confused by the question. "What do you mean?"

I hit him with Death's hypothesis as if it was already cold hard fact, because I was pretty sure it was. "Given what happened at the Sagrada Familia, you had to realize that with all that lost knowledge of angel speak, you also reacquired a piece of you you'd once thought would be better off stuck somewhere else. Namely, that you were kind of an asshat with anger issues."

He narrowed his eyes at me, but I kept going. "Now that you've found your craft experiment here in the In Between, what other bad behavior did you stuff away with it? And while we're up, what's the piece of you that the Shadow Court and Abigail stole?"

"I haven't encountered anything else. There's nothing here but Dee's formula. Hidden away in this place of…extraordinary beauty." He sighed with deep contentment, turning his gaze to the perfect far horizon.

"Fair enough," I allowed, though I didn't believe him for a second. There had to be something else here. Then again, maybe Armaeus simply didn't recognize that he'd changed yet again in some way. I certainly couldn't tell, at least not yet.

I tried a different tack. "So, what happened to Simon?"

"Simon," he murmured, as if he just now recalled he'd left the guy behind. "He helped me enter the In Between. He got me this far, then begged me not to go further. That there was danger, that he needed to map it, that…" The Magician shook his head like a bear coming out of slumber. "He got quite upset. I don't know why."

"Maybe because there was danger?" I asked, looking around Armaeus's grotto more critically. It was undeniably beautiful, like something out of a fairy tale, but now it was starting to frighten me. Armaeus clearly had no idea he'd left Simon in relatively dire straits, and that wasn't like any version of him. "Either way, we've got to get going. Pronto."

Armaeus flinched, then set his mouth in a stubborn line. "No, we don't. There is nothing in the outside world that we cannot accomplish from within this space, Miss Wilde. There's no reason to ever leave. And now that you're here, there is no reason for us ever to leave each other again." He smiled so softly it made my heart quiver, even as my brain raced to understand his words. "It would seem I have a great deal of remembering to do when it comes to you in particular."

"Yeah, well, this isn't the time." I resisted the urge to fall headfirst into the illusion the Magician was creating, for all that it was more appealing than the mess that lay outside these magical walls.

And then, of course, I figured it out. This *place* was what he'd stuffed away with John Dee's alchemical formula. This whole beautiful, terrifying place.

"You've created some sort of trap here, Armaeus, something that makes you want to stay more than it makes you want to leave," I said. "I have a feeling you learned how to create this mental bouncy house right around the time you discovered Dee's breakthrough. It proved too alluring for you, so you killed it. You stuffed it in the In Between where it could no longer tempt you."

That caught Armaeus up short. He glanced around, and it almost hurt me physically to see the possibility strike him all the more powerfully, because I was right.

"I'd created an escape," he murmured. "An escape I could not resist. How...foolish..."

He closed his eyes and slumped to the ground, all tens of thousands of dollars of suit, shoes, and ancillary bling sprawled out on the emerald green grass by a babbling sapphire stream.

"Uh, Armaeus?"

He didn't move.

"Armaeus."

I launched toward him, bounding across the swaying grass and vaulting the bubbly stream. Then I dropped to my knees beside him, pulling him into my arms. "Armaeus, dammit, wake *up*."

For a moment, I thought I'd lose him to the entirely different escape of a coma. Then his body convulsed, his hands lashing out. The idyllic tapestry of sky and grotto faltered, and I could once again see the cold stone walls of the In Between for the briefest moment. Armaeus flailed again, his face contorting, but the sky and grotto returned, seeming more vibrant than ever.

"A...a memory, Miss Wilde..." Armaeus gasped, speaking in my mind. "Just one. Some connection between us..."

I could feel his pressure on my mind, and I knew instantly what he wanted. Something, *anything* to hold onto, to give him the strength to fight this illusion, this trap he'd so thoroughly constructed. I had easily a hundred thousand memories I could share with him, and I knew instinctively that any of them would do. I picked the safest one I could imagine, simple and clean, the two of us in Paris in the springtime, outside Saint-Germain-des-Prés —

Then, to my horror, a totally different memory surged forth in my mind, bold and terrible and shining bright. A memory of a trap I'd fallen into in Hell, where I'd believed that Armaeus and I were together, forever, our yesterdays and todays and tomorrows perfectly entwined. I'd come out of that trap reeling, and I'd never spoken of it to *anyone* — least of all, Armaeus. In fact, I'd thought I'd buried that devastating experience so deeply, so permanently, that it would never *ever* see the light of day.

Now it was the only thing I could think of.

"*No*," I gasped, but even as I struggled to pull away, Armaeus's body jerked again, and I felt him seize upon my own traitorous thoughts, plunging through them like a fist through glass.

"What do you need from me to believe?" Armaeus asked, dropping a kiss on my forehead. Where his lips connected with my skin, fire blazed all the way down to my heels. "Don't you want to see what I've built us while I waited for you?"

"Stop it!" I growled, but I couldn't stop it, I couldn't stop any of this. Because Armaeus now saw, felt, and *knew* absolutely everything I had seen, felt and known during that cruel deception — because he was inside my mind, experiencing it even as I'd experienced it —

He held me as the sun dipped into the far western horizon, his lips on my hair, his arms tight as I sobbed the tears I had never cried for my mother, my lost life, my lost self. My heart felt so full of possibility in those moments, I thought it would burst — but it didn't, and the sun finally set and rose again, and there was more laughter to be had.

"Stop," I whispered, far more weakly this time, because I knew what was coming next, knew what I had kept from Armaeus since the moment of that betrayal in Hell, the moment where I'd thought I'd lost him forever—

"There is something you have to know…"

"Noooo…" I groaned, shaking Armaeus violently now, trying to break his connection with my mind, my heart, my precious, precious memory—

"I love you, Sara."

The words were so unexpected, so impossible, that it was all I could do not to fall off the teak bench. I opened and closed my mouth like a carp tossed onto the shore, but Armaeus didn't say anything further. He simply watched me with those unfathomable, impossibly golden eyes, eyes that seemed to see directly into me, healing me, making me whole. "I don't—I can't—"

"You can," Armaeus leaned closer then, his lips brushing mine. Something shattered completely inside me, the last little bit of resistance I had, and I crumpled against him as he pulled me close, his mouth firm and hot, his fingers gripping my shoulders, his lips rough and insistent on mine. "You do," he growled against me, then leaned back, his expression impossibly fierce.

And then he spoke again, only it wasn't the Armaeus of my memory speaking, it was the Armaeus lying in front of me, his eyes wide and staring, filled with shock and wonder. "You *are*," he whispered, reverently.

Without warning, a burst of energy exploded from me fully formed, spreading into huge, glorious wings of fire that arced up and over us, then collapsed and poured into Armaeus's body, setting him ablaze. The wild, frenzied energy consumed him entirely for a one breath, two — racing over, around, through him —

And then it was done.

A scant heartbeat later, we stood in the center of a roughly hewn stone chamber, bare except for a small table in the center. On the table sat a thin leather-bound journal, and beneath the book, a cloth embroidered with stars and planets. No more babbling brook, no more grassy plain, no more blue sky. Now, only stone and silence surrounded us.

Armaeus drew in a long, shaky breath. "I... Thank you, Miss Wilde."

I could only stare at him a long moment, mute with shock and emotion so thick I felt strangled. When Armaeus didn't say anything further, though, I finally, shakily, cleared my throat.

"You, ah, feeling better now?"

His lips quirked. "In a manner of speaking. There's much I have learned here." He reached out and picked up the book, wrapping it in the strip of embroidered cloth. He held it close to his chest, allowing his eyes to drift shut for the barest moment. Then he looked at me and shook his head. "And now I have something else, too. This memory of us, together."

I put up both hands. "Yeah, well, no. None of that actually happened," I said curtly. "It was a trick, a trap. I was in Hell, and I was being played — so it was all a lie. All of it. It didn't —"

"I understand," he said, his eyes still warm and wondering, his expression so gentle, I suddenly wanted to cry. "But I thank you for it nevertheless. Without it, I wouldn't have had the strength to break free of this trap I'd so neatly set myself. Without it...I wouldn't have understood a lot of things."

"Well...fine, then," I said gruffly. "But it didn't happen."

"As you say, Miss Wilde," Armaeus said quietly, a soft, bemused smile still softening his lips. "As you say. But now, I think we should go."

He gestured to the doorway cut into the thick rock, and together, we started walking.

CHAPTER TWENTY-TWO

We slowly journeyed back through the endless maze of corridors, the trip seeming to take five times longer than the way in. When we finally reached the green glow that told me Simon was right around the corner, Armaeus froze.

"What did I do here?" he murmured, stepping away from me.

I squinted at him, but there was no sugar coating the truth. "Ah…well, you left Simon pretty much in a coma such that Death had to watch over him while you were playing change-the-metal-into-gold."

"I left Simon in harm's way?" He echoed, aghast.

I sighed. "Well, perhaps not in harm's way, but definitely in its general vicinity. Simon couldn't come out of wherever you stuck him on his own. Death came to watch over him, but he didn't seem to be getting any better."

Armaeus shook his head. "Death is the bridge between life and the next plane. She has some grace with the living whose paths are not yet complete, but she cannot heal. That's not her job. It's mine."

I waited for him to say, *and yours as well,* but he didn't. He simply kept moving, and a few moments later, we reached Simon and Death. Death stepped away as Armaeus knelt beside Simon. Reaching out, he touched the Fool on the forehead. Simon abruptly sucked in a strangled breath, as if he'd been holding it this entire time.

"No!" Simon shouted as he looked up and grabbed the Magician by both shoulders. "Don't go in there, don't go in! It's dangerous."

"I'm already back," Armaeus assured him, but the revelation did little to improve Simon's demeanor. The Fool flinched, an expression of fear crossing his face. Then his glance shifted to me.

"What is it?" I asked quietly. "What is it you were afraid of?"

Simon shook his head, his eyes wide. "I don't know. I knew there was a trap. A terrible trap that he wouldn't be able to leave on his own. Not ever."

"A trap of my own making," Armaeus said thoughtfully. "One which will take much study when the time is right."

"Which would not be now," Death snapped.

He looked around until his gaze found Death, and nodded grimly. "What did I do?"

"You trapped Simon too, in the doorway to your little hideaway," she said flatly. "If you hadn't returned…"

Silence fell between us for a long moment, then I spoke.

"So…" I asked Armaeus. "Now that you've got Dee's little book of spells and everything, is there anything else that's coming to mind?"

He turned to me, and his eyes seemed to shift a little, his expression shuttering. "No. There's an awareness of a lesson I have yet to learn, a certainty of a sorrow I have yet to understand. No further. But I have regained the language of the angels as well as the secret of the transmutation of elements, and time is of the essence. I have gained all that I have lost and can take a stand against the Shadow Court."

Whoa, whoa, whoa.

I felt the wrongness of Armaeus's statement but proceeded as diplomatically as possible. "Well, you haven't gained *everything* you've lost, because you don't remember me. And if you don't remember the Shadow Court itself, including all the stories and problems and crises that led up to the point at which your memory was taken away, then we still have a problem, and we still don't know what we're up against."

"Fair enough." The Magician turned to Death. "I'll need to return to this place one day to resolve that which I could not resolve today. But for now —"

"For now, I'm getting the Fool out of here. And *you*…" She swung her gaze to me. "Be careful. I mean it."

At that point I was treated to my second experience of Death's mad transpo skills. After all, with Simon still groggy, there was no way we could trust him to make the jump on his own, especially out of the In Between.

Perhaps not surprisingly, Death traveled with the same economy that she did everything else in her immortal life. While Armaeus preferred to disappear in a puff of smoke and I lit myself on fire, Death simply was there one moment and gone the next…much like life itself, for far too many people.

The Magician exhaled. "I didn't think it would be easy to get rid of her. Which means she knows what's coming, and knows it's meant to be."

"Uhhh…what do you mean, what's coming?" I thought of Death's admonition of thirty seconds earlier, and my nerves prickled. "We should get out of here too. Why aren't we getting out of here?"

"Because there is more to be learned in the In Between, Miss Wilde. Far more. And I, once again, will need your help to confront it."

As if on cue, the walls shuddered around us, and where there had been rough but unbroken stone before, several fissures suddenly appeared in the wall running from the ceiling to the floor. First only as wide as my finger, then as wide as my fist.

"They're here," the Magician said, his words barely a sigh. He grabbed my hand and pulled me along as he began sprinting back down the corridor. *Down,* not up.

"Wait, who's they?" I spluttered. "Why aren't we *leaving*?"

"Because there's something I left here. Something I must find." Armaeus delivered this without breaking stride, the two of us racing through the darkened passageways as if the hounds of hell were on our heels. While it wasn't a pack of dogs, there *was* something pursuing us through the winding corridors. Something that chittered and rustled and yowled, moaned and cried. It was like amateur night at a death metal concert, and I was not a fan.

And it was gaining ground. "I'm serious! Who is *they*?"

Before Armaeus could respond, the corridor dumped into a box canyon. We stumbled to a stop, blocked.

With no other choice, we whirled around, forced to face our pursuers. And instinctively cowered back. The creatures lurching after us were more shadow than form and reeked with power. Lots of power. Extremely messed-up power. Even with my third eye peeled wide, I couldn't make any sense of the riot of crisscrossing currents of electricity and snarl of tangled energy. It looked like someone had blown up an Arkham Asylum dollhouse and then patched up the inmates with a staple gun.

"This is magic," Armaeus said, his tone rife with awe. "Broken magic."

"Broken?" I yelped. "What does that mean, broken?"

We took another step back, only to connect with the immovable wall of the In Between. Nowhere else to go. Meanwhile, the current of what Armaeus called broken magic hovered now only ten feet away, stopping apparently because we'd stopped, which was downright neighborly of it.

"Spells once formed in light and joy that were then used for ill purposes," explained the Magician, his voice still tinged with far too much awe and far too little fear, in my book. "My own failed spells, some of them, but far more spells and bits of arcane lore that I had stripped away from sorcerers who didn't possess the skill or discernment to wield such magic. Once, they were beautiful, full and true in the light of the world. But here, they are truncated and corrupted and false, reflecting all the twisted uses of magic that mankind has ever attempted to wrest into a new form for its own corrupt ends. They are—broken. And I could not fix them."

"Got it. Broken." And given what I was looking at, I could see what he meant. If magic had a physical form, it would surely be a wonder to behold. These…were not that. Spells that at one time had been things of beauty were now shrunken, misshapen, and deformed. And they were quivering toward Armaeus—the Magician, not me—as if he could somehow help bring them back to life. And maybe he could. But for him to have thrown all these bits and pieces of broken spells into the heart of the In Between like so much trash didn't feel right. All these spells were completely out of balance, the light stripped away from the dark or the light amplified to the point of being a punishment. I found myself staring in mute horror even as the wraiths finally reached us, and then I heard the first of them strike Armaeus...and he didn't fight back. There was only the briefest puff of air as he absorbed the broken magic inside him.

"What are you doing?" I gasped, but I didn't really need an explanation. He was absorbing the broken bits of magic—all of it—in hopes that within all the pain and misery, he'd find the missing piece of spell work that would make him whole again.

Unfortunately, that approach didn't seem like it was going so well.

"No..." groaned Armaeus after one particularly brutal hit. "*No.*" Another hit him, then another, and a sob broke free from his throat. Then he half screamed, dropping to his knees with an agonized gasp, and that was all it took for me. Turning to Armaeus, I threw both arms and a couple of spectral wings of energy around him and enveloped us both in a curtain of fire—and we were gone.

We crackled back into awareness a heartbeat later, both of us crumpling together on the cold rain-soaked concrete of the shipyard. Not my best location for a return visit, granted. But it certainly was top of mind.

I yanked Nikki's phone out of my jacket. The flashlight still was toast, but the rest of it seemed to be working. I'd take it. I scurried over to my borrowed motorcycle, which was somehow miraculously still sitting there. While Death, Simon, and the Magician had been stuck in the In Between for days, not much time seemed to have passed since Armaeus had summoned me there. Still, I had no idea where Nikki had chosen for our next lodging, or if anywhere in Hamburg was safe. I pounded out a text to her as Armaeus stirred on the ground.

"What...where?" he wheezed.

"We're in Hamburg, big guy. You can sort out all your problems in therapy later, but I can't afford to lose you right now."

"Miss Wilde." Armaeus shook his head, peering at me. Even from his position laid out on the ground, he looked...different. Better. "Just who exactly would you consider qualified to provide psychoanalysis on me?"

His tone was so cool, so supercilious, and so endearingly familiar, I nearly dropped my phone. "Ah, so *now* you're feeling more yourself?"

He offered me a lopsided smile that did funny things to my heartbeat. "It would appear that my mission to the In Between bore many gifts, above and beyond the extraordinary gift of John Dee's learnings. I now have the secret of alchemy, which is far different than I thought it was. I have, with your help, healed some very broken magic. And I have also learned...other things. Important things." He glanced around. "We're in Hamburg?"

"Where it's finally stopped raining, yup."

His quizzical smile broadened, and he nodded as he sat up fluidly, with none of the weakness I'd seen in the In Between. "Of course we are. The dead zones."

My phone pinged with Nikki's response. "You know about those?" I demanded as I looked down at my screen. "And do you have any idea where Avenue Am Sandtorkai is?"

"Near the Speicherstadt, yes. A good location, but there's one better."

Without further discussion, it was Armaeus's turn to play Woober driver. Abandoning the bike for good this time, we disappeared in a burst of smoke and a second later reappeared in the dining room of somebody's house, definitely not mine. I stepped away from the Magician and turned around, recognizing the quality of furniture, artwork, and decor in general.

"Ahhh… Have you always had a house in Hamburg?"

"Not me personally, but the Bertrand family has held a home here for over a hundred years." He paused, looking off at the far wall to concentrate. "Since 1852, in fact."

"That's…interesting timing."

"Indeed, falling rather late in Abigail Strand's tenure as Justice. I didn't buy the house personally, though I wasn't unaware of its existence as I was with the house in Paris. However, I'm not entirely sure whose decision it was to purchase in this particular city, now that I think about it. It would seem I should make a study of all such points of confusion in my recollection. I suspect it would make for very interesting results."

"You still don't remember anything about the Shadow Court?"

He grimaced. "I do not. The apparent purpose of my journey into the In Between was to recover the knowledge of Dee's alchemical process, reclaim an awareness of a trap I'd built for myself…a trap I would do well to destroy for good…and to achieve a sudden and unfortunate realization of the nature of what I released into the In Between a short while ago. Eight hundred years of broken and misguided spells, it would seem."

"Yeah, let's talk about that. A little more detail would be good."

"In my studies, I've come across an endless series of magic and spells that didn't do what their owners wanted them to do or, worse, accomplished their wielder's aims far too well. These broken spells have been entrusted to me for centuries upon centuries, so that no others may stumble across their madness unaware."

"Then why'd you suddenly decide to get rid of them? I mean, it was handy that the In Between portals were right there and open at the time, but there's no way you could've been thinking about airing out your gray cells while you were getting blasted by the Irish gods a few weeks ago."

"True, unless there was something in my memory storage that I knew was a liability. In my weakened state, I couldn't keep it protected. If I thought I was on the verge of death or being broken, I wouldn't want anyone to take advantage of my weakness and turn it against the Council."

"So sending all those spells to the In Between was your version of activating your ejector seat."

"Until I was better able to heal that broken magic, yes. So it would appear." He moved over to the bar, taking down the bottle of scotch. He eyed it thoughtfully before pouring glasses for both of us.

I accepted mine willingly, savoring the rich slide of liquor down my throat as Armaeus studied me. When he spoke, his voice was quiet.

"I have put you through a great deal, Miss Wilde. It was never my intention for you to suffer so much on my behalf. Had I realized the harm I'd be causing you…"

"You still don't remember me, do you?" I asked bluntly, gesturing at him with my glass. "You want to, but you don't. And the fake memory of Hell doesn't count."

He sighed. "I do not, not entirely. It's possible that I need to fully reclaim more of the magic I placed within the In Between before I can successfully reclaim all my memories."

"So the 'memories' you have about me now, about how I've suffered or whatever, aren't really memories after all, are they? They're whatever you were able to pull from my mind when you reached out to me for help and I let you in."

"Yes. But you see, I hope, the advantage of letting me in, as you call it." He eyed me over the glass. "I want to understand you, Miss Wilde. To understand us. I want to know everything I can about you in case it could serve us in the coming confrontation with the Shadow Court."

I twisted my lips. What he was saying made sense, but there was a complexity to it I didn't trust. I hadn't believed the apparition in the shipyard when he'd cast aspersions on Armaeus's feelings for me. I knew the Magician loved me. Correction. I knew that the Magician I'd *known* loved me. I also knew this man in front of me wasn't that same person. He was darker and edgier, and I'd seen only the barest hints of his new personality, or his new-old personality, now reborn within a far stronger being. I trusted the Magician I'd fallen in love with. But this Magician had not yet earned that faith.

And yet…I still loved him with every ounce of my being. Which made me more vulnerable than I wanted to be.

"We're going to have to find a workaround, I'm afraid." I drained the rest of my scotch and set down my glass. "Like I've said before, if you simply thumbed through my mind, those wouldn't be your memories, they'd be mine, clouded with all my hang-ups. Of which

I have many. Your interpretation of the actual events that created those memories could be entirely different than it was in the moment those events happened, and that misinterpretation could be deadly."

My explanation sounded good, even to me, but I didn't miss the quick pain in Armaeus's eyes or the sudden flash of loss that clouded his expression. He'd thought I'd give in to his reasoning. He'd wanted me to give in to it.

I wanted to give in to it too.

I glanced down at the booze refilling my glass. It now nearly reached the rim. "Getting me drunk isn't going to get you inside my mind," I warned him with a rueful smile as my phone pinged again. "That's Nikki. She's got the team with her. Should we join them or have them join us here?"

"Here," Armaeus said without hesitation. At least he sounded like the Armaeus of old, even if he didn't remember everything. "But they can't travel here directly from the hotel. Have them utilize conventional transport to an outside location I will provide while they're en route, then they can employ magic to transfer here."

I frowned. "You don't think they were watching us in the shipyard?"

"This house is warded. Anyone coming in or going out is cloaked, no matter where they come from. Still, tell them to use all precautions. I'll explain about the dead zones when they arrive."

"Yeah, I've already been introduced to one of those. There are more?"

Armaeus nodded. "Hamburg is an old city, full of secrets. I should have guessed the Shadow Court would be here. Now that I know where it is…the rest must in turn follow."

I communicated all this to Nikki, and her response was immediate. Roger, but change of venues needed. We've got Interpol waiting for a meet at 06:00, would rather not have them realize the Magician's back in town. Can he be discreet?

The Magician smiled, tucking away John Dee's prized journal into his jacket pocket and giving me a last, searching glance. "I assure you, Miss Wilde, you won't even know I'm there."

CHAPTER TWENTY-THREE

At Armaeus's insistence, the meeting place was none other than the warded location where he'd wanted everyone to meet before jumping to his family home, but it was hardly discreet. The Speicherstadt was one of the most well-known tourist areas in Hamburg, and though the conference rooms beneath the hotel we'd chosen were heavily guarded, how difficult would it be for an organization that had based its operations in this city for hundreds of years to watch it?

"Relax, Miss Wilde," Armaeus murmured. "All in due time."

Due time was fortunately not long in coming, as the doors opened a few minutes later to reveal Simon and Death.

"We're not staying for the party," Death announced before she barely cleared the door. "We just need the intel before I get Simon to Dr. Sells."

"I told you, I'm all right," the Fool insisted, sighing as she glared at him. "Look, I get it. I very well may die in the In Between at some point, but I didn't die this time, okay? I'm fine."

"It's still wise for you to be evaluated," Armaeus said. "You were under my care, and once again, I abandoned you to the In Between. I would advise not agreeing to go with me the next time."

"Are you kidding? I lit that place up with trackers like I *owned* it." Simon grinned. "I caught the full show of you and Sara facing down the hobgoblins of doom down there. It was *awesome.*"

The Magician leaned forward with consummate interest just as the doors opened again to admit Nikki and Kreios. Nikki had changed into her preferred Mod Squad attire for the meeting with Interpol—her hair styled in a dark chestnut sweep, her sleek black minidress barely skimming her upper thighs, with an inch of skin showing before her deep black thigh-high platform boots took over the show. Her gaze swept the room, pausing only briefly on Armaeus before settling on me.

"Dollface, you changed clothes." She grinned. "I totally approve."

I shifted uncomfortably in my chair, the expensively stretchy fabric of the new clothes Armaeus had suggested feeling completely foreign to me. My hair was slicked back into a tight bun, and I wore makeup. I also wore the totem of Guabancex, though it was tucked beneath my silky tank top. "I hardly think any of this is necessary."

"And I assure you, you're quite wrong," Kreios said. He sported an upgrade to his own Mediterranean Surfer Boy attire, with an elegant suit and dark blue shirt open at the collar, hints of platinum at his wrist. With their matching suits and feral grins, he and Armaeus could have been stand-ins for Shark Tank. "But what are we looking at?"

THE SHADOW COURT

"This is all I got, and it's not a lot," the Fool said. Death stayed close to Simon as he approached the table and slid into a chair with a little too heavy a sigh, and my gaze grew sharper on the Fool as he settled himself. Just how injured was he? He pulled out his laptop and opened it up, an image instantly projecting on the far wall. The logo of the Shadow Court, with its art deco crenelated crown.

"What you see there, that symbol—is nowhere and everywhere in plain sight. The Shadow Court is made up of a series of shell companies who are in turn linked to families so buried behind walls of security that it would take an army of bots to figure it out, and we simply haven't had time. But with history as our guide, and given their location here in Hamburg and the families who've lived and grown rich in this city, we got a little lucky. Because ordinarily, this isn't the town you want to be in if you're Connected. So there had to be some personal reason for it to make sense."

"The dead zones," I guessed.

Armaeus nodded. "The city of Hamburg was founded in 800 AD and eventually became one of the region's most vital shipping ports, with its access to the North Sea as well as inland trading routes. The city was a member of the medieval Hanseatic trading league and a free imperial city of the Holy Roman Empire, and because of its location and unusual governing practices, it has experienced both great freedoms and devastating losses. Much of the city was destroyed by fire. What was rebuilt after that was destroyed by flood, and what was rebuilt after that was destroyed by Allied bombs and economic attrition. Yet still, time after time, Hamburg rises from the ashes to recreate itself anew. Each time a little savvier, a little more hidden, a little more complex. The discovery that sections of the city were dead zones for magic was quite accidental, as one of the earliest guilds was a group of sorcerers who created magic-infused blades. Their wares sold well enough that they expanded — but the new location proved disastrous. It didn't take long for them to realize the reason why, and they charted the city carefully. But with the bombs, floods, and other natural disasters, the map lines keep changing."

"So how do you overcome one of these dead-zone things?" Nikki asked.

"You don't. You can only leave. At best, you can produce the smallest fraction of the abilities you used to have, enough to potentially facilitate your escape. Nothing more."

"But Connecteds still live here?"

"There are warded sections and large swaths of the city that are not afflicted. However, because of the mercurial nature of the dead zones and the number of natural and man-made disasters that have beset the city — don't think the two aren't connected — it proved impossible to maintain more than a small section of warded territory, especially on the rivers. The Alster and Elbe rivers are also extraordinary sources of energy into the city, and as such, Hamburg is a magnet for magic, albeit volatile magic."

"Why in the world would the Shadow Court maintain their base here?" I asked Armaeus. "It seems like a particularly hostile environment."

"A very good question. The answer is, because there is no safer place than a trap of your own making. And, too, Hamburg remains an important harbor, a hub of innovation and a symbol of worlds both new and old."

"Right," I muttered, thinking of the richly cultured voice of the apparition in the shipyard. That guy definitely would have a thing for tradition. "So we're looking for a single house, or perhaps more to the point, a single piece of property. It could be public or private, but it's almost certainly on the waterfront."

"We've got some possibilities," Simon said, "but my money's on this place."

He hit a few keys, and the scene on the wall changed to a nighttime shot of a building on the waterfront, lit up with lights, then the same building during the day. "It's nearby. It was a guild house back in the day, then a house of government, then a public house, and it's been a hotel since the postwar rebuild. This is another option."

A second image came up, a large and serene house on the hill overlooking the River Elbe. "Not near the city center, but protected like it's Fort Knox. It's been for sale for a couple of years, but priced so high that no one can seriously be considering selling it. From all accounts, there's no activity there, so I have a harder time believing it could be our guys, but it still trips my trigger."

Another image splashed across the wall, and Armaeus sat forward. "Why that one?"

"Well, other than the fact that it's on the same street as Casa Bertrand and it hasn't changed ownership since the 1500s, it has the second-highest concentration of psychic energy in the entire Hamburg region. If I was a suspicious sort, I'd say you bought the house down the street way back in the day strictly to keep an eye on someone, then forgot that was what you were going to do. No one realizes that the Bertrand estate owns your home either. It's gone through several apparent owners, all of them carefully screened, and they all check out. So...I figured something was up."

"I purchased the house in 1852, and then the Shadow Court disappeared from my every waking thought," Armaeus murmured.

"Pretty much," Simon agreed.

"Which leaves us where?" Kreios asked. "From what we have determined, Interpol has received several credible tips about an unusually high level of technoceutical drugs moving through Hamburg, drugs that are causing chatter all over the globe. But they want to speak with us. They wouldn't do that unless they needed information or assistance they could not access themselves. Their reliance on Detective Rooks has grown by the hour, only barely staying below the radar enough that he doesn't get targeted."

"What about operatives inside Interpol?" I asked. "They haven't noticed him?"

"They almost certainly have noticed him, but we've been moving very quickly to contain any threats as they appear and so far, so good. Once he briefs us this morning, that will change. He'll be the poster child for any recommendations or actions in the city. He'll be on the front lines."

I scowled. That wasn't exactly music to my ears. "Since when is Interpol on the front lines? They're supposed to provide guidance to local law enforcement, then law enforcement goes in and does the heavy lifting. What's different here?"

"The psychic element," Kreios explained. "Which Detective Rooks has already proven he can handle ably and without discernible reaction, while other members of the agency are having a hard time wrapping their heads around it. Local law enforcement in Hamburg will not be as reticent, but there are leaks in every government agency. If it isn't already known that Brody Rooks is advising Interpol, and where he comes from, and who he knows, it will be by mid-morning. He'll need to be protected."

"He'll need to be removed," I countered. "The first sign of trouble, I want him blockaded. He's not Connected enough to protect himself."

"He agreed to do the job," Kreios pointed out.

"And he'll do the job. But the job doesn't require him to get blasted off this planet this time around. So let's maybe not let that happen." I glanced at Nikki. "When does Interpol get here?"

"They're on the ground now. We expect them in thirty, and they'll almost certainly have a tail."

"Cameras all feed into here," Simon said, tapping the machine. "All you have to do is…" He faded off, and I looked over to see Death dart forward, catching the Fool before he could hit the desk.

"Go," Armaeus said before anyone else could speak, and Death laid her cool, pale hand against Simon's cheek—and they disappeared.

I turned on Armaeus, who pulled Simon's computer toward him and began typing, though the image on the wall didn't change. "Do you have any idea why—?"

"I don't," he said, his voice heavy. "It's possible there is something in the very nature of the In Between that's still sapping his energy. It's also possible that the monitors he put up are letting through more than simply images. Dr. Sells will need to do a full workup, but it's safe to say we'll not have the advantage of the Fool's insights during the coming challenge. Which is unfortunate."

"Not only the Fool." Kreios lounged against the far wall. "We're not meeting this challenge with the full Council, even those we trust."

"There's been no need to involve them," Armaeus said.

"It goes deeper than that," Kreios countered. He studied his longtime friend. "Armaeus, what is it you know about the Shadow Court that you don't realize you know? Because all this time, you've been making decisions based on gut instinct, but you shouldn't *have* that instinct if your memories have been completely erased. So you're going on something that is less than knowledge, less than memory, but perhaps more than your own intuition. And we need to understand it. Who is it you don't trust?"

Armaeus looked back at him steadily. "I don't know. There's no member of the Council who has betrayed us outright. But there have been times they have acted — out of bounds."

"Like Viktor. In Memphis, when I was a kid," I said flatly. "He was so far out of bounds, I can't believe you kept him on the Council." I couldn't help but think once more of the blond man's words in the shipyard. Who was he, and why did I feel like I'd met him before, however briefly?

Armaeus nodded. "That tendency toward a lack of boundaries is what I've focused on, in knowing who to trust. I feel there's…something important about it."

"The Magician always has a plan," murmured Kreios.

"Even when I don't know I do? Not a very good plan." Armaeus swung his gaze to me. "The Arcana Council is not made up of Connecteds who are solely good or even just, Miss Wilde. It's made up of those who are the strongest. In a way, we are our own dead zone, creating barriers that keep our own members from straying into a role where they could damage society. By and large, that's worked to keep us in balance, and when we've been breached — we've realized it quickly enough."

"What if you don't this time? What if that's the whole point?"

Armaeus's brows went up. "Explain."

"I was paid a visit tonight by a man I didn't know, a man I think I may have seen before, but—it was an illusion. A hologram. He wasn't really there. Hell, maybe not even a hologram—maybe his image was superimposed on one of my own memories to screw with me, giving a whole new meaning to deep fake. But I couldn't shake the idea I knew who he was."

"Show me," Armaeus and Kreios said at the same time. Even Nikki moved closer to me, and I reached out and touched her hand as I lifted my mental barriers enough to share the memory of earlier this evening in the shipyard. Armaeus stiffened with surprise, and Kreios started laughing. Even Nikki widened her eyes.

"What?" I demanded.

"I've seen him too," she murmured. "I can't quite remember…"

"Jarvis Fuggeren," Kreios said, shaking his head. "That's not the head of the Shadow Court. He's rich, but he's foolish, and the world is full of rich fools. He's also not nearly Connected enough. You met him at an antique gold show last year, where—"

My eyes widened. "The guy with the Nazi gold." I didn't remember him as being quite the idiot that Kreios presented, but my filters were likely different from those of a man who'd been kicking around since World War I.

"Exactly so."

Nikki's phone pinged, and her gaze shot to it. "Look sharp, we've got company. Interpol has hit the building."

CHAPTER TWENTY-FOUR

Armaeus vanished from the room in a whisper of mist. I barely had time to brace myself before the doors opened again, admitting a group of men and women, most of whose faces were set into steely masks of bureaucratic belligerence. All except Brody, in fact, whose face was set into a steely mask of long-suffering impatience.

"Thank you for meeting with us. I'm Agent Philippe Gustaf," the head of the delegation started, a gruff, square-built man with a voice as heavy as a concrete block. "We've asked to meet with you regarding a series of drug trafficking tips that have been flooding into our offices, centered in Hamburg, but let me be clear. Ordinarily, I wouldn't be wasting my people's time or yours with a personal meeting over something that could be handled via email."

I blinked. I had no standing in this meeting *and* I was sitting down, but I still leaned forward. "So why are you here?"

"To meet you all, face to face, and establish protocols. It appears we will be working together closely, and I like to know who I'm working with." He regarded me with blunt, unimpressed eyes. "Detective

Rooks insists you will be ideal assets to our efforts, and, as it happened, we were already scheduled to be in the city to be briefed on the drug trafficking situation. Unfortunately, we have business elsewhere, so this meeting will be brief."

I lifted my brows. "Elsewhere, meaning…?"

When Gustaf continued to stare at me with no indication of sharing more, Brody piped up. "There's rumors of an attack in Paris where Connecteds are involved. Sixth arrondissement. We've got very few details."

My heart skipped a beat. "The sixth is where Saint-Germain-des-Prés is located. Is that the problem?"

Gustaf grunted. "Why would you be concerned about that location? What do you know?"

"I don't—" I began, then caught myself just in time. The truth was, I didn't want to play this game of sit-on-my-hands with these people. I didn't want to involve mortals at all. But that was what was required of the Council.

The *Council*. Not the Shadow Court. They could get things done far more easily, according to Jarvis Fuggeren.

I shook off that thought. "Saint-Germain-des-Prés was the home church of a priest who did great work protecting Connecteds who were threatened with abduction or abuse. He also rescued Connecteds who had endured terrible trials and set them up in rehabilitation centers. He died a few months ago, but his work continues there."

Gustaf glanced at one of his men. "Under whom?"

"I don't know. I paid them a visit when they were in the middle of an operation a few days ago, but I don't know any of the top players."

Gustaf shifted in his chair, and his words, when they came, were blunt. "I would like to believe you, Ms. Wilde, but I don't. And the reason why is not what you may suspect. I do not believe you or your associates are involved with the drug trafficking network which brought us to Hamburg, but you should know that someone is going to great pains to make it look like you're involved."

I stiffened. Jarvis Fuggeren. I knew it as sure as I was sitting here. "What do you mean?" I asked.

"I think you understand me. With your past affiliations and current relationships, you have established a healthy network of operatives throughout Europe and Asia, and even into South America. You can move...certain items, very quickly." He didn't say kids, which I appreciated, but it was clear he knew a lot more about me than I preferred. "Now we have drugs moving even more quickly through Europe and Asia, and your name keeps coming up. As a blind, we know that, but it still begs the question. How would you do it? Move the drugs?"

"I wouldn't," I snapped. "The supply chain is where all drug operations fail eventually. There's always a weak link." It was the same with rescuing Connected children, though with far worse results.

Letting Gustaf chew on that for a second, I turned to Brody. "So what happened? Were there any casualties?"

"First, we focus on the situation here, because there *is* something happening, even if it is low level," Gustaf interrupted again. "It's very simple. We have alerted the authorities of the likely involvement of several locations in the city with the drug trade—locations, not families, institutions, or individuals. The sites we were given by the tipsters were very high level, and we do not want law enforcement to act unless or until there is sufficient proof. In short, they will set up surveillance, nothing more."

"Surveillance," nodded Kreios. "Nothing more."

"Who are these tipsters?" I asked.

"Anonymous," Brody put in, his gaze flashing to me. "But Connected. I did some research and—you'll probably be hearing about this yourself."

I blinked. That could only mean that complaints were coming in to Mrs. French too, back at Justice Hall. Yet another connection to Sara Wilde, I thought. If Jarvis was behind this, he was very good. "Got it."

"But these are only tips. Supposed eyewitness accounts of weaponized psychotropic drugs being disseminated at an alarming rate," Gustaf continued. "Nothing has been verified. We are given to understand that you have a great deal of confidence in your ability to ferret out mental terrorists, if that's what we're working with here, but we will need a little more concrete information for us to move forward."

"Like maybe the attack in Paris," I offered.

His lips thinned. "The attack in Paris is not in Hamburg. I would suggest it has nothing to do with the buildings and families singled out here. If we'd received some addresses in Paris, tips regarding drug transactions in that city, well, that would be a different story. I'm sure you can appreciate that we are not in the habit of accusing people of crimes they have yet to commit. The tips have indicated that a great deal of money and drugs is changing hands in and around Hamburg, but all such transactions are completely hidden and in no way match the shipping schedule of potential drug-laden boats, trains, and airplanes into the city. It's as if the contraband comes in, and, within mere minutes, a transaction is recorded in Germany, Amsterdam, beyond. It's not possible."

"Well, there is this thing called the internet…" I sat back, keeping my arms wide on the armrests. Gustaf was already defensive and suspicious. I didn't need to appear like his bad attitude was contagious.

"The tips include photos," Brody said. "Detailed descriptions of materials and packaging. The drugs are being transported to these other cities physically. We just don't know how."

"But you have suspicions?" I directed the question at Gustaf. This wasn't my first fractious tango with Interpol. With their two factions of exploit-the-Connecteds versus execute-the-Connected, I needed a better sense of which party Gustaf belonged to before I divulged anything helpful.

He stared at me hard. "They just show up here and poof, they're somewhere else. A whole lot of them, in lots of different places, with whispers of what they are and what they can do getting more elaborate by the hour."

"That…that sounds bad," I acknowledged. I didn't look at the Devil, but the implication was clear. Someone was teleporting drugs…and anyone that strong needed to already be on the Council. Unless, somehow, Armaeus had missed a sorcerer *that* powerful for all these years. That couldn't be right, though. Even if he'd forgotten the existence of the Shadow Court, someone would have noticed that level of individual psychic energy out there in the world. *Right?*

"And so we wait," Gustaf said. "For another shipment, for a crime to be committed, for anything that is actionable. We wait and we allow law enforcement to proceed, acting only as guides, and we allow any perpetrators due process in court."

I made a face. "If these guys are this sophisticated, they're not going to wait around for you to take them to court."

"And yet we are an international organization governed by international laws. We are also beholden to local law enforcement to execute according to the strategic guidance we provide. In order to ensure that execution continues to happen, we also need to play by their rules. I'm sure you can understand the implications of going in rogue in the middle of an operation without properly notifying all the agencies involved."

"I…" I shook my head, trying to quell my frustration. Was this guy even aware that all of his excruciatingly honorable protocols were exactly the delay the Shadow Court needed to close up shop? "Okay. So let's recap. Besides this little meet and greet, you're in Hamburg because you've received credible information about illicit and deadly drugs being shipped into and out of this city. Your response was to notify the local authorities and put them on notice that something may happen. Meanwhile, another attack in Paris, for which you have no information, has drawn your attention from Hamburg. How long until you return? And why aren't we all going to Paris?" I really, really was chafing under the Council's "you do you" policy when we could clearly run this operation so much better, but I knew I needed to cool it.

"Because that is not your place," Gustaf said quellingly. "Your job is simply to do as local law enforcement directs you, and nothing more."

I took in a deep, steadying breath. "Fair enough."

While Gustaf continued with his instructions, Nikki kept tapping on Simon's keyboard. Though the Fool was effectively out of harm's way in Dr. Sells's care, I could tell by the flow of information sliding across her screen that Simon was not exactly taking it easy in Las Vegas.

Unfortunately, Gustaf claimed my attention once again.

"Detective Rooks has filled us in on your activities since you were last in our system, Ms. Wilde. We do not wish to be at cross-purposes with either you or your organization. We are all here to work together. I am simply trying to understand how we may best do that while keeping you safe. You are all civilians."

I nearly bit my tongue off, but managed a smile. "That's certainly true."

My restraint wasn't lost on Gustaf. "I have it on good authority from Detective Rooks that you possess psychic abilities, yes," he continued. "Some might even say exceptional psychic abilities. But you must understand, information that we gather or results that are obtained through the use of psychic abilities will dramatically hamstring our efforts to bring these mental terrorists to justice. If we are going to get them, we need to get them with conventional ways."

My smile only broadened. "Of course." And I didn't even ask him how those conventional processes were working out. For which I deserved a medal.

"Furthermore, we—"

"Sara—what the hell. That's you." Nikki's bark of surprise drew everyone's attention, and with a stab of her finger, she switched the projected image onto the wall. We were looking at live feed of a busy Parisian square, which I knew at a glance was the exterior of Saint-Germain-des-Prés. And the woman holding an ice pack against her face...

I stood up. "What the hell is happening here?" I asked sharply, bolting up from my seat. "What was this attack? Who's involved?"

"Perhaps the better question is why does that woman look exactly like you?" Gustaf snapped back. "Who is she?"

"Emma Fearon. She's a volunteer. Who is putting the camera on her?" I demanded, pointing at the second image in Simon's collage of input feeds. "That is not standard video feed. That's the feed from a scope, like from a sniper rifle or a —"

Even with the sound turned down to a bare murmur, the sound of a rifle shot was unmistakable in the primary feed, and the camera slewed away crazily as a spray of blood blanketed the face of Emma Fearon. The scope camera remained trained on her forehead as she jerked back, stumbling away from the first cameraman, who had clearly been shot directly in front of her. She turned her startled face toward the camera, the glamour of my face now wiped from her image, and her own glamour barely remaining intact, such that I could almost see her one working eye going wide with horror...

The screen went blank.

"What the *hell*." I took several steps toward the wall, which suddenly went blank. Meanwhile, the phones of every single operator including Brody started a cacophony of buzzing, whirring, and rings.

Gustaf stood. "As you can see, the situation in Paris has escalated. We are leaving now. There will be no further action on the potential charges in Hamburg unless and until something else happens here. You are welcome to join us in Paris should you feel your presence will be a help and not a hindrance, but make no mistake, you are civilians and *will* act as such." He stared at me. "The young woman possessed your face, Ms. Wilde. Clearly with your awareness. There will be an accounting for that, you can rest assured."

"There's definitely going to be an accounting," I said. I looked at him sharply and then at Kreios. "Is she dead?"

Kreios shook his head almost imperceptibly.

"That's a negative," Nikki said as her fingers raced over the keys. "The cameraman is critically injured, but officers on scene believe that was intentional, that the sniper was not shooting to kill but to make a statement. The shot is too precise in too narrow a space for it to be anything else."

"Right." I scowled at the wall, now only covered with three separate feeds instead of five. I barely kept from crawling out of my skin as Gustaf went through the rest of his notes, asking questions about the Hamburg operation, the families involved, and constantly receiving updates from Paris. Finally, they stood.

"We'll be in touch. If we receive word that there is any change at this location, we will notify you and return. Until then—do not interfere."

Brody didn't even bother making eye contact with me, for which I was grateful. He would keep me up to date on anything that was necessary, and he'd remain safe in his cocoon of Interpol agents. I couldn't ask for anything more.

Except being able to do something.

"You cannot seriously expect us to sit around and wait for something bad to happen before we do anything," I accused Armaeus, who rematerialized the moment the agents had cleared the room. "The Shadow Court has done everything but send us an engraved invitation to sit ringside as they turn the technoceuticals up to full blast."

"We're operating within the system," the Magician said. "The system is not always as efficient, but it's run by mortals. They have the right to self-determination."

"You mean they have the right to get dead. You know the Shadow Court was well aware of who we were with and what we were talking about that whole time. They were also on the ground in Paris, ready to pull a trigger at the exact moment it would have caused the most damage. Once Interpol gets to Paris, they won't find anything. The action will have moved on. We're wasting our time."

"We cannot move against the Shadow Court without proper information, and that's coming," Kreios said. "We're too close to learning the truth about what Abigail did and how she did it. Once we have that, the memories will be restored to those who matter, and we'll be at full strength to act. Other truths may come out as well. Important truths."

"But why would they let that happen?" I protested. "Think about it. They've been ahead of us at every step. They have to know we're close to unraveling whatever spell Abigail put in place. So then what? The Council's going to remember what the Shadow Court is, but so what? How many people would that be? Two? Three?"

Nikki leaned back in her seat. "The Magician. Death. Eshe. The Hierophant. And, technically, your dad."

"Fantastic. Five people on this planet who might care, and let's face it, the Hierophant, Death, and Eshe won't give a crap. And Dad probably was barely aware of them when they did exist. Which leaves only one player who could cause them problems." I turned and looked at Armaeus. "You. Why aren't they trying to take you out? Why are they messing around in Paris?"

"Even compromised, I'm hardly an accessible target." Armaeus steepled his hands, resting his elbows on the table. "Still, it's an interesting point. If I'm the only one who knows the history of the Shadow Court after all these years, what relevance is that information? Why are they concerned about me unraveling Abigail's spells? If they drew no attention to themselves, they would earn me as an enemy, but not a focused one."

"Unless…" I frowned. There was one part of this that'd never made sense to me. Abigail had been a very conflicted soul, sure, but the nature of conflict was, well—conflict. We knew that she'd taken the Shadow Court from Armaeus's memory, but had she taken something else too, much as he'd stripped away the harsher elements of his personality in his bid to become a better Magician for a changing world? Something that would keep the Shadow Court in check? A last-ditch protection to help her sleep at night after her betrayal of the Council?

And did the Shadow Court know that bomb was still out there, waiting for someone to detonate it?

"Um…those spells that you stuffed into the In Between," I said, turning to Armaeus. "Were they all intact when we encountered them a second time? Did you recognize all of them?"

He frowned at me. "Those spells were the sum total of every failure I ever encountered as Magician. Those I made myself, and those I'd liberated from other souls. I could not take back all of them. You removed me from the In Between."

"But you recognized them. All of them. You were able to say, 'Oh, that one, yeah. You bastard, I got you.' Every single time? There weren't any that *should've* been there but weren't?"

He glanced toward the wall, clearly thinking. "I fail to see the relevance…"

"You think Abigail Strand removed certain broken magic from Armaeus along with his memory of the Shadow Court?" Kreios asked. "Magic relevant to *constraining* the Shadow Court?"

"I mean, it's possible," I hedged. "She had to have done something as a backstop in case she was making the wrong choice. She was a good person who had a very healthy dose of self-doubt. She would've had something in place."

Nikki made a face. "But will that help now? I mean great, you've remembered the Shadow Court existed, and maybe there was something back in the day that could stop them, but let's face it, this intel is a hundred and fifty years old. We still can't find the Shadow Court even though we know they exist. What's to say the old trick to box them up still works either?"

"Fair," Armaeus allowed. "But even if it doesn't provide the whole answer, it could provide clues to that answer. I need to return to the—"

"No." Kreios and I responded at the same time, but it was Kreios who kept talking. "You collapsed, Armaeus. Simon could see the whole thing, even compromised as he was. You are not strong enough to take on the sum total of your broken magic. Not yet."

"Miss Wilde is not going back there alone," Armaeus argued. "She's not—"

"That's not necessary either." I cut him off before he could remind me again of my lack of skills and force me to throat-punch him. What was his *deal*, anyway? I needed the old Armaeus back who thought I could do anything. He'd been pushy, but he wasn't infuriating. "We don't need the In Between. We need the library at Justice Hall. That's where Abigail would have stored

269

information about a spell that would stop the Shadow Court even as she cut the Court out of your awareness. That may even have been how she learned about such a spell. Are there any complaints against you, Armaeus, that you know of?" I'd actually never considered the possibility of the *Council* behaving badly and drawing the ire of an abused Connected before. It…certainly bore looking into.

Armaeus inclined his head. "I can't imagine any, no. Nor would Justice keep them on hand if there was. There would be no value."

"Maybe, maybe not."

I thought about the pitch Jarvis Fuggeren or his doppelgänger had made to me. He couldn't seriously think that I'd come over to the dark side, but what if that wasn't his play to begin with? What if his entire point was to sow discord between me and Armaeus, and…then what? Kill Armaeus? I'd like to see him try. Kill me? That also seemed like a less than brilliant move. I'd helped push the gods back into their places, and I had the weight of the Arcana Council behind me. While no one was untouchable, I'd give anyone a run for their money these days.

"Sara." Nikki's voice recalled me to the room, but she wasn't looking at me—or at her screen. She was looking at the wall. The wall which was once again filled with images of people milling through the courtyard of Saint-Germain-des-Prés. Only the view of these cameras wasn't at all from the nearby handcams of news outlets or video streamers. It was an image from a rifle scope, like the one we'd seen fixed on Emma's face.

Only it wasn't solely on Emma's face anymore.

A large, hulking Mongolian in military gear stood talking with police officers just outside the main steps to the church, imposing in his might. His face was careworn, his expression grim. It was the head of security of the House of Swords, General Ma-Singh, whom I'd requested to come and provide security. Beside him, half blocked by him, stood Emma, wrapped in a silver reflective blanket.

A second scope image turned on, both the enormous Mongolian and the petite Frenchwoman directly in its sights. Until Ma-Singh shifted his position, placing his body fully in front of Emma's. He was protecting her, as I'd asked him to do, unconsciously creating a barrier of perfect safety between her and the rest of the—

The violent report of guns firing echoed loud enough to be heard on the other side of the veil.

"No!" I gasped, my hands going out as horror rocketed through me. No one—*no one*—Could be hurt again because of me. *No one!*

But I was too late.

CHAPTER TWENTY-FIVE

I want it. All of it. Now."

I didn't even try to temper the rage in my voice as Mrs. French scurried away. I was left staring at the trio of Abigail Strand's young librarian assistants. They had no idea what they were looking for. To them, it was a game. To them, after living in this library year after year, decade after decade, century after century, the world on the outside must have taken on an ephemeral meaning, abstract.

I hadn't told them their search was a matter of life or death. They wouldn't know what that meant either. But the fact of the matter was, Ma-Singh was in critical condition in a hospital because I'd sent him into a battle I hadn't fully understood, and Emma Fearon was one room over, traumatized to the point of immobility. They'd both recover—Armaeus had assured me of that, had sworn it to me as if his own life depended on it—but I'd failed them both. Again.

I wasn't going to fail anymore.

"We *have* found several mentions of rogue power, ma'am." The tallest boy, Bobby Haymoor, said, his eyes wide beneath his mop of unruly hair. "And I do know there are complaints against the Magician—this

Magician, anyway. The one in office now. I've only seen him a few times…"

I grimaced. Something else I would be taking care of, but I couldn't focus on that right now. I couldn't focus on much of anything beyond the face of young, brave Emma Fearon and the irrepressible, larger-than-life Ma-Singh. Two people who'd believed in me. Two people I'd—

Stop it. I pushed the useless thoughts away. Back in the conference room in Hamburg, I hadn't waited for anyone to act, to talk. I'd simply returned to Justice Hall to finish what I'd started but had left to other hands to complete. As I did everything. As I refused to do anymore.

"Here we are, here we are," Mrs. French called out, announcing her return before she opened the door of the library and stepped through, her arms full of cases and books. Three more assistants followed directly behind, a wagon trail of information. "There's quite a bit, though. We've read through it, but nothing popped out."

"If she left it, she wanted it to be found, whether she wanted to admit it to herself or not," I said. "Spread it out on the floor, nothing overlapping."

I thought about what I knew about Abigail Strand as the boys and Mrs. French scrambled to complete my request. The last Justice of the Arcana Council had endured a condition once known as multiple personality disorder, now known more commonly as dissociative identity disorder, brought on by the trauma of her young life. She was a gifted Connected and had been cruelly used in experiments by a Connected she'd trusted. A doctor of science, a man of refinement and good manners. He'd been so much better educated than the young Abigail, so much more sophisticated, that she'd been out of her depth, willingly submitting to his experiments to tease out greater and greater abilities from her, abilities that lay beneath the fragile crust of her mental barriers.

In some ways, she and I were all too alike. But while I'd drawn the interest of Armaeus, who'd only wanted me to reach my highest potential, Abigail had drawn the attention of a predator. And while I'd been able to keep people from crawling around in my mind, once I made up said mind to do so, Abigail had been forced to slip into other identities to cope, always deferent, always hiding. Until she'd turned on the bastard and killed him flat.

Armaeus was the one who'd discovered her that day. He'd felt the disturbance in the psychic balance on the planet, and he'd investigated. By the time he'd reached Abigail, her tormentor was dead, and the Magician was left with an unreasonably powerful Connected whose mind was barely intact. He'd elevated her to a role on the Council to give her the protections she'd needed, and to protect the world from her. The accession had been good for Abigail, he'd believed. She'd seemed far happier, balanced, and productive. Right up until she died three years later, under circumstances that no one to this day fully understood.

"Who got to you, Abigail?" I murmured, staring at the cases before me. "And what did they convince you to do?"

Mrs. French, eyeing me worriedly, started speaking. "Justice Strand was a good woman, a brave woman, Justice Wilde. She wouldn't willingly harm anyone. She only wanted to protect them, she surely did."

"Protect them." I nodded, my gaze still on the cases as I continued murmuring my thoughts aloud. "And the Shadow Court could do that, couldn't they, Abigail?"

274

"Well, I do say she didn't tell me much about the—oh, my head." Mrs. French murmured, lifting a hand to rub her temple. I didn't miss her pained sigh, and as I studied the cases and coffers, I flicked my third eye open and braced myself for the light show.

I wasn't disappointed. A clear third of the cases were shooting off rockets like the Fourth of July, and the rest of them glowed with barely suppressed power.

"What am I looking at?" I asked more loudly, pointing to a set of the brightest boxes, all crowded together.

Mrs. French dropped her hand from her temple and obligingly sank to the ground, her heavy Victorian skirts billowing out around her as she picked up the first box. "These are complaints that came in during Justice Strand's time here. It's why we set them aside like that. But the boys couldn't open them, the dears. They thought they could at one time, were sure of it, but they might as well be solid blocks of lead now. I mean, good luck with it yourself, but—oh. Oh, well, then."

The case now lay open on her lap, surrounding her with a corona of light.

"Ahhh...how're you doing over there, Mrs. French?" I asked as the light flared, making me take a step back. The shard of Nul Magis in my hand throbbed, and I wondered, fleetingly, if I could quell Abigail Strand's wards on these boxes. Unfortunately, I didn't want to do anything to harm Mrs. French—and there was too little I knew about the nature of Abigail's abilities. She already appeared to be far stronger than we'd given her credit for. If my attempts to remove the boxes from Mrs. French or open them on my own triggered some other fell magic...I wanted no part of that.

I closed my fist around the Nul Magis, willing it to simmer down.

Meanwhile, Mrs. French fished a delicate scroll out of the case and squinted at it. "Quite all right, quite all right," she said absently. "This one is centered in a small town in Austria near Salzburg and dealt with—well, a rather unfortunate incident, a little hamlet that had been quite completely burned to the ground by the Magician."

I blinked. "Burned to the ground?"

She nodded, still seeming totally distracted, almost mesmerized by the contents of the case. "Very sad. The complainants weren't Connected, but they were entering their plea on behalf of the Connecteds who'd died, it seemed. One of the richest families in the area, known for their largesse, helping the community thrive, and all that. So...so very tragic. To see them go up in flames like that was devastating for everyone, and they begged for help."

"Help for what? It was a rich family that was harmed. How did that impact the others? Were they employers?" I couldn't imagine an Armaeus in any incarnation burning a mortal dwelling to the ground, certainly not in the 1850s, when society had evolved enough to report such things in the news. Someone would complain about the disaster—someone clearly had complained, and if Armaeus was to blame...he should have been brought to Judgment.

But Abigail hadn't done any of that. She'd left Armaeus in his role, intact, and, what...merely wiped the memory of this crime clear from his mind?

"Well, that's a good question, because..." She kept scanning the page. "Oh, here we are. It was a mansion owned by Maximilian Fuggeren."

I stared at her, my third eye flinching against the sudden flare of light. "Fuggeren? You're sure?"

"Quite, quite," she said, continuing to read the documents with a reflective look on her face. By now, she was completely surrounded by the fiery light. "And I will say...I remember this one, now. Justice Strand went personally, and she returned—well. I would almost have thought she was in love, as happy as she was, though it wasn't quite romantic love, more...I guess admiration. She said it wasn't the Magician's fault, exactly, though he'd done a bad thing. Very bad. Very wrong. That he wasn't himself. But we can't always be ourselves, can we? There has to be forgiveness and grace, and the Magician was not about either of those things—couldn't be, in his role. He was all logic and certainty and balance. But we're not balanced souls. We, all of us, have our darker moments that are ours to have and right and true and deserved to hold sway, and he needed to step out of the way of the shadows and let them be..."

She broke off, rocking a little, and I narrowed my eyes on her, trying to parse her words into something resembling coherence. "Ah, Mrs. French?"

"I'm quite all right, quite." She sniffled. I realized to my shock she was crying. I stepped forward—and was pushed just as quickly back by the flare of light from the other cases. The sudden pain that erupted within me took my breath away, but Mrs. French seemed not to be afflicted in the center of the flames arcing over the cases.

I hissed out a breath, battling the pain. "What about the others?"

"Oh...oh, those." Mrs. French obligingly dabbed at her eyes and pulled the other boxes close. She popped open the second box, a case of shiny gold, without issue. "This one was before, a complaint—oh, well. Not against the Magician, but against a young sorcerer, also in Austria, also…hmmm. Well, he's a fine-looking man, now, isn't he. Blond and bright. *Denarja* was his name, just that one name, but it's a fine name as well."

"It means money. In Slovenian," I offered, but Mrs. French still seemed in full swoon as she read the slips of parchment in the case. "What did he do?"

"He did nothing wrong, you can be sure of that," she said staunchly, though her eyes didn't stray from the picture and pages she clutched in her hand. "There's a second note here, in Abigail's own hand. Denarja was a fine man, a beautiful man, and he did warn Justice Strand of what was to come, he surely did. Warned her and begged for her grace, he did, not for himself. Not for himself. But for the Magician. For what was to come."

"Did he now?" My disbelief warred with my anxiety, but there was no doubting that Mrs. French fully believed what she was reading, was in the moment and swept along by the pageantry of what was playing before her eyes. "If he did nothing wrong, what was the complaint?"

"Not a complaint at all," she sighed. "She tells it plain. He wanted to catch Justice Strand's eye is all. Catch her eye and tell her how strong she was. Oh, what a flattering fellow."

"Right." I gradually figured out that most of the energy that was pulsing up from the cases was coming from Denarja. He was the lure that had pulled Abigail in, and she'd never been able to part with the case. But why wouldn't she have removed the Magician's crime entirely if this guy pleaded for grace on behalf of the Magician?

And why couldn't I get any closer?

I tried again, and once again, the pain that ricocheted through my body had the force of a lightning bolt. It had a curious nature as well, sharp and cutting, almost furious. My eyes went wide. Jealousy? It felt like the incarnation of jealousy, keeping me from approaching the case. The case of Denarja somebody or other, a sorcerer of Austria, who'd developed an almost guru-like hold on Abigail. One aspect of Abigail, anyway. He'd exerted a hold on her so strong that she'd, what, forgiven the Magician for a crime against a mortal? Or against a Connected living in a mortal's home—but even that made no sense. Even if the Magician had acted improperly, there shouldn't have been any evidence left behind, not for long. Armaeus was a champion at cleaning up after himself.

I focused on Mrs. French again. "What about the third case?"

"Same as the second," she said without taking her attention from the picture of Denarja. "Came in exactly at the same time, two different complainants."

"Can you read it for me?" I asked after a moment, when I realized she had no interest in looking anywhere but at the case of the sorcerer.

"Oh, if I must," she said crossly. She leaned over and picked up the third box, but the clasp wouldn't budge. "Nothing doing. It won't open."

"Try harder," I blurted as her attention moved back to the second case. Her head came up with a sudden snap, and she scowled at me through the curtain of fire that she couldn't see but that had leapt up between us in fiery anger.

"There's nothing to *see* in that one, Justice," she practically snarled. "Abigail tried to toss it, tried to have all of us toss it, but it wouldn't toss. Some of the cases are like that, sticking around where they're not needed anymore, but she's got the whole library now, doesn't she, for troublesome cases like that. Plenty of room."

"She wanted to destroy it?" There went my theory of Abigail keeping something to help the Council against the Shadow Court, unless she thought Denarja was that guy. I wasn't feeling that, though. And there was something about that third box…

"Who issued the complaint?" I pressed. "Is there any marking on the box, anything at all? Because it looks like it's…um, kind of melting."

"It's doing nothing of the sort," Mrs. French insisted, no matter that, in the flare of heat surrounding her, the surface of the box was practically bubbling. Where it had started out as a plain black box, now it was glowing a fiery red, and beneath that, a cerulean blue was peeking out, neon bright. I struggled to move forward through the curtain of fire, but once more, I was rebuffed. My own hands lit with blue flame, but the pressure against me only seemed to increase. Abigail had been a Justice, like me. She'd come to her role with powers of her own, psychic abilities I knew very little about. She was blocking not me personally, but quite literally the position of Justice. The position she had to have suspected would be filled once again after she had passed on. One of her identities must've realized that she was not strong enough to stay in that position forever, immortality or no. And her guru, her guide, must remain safe.

But there was this other box…

"Keep trying to open it, Mrs. French," I urged. "It's important. If you could let me know at least who had launched the complaint, that would be so helpful. Then I'll leave you to your research on Denarja."

"Oh." Mrs. French's eyes widened with absolute delight, and she focused more closely on the box in her hands. "Well, perhaps if I just—"

Disregarding entirely the flames that licked and roared over the surface of the box, Mrs. French drew her fingernail along one seam, cackling with delight as something appeared to give way. "Well, now, that's more like it," she said, eminently pleased with herself. She bent closer to the box, ignoring the searing heat, and pressed the surface harder. "Justice Strand always did tell me that I had a gift, beyond my own long-lived ways. She said I never gave up, even when I should. I was just too inquisitive that way."

She smiled absently as she fiddled with the box. "She didn't pay me much attention, you know? Appreciated what I had to offer but never asked me to do much more, when I was always so willing to do anything for the woman. She was such a precious soul, such a grace."

"She was lucky to have you," I murmured, my attention fully on the box.

"I was lucky to have her, you mean. She trusted me." Mrs. French sighed. "That's one other thing she would say. Bless my soul, I haven't thought about it in years. But she always told me she knew she could trust me. That no matter who she was in any given moment, my genuine affection for her would never change. She was never afraid of me."

I grimaced. Mrs. French obviously didn't know that Abigail had warded her, though clearly those wards were fairly light if she was able to get even as far as she had with the box in her lap. Had Abigail assumed that Mrs. French would never get this far? Or if she did, that there'd be nothing to worry about?

"Oh!" Mrs. French finally said, and I could hear the lock pop, the report as loud and abrupt as a thunder crack. I winced, thinking about the poor residents of the Palazzo Hotel beneath me and wondering how much of that psychic boom had been heard in the floors below. But I still couldn't get any closer to Mrs. French. I could only watch as she sat back abruptly on her skirts, looking for all the world like a butterfly perched on a mushroom cap, and stared up at me with wide and startled eyes.

"Well, bless my *soul*," she breathed with total shock. "It was Cassius D'Angelo. He's who leveled this complaint, Justice Wilde. I didn't even know that was possible."

"What are you talking about?" I'd never heard the name Cassius D'Angelo before, but the way Mrs. French spoke it, it was clear she did. "Who is Cassius D'Angelo?"

The brightly burning streams of energy suddenly guttered out, and a stiff breeze rocked me back on my heels, hot as the blast from the furnace. Before I scarcely drew in my next breath, there was another figure in the room with us, looking as dashing and self-assured as he always did, from the tips of his long, tawny locks to the soles of his battered beach sandals.

"I never do tire of saying this." Aleksander Kreios sighed with deep and obvious pleasure. "But speak of the Devil, and he shall appear."

CHAPTER TWENTY-SIX

W ho — what?" Mrs. French sat on the floor with cases scattered around her, her expression entirely bewildered.

"Cassius D'Angelo was the Devil in 1852." I didn't pose it as a question, and the Devil didn't bother nodding, just gave me an indolent shrug.

"You can't hold me accountable for my forebear's actions, but what did he do now? He was a colossal ingrate by all accounts. He came from Sardinia in the late 1700s, when the country was constantly at war, and he never could shake that off. He lasted until 1878, when he waded into the wars of the Ottoman Empire and was killed for his troubles. Nasty bit of business there, from what I'm told. He went down in Austria. The Magician got to him too late to save him, but not too late to incinerate his torturers."

"Torturing the Devil." Mrs. French crossed herself. "Who would've thought it was possible?"

"So the Magician couldn't save him, but he tried? Which meant — I mean, if he and Cassius weren't friends, they were at least allies."

"Strong allies," Kreios confirmed. "Cassius didn't agree with Armaeus's penchant for balance, but then —

who could? They were at odds a great deal during the last twenty years of Cassius's life."

"Last twenty years…" I turned to Mrs. French. "What was the nature of the complaint he sent to Justice?"

"A complaint?" Kreios's elegant brows arched. "How interesting."

"I…ah…a moment." Mrs. French grew flustered again, as if she was surprised to find the box still in her lap. She picked up a single card from a bed of red-and-white material. The card contained very few words from what I could tell, and she frowned down at it. "It's in Latin. 'For shame, Magician. You see only the lock, not the key.'"

"The lock, not the key?" Kreios echoed. "I can't say he was wrong, but what does that mean?"

"And how does that constitute a complaint?" I complained. "Is there anything else in the case?"

"Not at all—well, no, that's…" She pulled out a tuft of red velvet—and kept pulling. No sooner had she cleared the first strip than another nudged up, this one in snowy white. Then a third, once more in the same deep crimson of the first. The material seemed to grow exponentially as it cleared the case, until in a very short time, Mrs. French was surrounded with a luxurious pile of confetti in yards of rich red and white velvet. And then she pulled out something different.

"Bless my soul," she whispered as she held the item up.

"It's a key," I said flatly. "Give me that."

I moved forward and took the key from Mrs. French's unresisting hand, but even with the careful scrutiny of my third eye, I found absolutely no energy signature emanating from it. It was a flat dull skeleton key, fashioned out of some sort of metal. "What is this, lead?" I asked, handing it to Kreios. The Devil took it without hesitation.

"So it would seem," he agreed, turning the key over in his hand. "It may mean something to Armaeus, but not to me."

I frowned, something niggling in my brain...something about a key... I turned to Mrs. French. "When did this complaint come in, again? Before or after Abigail's run-in with Denarja?"

"Who?" Mrs. French blinked at me, and I sighed. Whatever magic had been caught up in these three cases, it was strong and beguiling, even a hundred and fifty years on.

It took only a brief explanation to bring Kreios up to speed on the events of 1852 and the tale of Armaeus incinerating a hapless hamlet, but the Devil was equally taken aback. "I can tell you, in all the time I've known him, Armaeus never destroyed any outpost like that where there weren't actual outright enemies to the Council. And even then—no mortal structures were destroyed in any way that could be laid at his feet."

I squinted at the material lying at *our* feet. "Red and white—that could be the Austrian flag, right? The hamlet was in Austria. What does that have to do with the key?"

"The key is a symbol," Kreios agreed. "You only see the lock, not the key."

"Lock lock as in block? Or lock as in portal or keyhole? It could go either way." I scowled, frustrated. "We'll have to ask him."

"That...is somewhat problematic," Kreios said. "After you left, Armaeus faltered again. It was almost as if he'd been holding it together on sheer willpower alone and could no longer. He became disoriented and started mumbling to himself in full conversations, as if

285

there were several stories being told to him at once, and he couldn't follow the right track."

"The angelic communication," I said. "He hasn't shut it off. He needs to shut it off, but he won't."

"Most likely, but it presents a problem. This key, whatever it is, may be the last trigger required for him to understand not only the existence of the Shadow Court, but also how to fight it. Or it could completely unhinge him."

"Or it may mean nothing at all," I countered. "Cassius wanted the Magician to fight. If he leveled a complaint, it follows that there was a fight to be had, and Armaeus didn't take it on."

"Or he didn't finish it," Kreios agreed.

"I've got the date now," Mrs. French piped up. "Eighteen fifty-two, right after this box here…"

She picked up the golden box, the one that had contained the missive from Denarja. "Don't open that," I blurted, and she dropped it just as quickly, blinking at me.

Kreios regarded me curiously as well.

"Sorry," I offered. "That one had some sort of mesmerizing spell built into it. You open it again, we might be here all night."

"Well, I say," Mrs. French murmured, but she tapped the third box. "The Devil's complaint also came at the same time as the complaint against Armaeus, leastwise by the dates on the box."

"So all three could have been linked to the same incident. Denarja contacts Abigail, Armaeus blows up the house of this Austrian lord, the Devil issues a complaint."

Kreios snorted. "Explosions seemed to make Cassius happy, though. Why would he have any issue with this one?"

"Maybe he blew up too little? Maybe he blew up the wrong thing?"

"You see the lock...not the key," Kreios mused. "And he sent this complaint to Abigail. Which she promptly ignored."

"That's not quite right, beggin' your pardon, sir."

We all turned to see Bobby Haymoor standing at the door of the library, the others hovering behind him, ready to bolt. He looked at Kreios with wide, admiring eyes, and the Devil immediately picked up on his sense of wonder.

"By all means, share what you know," Kreios said, in a voice as gentle as a sigh. "Whatever the truth you most wish to speak."

"I..." Bobby took a step forward almost without seeming to realize it, then straightened. "We knew there was something off about some of the boxes Justice Strand had us sort, right? I mean, you've seen the library. It's chock-full to the brim of cases she'd completed, petitions she ignored, and those she refused to touch for reasons only she knew. And no matter how many shelves we filled up, there were always more shelves to go. You can't fill Justice Hall. There's always room for those who seek it, you see?"

"I do," Kreios said. I merely stared at the boy. He'd spoken more to the Devil in the last thirty seconds than he had to me in five months.

"So when Justice Strand wanted us to discard some of the boxes, well, we didn't quite know what to do. Some we burned easily enough. Those were cases that were solved, you see. But those that weren't, sort of didn't want to go. They took longer to burn, made us feel bad."

I grimaced, imagining their conflict. All those cases waiting to be heard, and those that never got their own say thrown into the fire. The boys owed Abigail their lives, and she had provided them safe haven. But they still had their own sense of right and wrong.

"Those were the old cases," the boy continued. "The new ones she threw on the pile of discards, we knew hadn't been solved because they came in on her time, you see. And we didn't think it was quite right since it wasn't a situation of an old crime finally getting its Justice. These were people who were still alive. They still could have their wrongs righted." He pointed to the case Mrs. French still held in her hand, cushioned by all the yards of red and white velvet. "And that one she outright panicked over. She tried to destroy it herself, only it wouldn't budge. She couldn't open it either, was the problem. She couldn't get rid of it, couldn't solve it. She…well, she spoke to it in different voices, pleaded with it. But nothing doing. It wouldn't budge. Finally, she just gave it to us and told us to take it out of Justice Hall, out of her sight. To keep till it was needed, though she never did explain that."

"That was in her quiet voice," squeaked one of the boys hovering in the doorway.

"Right, yeah," the first boy said. "That voice, we'd never heard before or after. It sounded…it didn't sound right. Not quite scary, but—not right. We took the box away and promised her we'd get rid of it, but of course we never could. Then we…" His cheeks colored. "Well, then we sort of forgot about it altogether until recently. Even then, it's not so much that we remembered as we remembered we forgot."

The Devil didn't actually shoot me a glance, but I felt his interest veer toward me anyway. His eyes, however, stayed on the boy. "Did she ask you about the case again? This particular one?"

"She didn't, no, sir. Not as I can recall, anyway. Honestly, she didn't even know it'd come in until, what…a few weeks after it arrived?"

"A month!" came another voice from behind the door, and a towheaded boy peeked around the corner. "Beggin' your pardon. But it was a month. My birthday month."

"That's right, a month. She left for several weeks— longest she'd ever been away. When she came back, she was like a new person. Happy, even singing, like the weight of the world had been lifted off her shoulders."

"She was in love," Mrs. French said, but her voice was uncertain, as if she'd hit upon the answer only to realize it wasn't quite right.

"No, no, she was already that," her young assistant countered. "Temperance Simms swore us to secrecy. This wasn't love. This was…more like she was cured, it seemed. Cured of her, ah, changeability. Or we thought so, anyway. Till she saw that box and fell apart again."

His expression made my heart crumble a little, and I suddenly connected the dots. "Abigail had been helped by the Shadow Court. She'd already been vetted by them, and then the situation with the Magician and this hamlet drove them to meet with her. Then Cassius's complaint frightened her, but she couldn't get rid of it. She had to do something else."

"I don't know, ma'am," Bobby said, lifting his shoulders. He still looked dejected, and I pulled my hands into fists, feeling the pulse of the Nul Magis in my right hand. Sometimes, having all your memories back wasn't all it was cracked up to be. "I only know that when she saw this new complaint, the one she couldn't open, she was distraught all over again. The rest I've already told you."

289

"You've been very helpful," Kreios assured Bobby, and he extended his hand. The other boys yelped and disappeared behind the open doorway to the library, but Bobby blinked, then stepped forward. Slowly at first, then with a little more verve, until he reached out and shook the Devil's hand.

"Thank you," Kreios said. "You'll find in life it's better to know the truth and be sad than to be happy with your head in the sand. You did well."

The boy's eyes shot wide, and a smile of shy excitement burst across his face. He shook Kreios's hand again, hard, then he turned and dashed back through the door of the library.

"Well, I…" We both turned to see Mrs. French with her hands to her cheeks, tears leaking from her clenched eyes. "That was very kind of you, sir. Very, so very kind."

"Shhh," Kreios said, lifting his hand.

Mrs. French immediately straightened, exhaling a sharp breath and looking around as if she didn't quite know where she was. "Right-o! That was something. So. I'll be cleaning up the lot of these, then, if you're done?" Without waiting for a reply, she hauled herself upright, shaking off the yards of red and white velvet, and began bustling about the room.

"What are we going to do now?" I asked. "If you give Armaeus the key, and it's more than a key, how can we let him go off to fight the Shadow Court? He's not stable, even if he's suddenly granted the insight he needs to beat them."

"He's not stable," Kreios agreed. He looked at the key, holding it up to the light. "I don't believe there are any magical properties to this key whatsoever, or any markings of a more mundane sort to indicate that it might have actually gone to a lock."

"A key with no lock? What, was Cassius some kind of Riddler-in-training?"

Kreios snorted. "I don't know. He wasn't my immediate predecessor, and I had troubles of my own to solve when I ascended. But I've spoken with Armaeus about all the past Devils he served with, and his memories of Cassius were always a little...fraught. It will be good to see what his reaction to the key is. A key, not a book. After the lost chapter of the Zohar and the journal of John Dee, I rather expected it to be a book."

I hadn't thought about that, but he was right. "Maybe the key unlocks a book Armaeus forgot he had?"

Kreios pursed his lips thoughtfully. "Perhaps. Or perhaps Cassius was clever enough to realize he couldn't write anything down in this instance. Words leave a mark, but the whisper of truth baked into forged metal? Something else entirely. Either way, you're right. Armaeus is not ready to fight. So any revelations this key will bring us won't help in this immediate battle, the one the Shadow Court is setting up so assiduously."

I sighed. "I was afraid of that."

Kreios, however, kept going. "Which means you'll have to fight it alone while I go present this key to Armaeus."

"Wait, what?" I squinted at him. "I mean, yay, fight—but why me in particular? And why alone?"

Kreios smiled. "You, because the Shadow Court is clearly baiting you. There's something they need from you."

"I don't know about that. They pretty much know things about me I've forgotten myself."

"Ah, but as you told Armaeus—yes, he told me— learning someone else's past isn't memory, it's history. They think they know you, and they will leverage that knowledge, but their logic is faulty if they think they know you better than yourself. And you will stand alone because we cannot trust the full Council in this fight, nor do we want to betray our hand about that. We don't know who the Shadow Court has compromised, if anyone. We will need time to ferret that out, but time is something we do not have. Armaeus cannot stand for the Council because he cannot stand for himself. Right now, he is existing in a state of suspended animation, with pieces of him still lost, and those he has found—unfamiliar. Foreign. Like bones healed improperly that need to be rebroken."

I pulled a face. "That…sounds awful. But, fair enough. So how exactly do you expect me to defeat the Shadow Court by myself?"

"I don't. I expect you to fight them."

"But I've never really learned *how* to fight. Not properly."

Kreios's smile was rich and full. "Fighting is life, Sara Wilde. You merely need to want to live. Do you want to live? Do you want Armaeus to live?"

"Of course I do," I muttered, rubbing one hand over my eyes. I couldn't remember the last time I'd slept, but it seemed like…too long ago. "Armaeus has to live. I have to live. There's no other way."

Kreios nodded. "Then you'll know how to fight when the time comes."

"You better be right," I said as I heard Mrs. French's startled exclamation, followed by the staccato clatter of a dozen new canisters sliding home in my office. *Thump, thump, thump.* Complaints, I knew instinctively. Complaints against the Shadow Court, or at least the drugs they were pumping into Western Europe. *Thump, thump, thump.* "Because apparently, it's going down now."

292

CHAPTER TWENTY-SEVEN

I crackled back into awareness at the shipyard in Hamburg, my favorite place in the city by dint of the fact that I'd now been there multiple times. It was midmorning, but though the place was a beehive of activity, I mercifully did not incinerate anyone on arrival. My borrowed motorbike was, of course, long gone, but a squat, gunmetal-blue container truck with official-looking lettering on the side trundled by me as I sucked in my first gust of Hamburgian oxygen. I stepped up on the truck's back bumper and clung to its ladder on impulse, if only so I wouldn't be left standing in the middle of the yard.

This wasn't a good long-term strategy, of course, but it did give me a second to get my bearings. I scanned the shipyard wildly as the truck bounced along, splashing through puddles and drawing no attention whatsoever, even with the leather-jacketed stowaway on its back. Sadly, nothing immediately popped up as "this is your next step." When the truck took a hard right into a sea of pallets and container boxes, I traded one ladder for another, hopping off the back of the truck to clamber up the nearest stack. Better views up high, I reasoned, and I wouldn't be quite so noticeable.

When I reached the top of the pallets, I did a quick scan around. Seeing no one, I went flat on the wooden surfaces and pulled out my phone. Could the Shadow Court and their goons track my phone in the city? Could they pick up a call if I tried to contact Nikki? I had no idea, but I punched in her number anyway as I stared out over the Great Container Sea. If I needed to bring the party to me, at least I'd found a really great dance floor.

She answered on the first ring. "Dollface. Where are you?"

"Shipyard, but probably not for long. Anything happening?"

"Not a damned thing," she confirmed. "No word out of Paris that we can get, everything locked up tight. They're calling it a domestic terror attack, but we know that's not right."

I tightened my jaw. It wasn't right. It was a message, and one delivered just to me. The Shadow Court was going to continue to push and push until I pushed back. Not a problem anymore. "And local—you track how they're getting drugs out?"

"That would be negative. The port of Hamburg has been rocking with shipments this whole week from a laundry list of Connected bad actors, and the whole thing is running slick enough that you know it's business as usual. They've been doing this a long time, which means we just sort of stumbled into their supply chain. So the drugs…"

"Are already out there. Whatever this new batch is, it's just the latest flavor."

"But it's big, and it's causing a lot of buzz. We're getting the idea that these tips are coming in from Connecteds who are actually part of the supply chain, who're suddenly getting cold feet with what's now getting fed into the system. Now that we know what to look for, Simon's been jacking his IV drip with enough caffeine to fuel some pretty epic search algos on the arcane web. There's enough of these new drugs everywhere from global powerhouses to Third World powder kegs to make a pretty big boom if they get released into the general populace. We still don't know how they're using these technoceuticals either. Weapons, gotta be, but against who?"

"Against everyone," I muttered. Something shifted in the far distance, the lightest flutter, and I scowled. I couldn't see anything, but that didn't mean it wasn't there. Not with the Shadow Court's speed demons or whatever they were. "I gotta roll. Keep trying to track down any actual illicit drugs we know about that are shipping in the mix. It's the only way we'll be able to get Interpol to act."

"Roger that. What about you?"

"I'm going to—oof!"

My phone went flying as the first wave of bodies hit me, three operatives appearing as if out of nowhere, blasting into my side. The phone skittered over the edge and went soaring into space, so I mentally checked the device off my "things to break" list and rolled up to my feet, zigging out of the way in time to miss another flying leap. That guy also went over the edge, so I added him to the same column as my phone.

That left the two initial bad guys squaring off against me, but neither of them opted for dodgeball as their game of choice, instead going for their guns—

I blasted them.

I didn't even think about it. I didn't care about anyone noticing me. I didn't care about how badly I hurt these asshats. My hands came up as if of their own accord, and my version of gunfire shot across the open space of the pallets and lit their bodies up with electricity, a full-on taser strike without all the silly string to clean up. They were jacked up to the point of levitation, then collapsed, quivering on the surface of the Container Sea, down for the count. Which was good, because no sooner had I leapt over them than a shout sounded in the distance. I whirled to see an entire wave of goons reach the top of the pallets and storage containers — and take off after me.

"Crap!" I had no idea how much electrocution juice I had left in my tanks, but it wasn't enough to fight off the swarm vomiting up from the alleyways between the pallets — and I immediately got the sense that no matter how many of these asshats I took out, the Shadow Court would just make more. Maybe to tire me out, maybe simply to piss me off. They didn't expect this to be the actual fight, just the first course.

They were still playing games.

With a roar, I flicked open my third eye and noticed a similar chaos of energy circuits that I'd experienced at the Sagrada Familia. This army were all Connected — or Connected enough — and they were linked to each other, moving together as a single unit and directed from a single point of origin. That port of origin was what I needed to get to. I couldn't run away from this, not forever. They'd simply keep hunting me down or killing people to get my attention.

I had to run toward it.

Taking advantage of the five seconds it had taken me to put all this together, the next wave of supersonic attackers hit me square. They were moving too fast to use guns, and I thrust my hands out to either side, pummeling them back with a wave that I deliberately focused on the same electroneural networks that were binding them together. They erupted in a roar, some of them literally catching on fire, but there was nothing I could do about that right now. Instead of running this time, however, I followed my surge of energy forward. The throng of bad guys parted like the Red Sea, all of them flailing, jerking, and grabbing for me, screaming and crying and gasping with agony, the entire chaotic scene looking like Dante's hell or the last panel of a Bosch triptych, played out under the bright and cheerful Hamburg sun.

But I kept moving. As I passed body after screaming body, I felt the Shadow Court soldiers' energy blasting out to me, saw their eyes, touched their faces—mostly to shove them away from me, but I also needed an image, a picture, a place, a location. I needed that location to be strong enough that I could fix on it—fix on it and embed it in my mind and believe that I'd been there before. I needed to believe so desperately that I could reach it again that even having never been there, I could flash myself into existence exactly where I needed to be. As I moved, I also yanked weapons away from my damn-near-electrocuted assailants—a knife, a gun, another gun, a switchblade, stashing them on my body. I didn't know what I'd need later, but I believed in being prepared.

I finally got through the wall of humanity and hurdled over a makeshift alley, the space beneath me still crawling with more Shadow Court flunkies racing up the walls. I blasted another sheet of electricity into the space between the pallets for good measure, then looked up—and out.

Three more sets of assailants were hauling their bodies up and out of the shadows beneath the Container Sea, and they all were coming for me. From different directions.

"No!" I gasped as a hand locked on my ankle and yanked my leg out from underneath me, flipping me

297

hard to the surface of the pallet. I grunted as pain shot through me and blasted the asshat who'd gotten to me, but he barely staggered back. Meanwhile, the seven circles of hell were closing in, and unless I detonated a nuclear bomb, there was no way I was going to get this wave off my back. They'd take me, and that was not going to happen.

Then I recognized him. It was the guy from the motorcycle that first night in Paris, and the guy standing on the corner during the downpour in Hamburg. The assassin who kept turning up like a bad euro. But this was no drone, dammit. This was someone I could work with.

This was someone I could use.

"You!" I spit out, and instead of a defensive maneuver, I sprang toward him, wrapping my legs and arms around him as he grunted in surprise. I pinned my third eye wide and stared straight into his stony glare as I caught us both on fire—

And flashed to the first image that sprang up in my mind.

We crackled back into existence on a cobblestoned street that I vaguely recognized as being part of the Speicherstadt area, and sprang apart. None of the horde came with us, but before I could get my bearings beyond that, I sensed more than saw the guy's hand arching out, the flash of the blade. He was going to knife me right across the neck, the same move he'd done to Nikki.

Nikki. Drawing on the deep pool of rage, I wrenched my body back, tumbling ass over teakettle with a speed and grace I didn't know I had in me, whirling like a dervish. Something hard and metallic cut into my chest, and I gasped, assuming I'd been hit, but the guy was nowhere close enough to me to be able to hit me like that. I caught a glimpse of gold as I glanced down at my shirt and thought—Guabancex. The storm goddess token had finally made herself known by stabbing the crap out of my sternum.

"Not the time." I ducked to the ground, missing most but not all of the flying attack from the assassin. The parts of him that did hit me, though, were a doozy. My entire body lit up on fire as I received the same kind of dose of electricity as I'd been doling out on the pallets in the Hamburg shipyard and, lethal weapon or not, that shit hurt.

"Enough!" I barked to no one but my own hesitation, and I blasted him before I even caught my own breath. Only now my energy was stronger, harsher, spilling forward not in clear blue but in a murky red and purple haze. It was energy born of the spray of Nikki's blood, the brightness of the reflective blanket wrapped around Emma Fearon, the startled eyes of a Mongolian general who'd done nothing but do what I asked him to do, to serve and protect and—

"Enough!" I roared again and leaned into the blast of magic, blowing the man clear across the street. Somewhere, a car screeched its brakes, and then the sound of a crash and explosion sounded, but I was well beyond caring about that. I kept the red-and-purple fire flowing from my hands steady as I stalked toward the man, whose guns came up—and they were no ordinary guns—and blasted at me full-bore.

The fire I hurled back at him, however, roared straight up toward the sky, blocked by some kind of temporary wall of power that was enough to stop me in my tracks.

That was all the time the guy needed. He flipped over onto his feet, staggered upright, and was gone. I'd never seen anyone run so fast.

Other than me.

I took off after him at full speed.

CHAPTER TWENTY-EIGHT

I had to hand it to the guy, he could absolutely motor. My unnamed nemesis turned once, then again, and then a third time, weaving through the streets of Hamburg like a man on a mission. I was gaining on him, though. It felt good to run, to race so quickly over cobblestones, asphalt, and concrete that the world became a blur and I was safe in a cocoon of action for at least a little while. We burst out into a bricked street that ended abruptly at the edge of some sort of canal. The assassin in front of me started flagging abruptly, and I poured on the speed—realizing too late what he was doing.

I ran smack into a vat of gravy.

Instantly, my arms went out, flailing in exactly the same way the goddess Guabancex had been rocking it hurricane style in the minds of her believers, and managed not to face-plant into the bricks. But there was no doubting that I'd hit a dead zone. My fingers didn't kindle with electricity the way they needed to, and the fire in my belly had more to do with raw panic than anything more useful.

I rolled away and scrambled to my feet, staying in a crouch, yanking one of the stolen guns from my waistband and bringing it up in both hands. The assassin did the same thing, and we circled each other warily, trapped between a large, gorgeously bricked building and the picturesque waterway, but he hadn't shot yet. I eyed his weapon and figured maybe it was a teched up gun. If that was the case...was mine too? Maybe I should've gone for the knife.

The guy stepped toward me, and I realized another problem. I had Great and Awesome Powers in the body of a five-foot-six American woman poorly trained in hand-to-hand combat. I wasn't John Wick; I couldn't do anything with a pencil other than tank the SATs. And this guy knew that—knew it! Which was why he'd brought me here.

"You wanna die fast or slow? You're kind of boring me with this dance," I pointed out, because if nothing else, at least my mouth was still supercharged.

His gaze flickered, but only slightly, and I sighed, layering on the line of bullshit like graffiti on an overpass. "You know I've got tactical gear on, and you know my skin's been treated with straight-up non-Connected body armor. Say what you want about our breakfast bar, the Council's got way better toys than you do."

"Body armor," he sneered, and I edged farther to my right. When had I entered the dead zone? Had it really been across the street or was it closer? And what were the parameters of it? I flicked my third eye on, trying to get my bearings, and squinted. My third eye still worked, sort of, but it was definitely going to need bifocals if I planned on spending any amount of time in dead zones. Nevertheless, there was a definite bowing in the energy field brownout—the zone didn't fall along exact lines. If I could just get close to that wrinkle of energy...

"I suppose you'll tell me your saliva is poisoned too?"

My regular gaze sharply refocused on the guy as we circled each other, and I could tell immediately he was getting closer to me. He knew what he was doing. He only needed to have a few steps' jump and he'd be able to take me down flat. His body weight and obvious training would totally win out in that confrontation.

A rhythmic whooshing noise rattled the street beneath us, and I almost lost my balance. The assassin took a step forward. I fired my borrowed gun.

The bullet missed, but it still had the effect I wanted it to. The guy stopped and backed up a half-step sideways, suddenly far warier. "Guess you didn't outfit your whole gang with your newest and fanciest pistols," I said, taking full advantage of my turn to sneer. "There's still value in going analog, looks like."

"How do you know my gun isn't analog as well?" he countered, once again doing his crab walk to the right, circling in.

"Maybe because I'm still alive?"

"Fair. But I know something else about you, Justice Wilde. You never finish the job." Then, moving faster than he really should have given the lapse in our psychic abilities, he reached into his pocket and withdrew something bright and fierce—a blade, I thought, a knife—and I did the only thing I could. Locking both hands on my gun, I sprayed the man with bullets in one fierce sweep to the left, then the right. The Shadow Court's assassin stumbled back as if the stuffing was knocked out of him, and I screamed and rushed forward, knocking him the rest of the way to the ground as I straddled him, then pistol-whipped him once, twice, with my gun, blood spraying across the wet bricks.

Unfortunately, Captain Nemo was apparently wearing a bulletproof vest, and he was no slouch in the self-protection department. He twisted beneath me, scissoring his legs, and suddenly, he was on top and I was sprawled out over the pavement, sucking wind. I yanked one of my stolen knives out of my jacket, and he knocked it away as if I was his six-year-old little sister, then drove his own blade deep into my shoulder.

"Aigh!" I screamed, and though we were admittedly in a psychic dead zone, the exigency of my pain blew through at least a couple of those barriers. I could feel the tingling of power, however faintly, as the whooshing repeated far beneath me in the bowels of Hamburg's subway. Bringing my hands around, I clapped them to either side of the assassin's head, effectively boxing his ears. I didn't bother reaching for another knife but instead pulled out the blade he'd sunk into me. Warmth spread out over my shoulder, not all of it blood. Apparently, my sudden spurt of healing energy at least managed to cauterize the shit out of the wound, even if it didn't fully heal me. I'd take it.

The guy once again slashed out at me with a new sharp and pointy object, and this time when I saw crimson, it wasn't the memory of Nikki's arterial spray but my own actual blood. The pain was overwhelming, followed by a ferocious fire that seemed to blossom up from my heart and billow out. Once again, I didn't feel entirely healed by the internal wave of haterade, but the adrenaline that jacked through my bloodstream helped convince me that didn't really matter anymore.

"Enough," I gritted out, and with a strength neither one of us expected me to have, I head-butted the guy right in the nose, breaking it and then following his flopping body backward, clawing and screaming and punching as if I had been trapped in a schoolyard brawl with a bully who wouldn't back down. I saw nothing but a curtain of dark purple haze in front of my eyes, with steaming red smoke and sizzling blue energy bursting forth in trickles and shots, not full on, but enough—enough!

The man flailed upward, and I rolled to the right—directly into a golden beam of sunlight that was so invigorating, I could feel all my senses fire—

And then the bastard punched me right across the jaw, sending me sprawling back into the darkness of the dead zone. *Damn, that was fun while it lasted.*

The whooshing in the street beneath me made all the hair on my skin stand on edge again as the entire surface vibrated in three quick bursts, then the guy was on me once more. I scrambled to get away, to get back to the safe haven of the street corner, but he was faster. Faster, bigger, and with something to prove.

I tried to dig down deep into my gut for the same fury that had propelled me the last time, but it was far more difficult. I lurched forward and he grabbed my ponytail, whipping my head around. It was only by using my momentum to propel my feet in an arcing circle that I was able to get in a glancing kick to his temple, allowing me to wrench myself out of his hold and hit the ground.

My hands connected with the bricks, and the whooshing hit again, and I realized—it was warm. The street's surface was unnaturally warm. There was energy there. Deep underground, but energy. Just as in one breath along the streets of Hamburg there was no dead zone, and the next there was, it seemed like at ground zero, I was shorted out, but below us—below us, something was happening that was being powered by Connected energy. A *lot* of Connected energy. And if there was something below us, then it followed that as below, so above—

The beauty of this mental construct was forcibly shattered as my head connected with the very hard, very dead-zoned pavement, and I bounced up, curling into a ball of self-protection as the assassin kicked me hard in the rib cage, driving the totem of Guabancex once more into my skin. The sudden double shot of pain spiked my rage meter again, giving me the energy to get the hell away from the flurry of kicks. I jacked to the right, rolling several feet into the center of the street— away, unfortunately, from the edge of the dead zone. I didn't stop until I crashed into a parked car, then flinched away as the asshat flung a knife at me that connected with the metal and clattered to the ground.

Using the last bit of sheer willpower I had, I hauled myself up against the car, dragging myself up onto the hood with my arm, still-numb from the asshat's knife to my shoulder, trailing behind me like a weird, S-shaped noodle. With my other hand, I wrenched the totem of Guabancex out of my jacket. I had no more energy myself. I had nothing left to give. I didn't even know if what I was about to try would work, but the Shadow Court hadn't been the only thing to follow me out of the jungles of Guiana. The wind had followed me as well. From eddying breezes to rushing wind to pounding storms, Guabancex had been making herself known to me, and if she still wanted to catch my attention, now would be a really great time to show me how much she really cared—

The knife that ripped across the street and buried itself in my thigh was brutal and wide bladed, and my eyes popped open, a curtain of dark purple haze once more in front of me.

"Enough!" I howled, half in agony, half in fury, and with a violent burst of my own residual Connected energy, I planted the leg that wasn't gushing blood on the windshield and launched myself off the hood of the car — out into the open air.

Above the dead zone.

There was no lightning, no thunder, just a roar of hurricane-strength wind so strong that it practically levitated me off the ground and sent the assassin sprawling. Signposts bent and broke free, rocks flew off the ground, bricks loosened and dislodged, all becoming shrapnel that roared through the tight space in a raging storm. Energy rushed back into me, healing me with fire and light, and I flung my hands wide, sailing on the gusty torrent until I crash-landed once more, this time into the body of the assassin. He'd clearly had the breath knocked completely out of him as he bled from a dozen different places, his arm sliced open by a Stop sign now lying a few feet away. Worse than that, he was bleeding out.

"Oh no, you freaking don't," I hissed, covering him with my body long enough to shoot him full of healing power as well, as the roaring wind lifted off us both and rushed up into the sky, the vortex of destruction dissipating almost as soon as it began. The assassin was unconscious, but he would live. He might not *want* to live after Gamon got done with him, but he'd live. And we'd have the added benefit of more information about the Shadow Court. I was kind of a pansy when it came to getting the information I needed out of people, but Gamon, Judgment of the Arcana Council, had once been an agent of Mossad. She'd get the job done.

Meanwhile, I collapsed on the bricks, sucking in oxygen as the storm raced away above me. Thunder cracked in the distance, and lightning, but none of it compared to the rhythmic rush of energy beneath me.

Whoosh, whoosh, whoosh.

Thump, thump, thump.

I felt the energy of the city street beneath me, the energy of the Connecteds of this city, pulsing like a living thing. I didn't know these people, their troubles and their hopes. I didn't know them; they didn't know me. But today, I'd stood for them anyway. I'd used not only my magic but the same grit and determination that had kept me alive as a seventeen-year-old girl with a Tarot deck in her backpack and her home in fiery ruins, the same resourcefulness that had taken my twenty-two-year-old self down tunnels and into bunkers and long-forgotten caves, searching out relics to sell to keep Connected children safe. I wasn't just some righteously mighty member of the Arcana Council, weaving the energies of the world — I was still that little girl, still that lost young woman, still that brokenhearted loner who'd lost the mentor who'd first shown me how to use my abilities for the greater good.

Whoosh, whoosh, whoosh.

Thump, thump, thump.

I peeled open an eye, staring at the beautiful building in front of me as the cobblestones shook beneath me. I realized, blearily, the letters that were written across it, in English, oddly enough, said HAMBURG PORT AUTHORITY. And I finally made the connection of how the Shadow Court was transporting its drugs so quickly and efficiently that they were in the port area one moment and gone the next.

Whoosh, whoosh, whoosh.

Elon Musk's hyperloop tubes, the technology stolen and repurposed by the Shadow Court. Hidden deep underground and extending for hundreds of miles, this magically enhanced supply chain could deliver its contraband from the storied port of Hamburg to the distant heart of Europe, as efficiently as the pneumatic tubes in Justice Hall.

Thump, thump, thump.

That wasn't the only connection I made either.

I closed my eyes and lay on the ground and let my mental barriers ease…and suddenly, he was there.

I've got you, Miss Wilde, Armaeus said in my mind, his voice filled with wonder and surprise — and a fierce, unmistakable strength I hadn't felt in him for far, far too long. *I've got you.*

CHAPTER TWENTY-NINE

S o…does Elon Musk have any idea his hyperloop invention has been co-opted?" Nikki stared at me over the top of her laptop, while the screen of the machine next to her shifted, Simon's face coming into view. We were sitting in Armaeus's conference room back in Las Vegas, and it was almost like old times. The wide view of the Strip stretched far beneath us, baking in the summer sun, and Nikki, Armaeus, Kreios, and I were ranged around the table. Simon spoke from his hospital room at Dr. Sell's clinic, but at least we were all in the same city again. Progress.

"Well, other than the fact that someone was using it to pump Europe full of technoceuticals, I think he'd think it was *awesome*," the Fool declared. "I mean, are you kidding me? A fully functional hyperloop using his specs that jettisons canisters of organic materials and nanotech halfway across Europe in the blink of an eye? That's man-made ingenuity right there, no Connected ability required."

"Well, there's some Connected ability required," Armaeus corrected from his position next to me. "The energy source, for one. The electric propulsion system Musk is testing now is nowhere near adequate for large-scale loops. For that, psychically enhanced circuits are required. Musk will get there, but it will take time. And the money necessary to build the loop remains problematic. Not everyone is able to co-opt ancient cave systems and little-known aqueducts and abandoned subterranean passageways to transport canisters not much larger than the pneumatic tubes employed by Justice Wilde. The hurdles to putting the hyperloop into play for human transport, in a predominantly aboveground, highly regulated tube system, remain significant."

"And it looks like the Shadow Court's gonna be encountering some of those hang-ups as well," Nikki put in. She tapped several keys on her laptop and grinned. "Brody reports that Hamburg's finest found the technoceutical launch zone directly beneath the port authority's main building. Apparently, there's an entire rabbit warren of corridors and passageways beneath that building and throughout Hamburg that've been used by the richest and most powerful traders throughout the centuries as a secondary shipping route for the most precious and illicit cargo. The Shadow Court, whoever they are, just took it one step further."

"Whoever they are," I said grimly. I sat at the end of the table, a glass of scotch untouched beside me, hunched into my jacket. In my lap, I clutched the totem of Guabancex, bringer of storms.

Almost as if I'd summoned her, the wall of Armaeus's conference room shuddered, splitting wide. The dark, fierce figure of Gamon stalked through it, her face grim but satisfied.

"He's dead," she said summarily. As usual, Judgment of the Arcana Council looked like the warrior she was, clad in full leathers and heavy, scuffed boots, her dark skin heated from exertion, her long dark braid of thick hair lashed away from her face. With her high cheekbones, chiseled features, and flashing dark eyes, she'd command attention in any room, but her air of brutality would send gazes flinching away just as quickly.

"Dead," I echoed. "My fault or yours?"

Her smile flickered ominously. "I may have helped it along a little bit, but you did a number on him. He didn't die in vain, though. He knew more than he thought he did, in the end."

As I grimaced, trying not to imagine how that interrogation went down, Gamon peered around the room until she saw Simon's face on the screen. "I sent you the information. Names, places, connections. Our guy wasn't at the top of the food chain, but he paid attention. The Shadow Court will give up its secrets soon enough."

"Excellent," Simon said, his glee making up for the fact that he was still bedridden. "We've also got a ton of information from Mercault, who's thrown the entire House of Pentacles behind our efforts to search and destroy these guys. Now that he realizes who the Shadow Court is and what their game's about, he's *pissed*. Apparently, they've been disrupting his own supply chains for the past year, but he couldn't figure out who was behind the problems he was having. And, I suspect, he feels kind of bad about throwing you under the bus, Sara."

I rolled my eyes, and Simon grinned. "Then there's the Hamburg crime scene. We've got an entire pile of data and evidence we've recovered both at the drop site and the terminus points for their drug network. We got people, places, entire lives we can poke through."

I eyed him. "I thought Interpol was keeping this all under wraps."

"They are, technically speaking. But everywhere Brody goes, I go. And Brody's done his level best to go everywhere we want to be since Armaeus scraped you up off the pavement."

Beside me, the Magician shifted, as if hearing his name spoken aloud was the only thing that could have stirred him from the mental labyrinth he'd currently lost himself in.

"What of Jarvis Fuggeren?" Armaeus asked.

Gamon shook her head. "Our guy had nothing on what he called the high court, which presumably Jarvis is part of. His orders came through people lower on the totem pole." She grinned, and the look was feral, dangerous. "*Those* names he did give up, though. So we can start there."

"We've got eyes on Jarvis too," Simon confirmed. "He's not trying to hide, though he hasn't hit our radar screens in more than a year. He's still making money, hobnobbing with anyone with either the privilege or the coin to throw a party, and generally living large off his ancestor's good business sense. Ordinarily, that would make me like him less as an evil overlord, but there's the drug component with this job. Rich, entitled guys love nothing more than making their coin off the drug trade. It's easy, they don't get involved, and the money keeps pouring in. None of it gets traced to them, and there just aren't a lot of decisions in this kind of business. It's about as turnkey as you can possibly get, even with the psychic component. Especially with the psychic component, since Jarvis can sample all the newest products and then decide whether or not he wants to share and with whom. It's a megalomaniac's wet dream."

Nikki snorted as I shook my head.

"Do you think they planned all this—drawing us out, showing us the drug trail, tricking me into the fight…a fight that I didn't even win, not exactly?" I asked.

"You won, Miss Wilde," Armaeus countered, but I waved him off wearily.

"Not really. We didn't knock out the Shadow Court, we only cut off one of their drug routes. Someone took a potshot at our own people—people I put at risk— because they were five steps ahead of us the whole way through. I collared the assassin, but we don't know if Fuggeren is a player in all this or just another convenient stooge, and you still don't have all your memories."

Armaeus nodded with a wry smile. "Put another way, you succeeded in single-handedly defending the interests of the Council without betraying the alliances—positive or negative—of any of its current members, or putting its temporarily enfeebled leader at risk. You identified a cancerous technoceutical distribution network trafficking poisons so deadly that even members of its own blighted supply chain were panicking and leaking information to Interpol and to your own office at Justice Hall. You ensured that not only could law enforcement move forward with shutting down this illegal hub, but that the Council was able to get our hands on at least some of the product, which will allow us to test it, break it down into its component parts, identify how it might be used. And, if necessary, reverse engineer it."

"Ma-Singh nearly died, Armaeus," I said, and it was my turn to stare at the far wall, caught in my own endless loop of self-judgment. "He was in the wrong place at the wrong time because of me."

"Yes," Armaeus said simply, and something in his voice made me look his way. Armaeus was staring at me with such naked emotion on his face that I blinked, my breath suddenly stalling out. "You would stop a bullet for any one of us. Step in front of any train. Endure any fire, break any bone. You would give chase when there was no catching your quarry, and you would lead away pursuers when there was no way you could outrun them. You would do all these things without a second thought, Miss Wilde. I've met you again only a few short days ago, and I know it to be true. There is no other human I've encountered in my life more willing to sacrifice herself in a moment of need, or more negligent about the value of her own life. And when people like General Ma-Singh see that in you, shining forth like a beacon in the darkness of this current war against ourselves, they gladly step forward too. Some, like Ma-Singh, because they can. Some, like Emma Fearon, because they must."

His voice dropped off, and when he spoke again, his words wavered slightly. "Some like Detective Rooks and Miss Dawes here and even...even myself, because they see in you something that makes them believe in the strength, the hope, the possibility that lies within every Connected soul. That it's worth taking the risk, fighting the fight, building the bridge. Because of you, Miss Wilde. That is the grace you give."

On the other side of the table, Nikki sniffled. "I mean, whatever. I don't like you all that much, dollface." Even Gamon made a slightly strangled noise deep in her throat, before stepping back through the doorway in the wall, and disappearing from sight.

"But you don't even know me anymore," I whispered to Armaeus, not knowing what else to say.

If anything, his manner only grew more intense. He leaned toward me, never mind that Nikki and Kreios were sitting not five feet away, never mind that Simon was still staring transfixed from his computer screen.

"I don't know you. I've only just met you. The key of Cassius D'Angelo revealed a great many things—but not that. Not you. But I know what I saw as you faced down a horde of pursuers who attacked you in the shipyard with a single-minded obsession to take you down. I know what I saw as you grappled with the assassin of the Shadow Court, facing him with equal courage whether you had the benefit of your magic or not. I saw you as the idea struck you of how you could defeat an enemy who had you dead to rights. I witnessed how you would not give up. And I watched you summon a god to your aid...a god who willingly responded."

I clutched the totem beneath the table. "I can explain that."

"My dear Miss Wilde," Armaeus chuckled wryly, shaking his head. "Your days of having to explain yourself to me have long since passed. You have given me a gift far greater than I would have ever thought possible."

"Ah...I have?"

His expression softened, but his gaze held me fast. "Down in the darkness and deception of Hell, caught in a trap you didn't know had been sprung," he murmured, and my breath froze in my throat. I knew what he was talking about, but I couldn't seem to summon the words to make him stop. "Lost on a faraway shore, you—loved me, Miss Wilde. You opened your heart and revealed a truth and a depth I had never before understood. A truth and a depth that changes everything. For the Council. For the Connected. For me."

I could do nothing but stare at him for a long second. "That wasn't truth," I managed, finally. "That never happened."

"It was truth," Armaeus countered. "You can, you do, you are. It is, always and ever, your love."

My eyes flared wide. "I remember those words. Brother McCullough—"

"Spoke the truth the angels most wanted you to hear, a truth I still couldn't grasp. You are the key, Miss Wilde. The love you give and give and give from deep within yourself, this gift that never wavers, never fails…it is the source of your strength. Father Jerome understood that. Ma-Singh understands it. Everyone you've ever known understands it, except you. And, until now…me."

"Well, I still don't understand it," I managed, my brain seriously on the edge of shutting down.

Armaeus's expression turned infinitely gentle, his gaze never leaving mine. "You will. Perhaps it took me forgetting who you were to see the truth of who you are. Perhaps I'd never truly seen you in the way I always should have. There is so much still left for us to do, to understand, but now I wish…"

He paused, his jaw tensing briefly. "I wish only that we might have the opportunity to get to know each other again—differently from before. Better, perhaps, in the end. I would like that, if you'd be willing."

I bit my lip, searching his gaze as I nodded, and Nikki hiccupped on a cough. Even Kreios may have sighed softly across the room.

"I'd like that, too," I whispered, trying to keep my voice steady.

Armaeus's smile was once again so familiar—and so different. Deeper, fuller, more earnest, yet more vulnerable than I'd ever seen before. He leaned forward and lifted one hand, then the other, touching his long, elegant fingertips to either side of my face.

"Then I would like to begin again with you, Miss Wilde," he murmured, still searching my eyes. "For I…I will love you, ever more."

For a long, fraught moment, I stared back at him, unsure of everything he was asking of me, unsure of everything he was offering. This was the Magician of the Arcana Council, a man I'd known and lost and found again, a demigod who was more and less than what he'd been before, a being whose heart had beaten lockstep with mine, whose arms had cradled me close, whose hands had healed me, body and soul. He was the same, he was different, he was the beginning and my end. And he was all I'd ever want, however I could get him, in this world or any other. I may be this key he spoke of, but he was mine as well.

I nodded quickly, tears slipping from my eyes.

"Sweet Mother Mary on a tricycle," Nikki breathed.

Then Armaeus tipped his head to mine, and began us all over again with a kiss.

~~~

Thank you so much for reading THE SHADOW COURT! If you enjoyed this book, reviews are the life's blood of an author, and I would sincerely appreciate yours wherever you bought this book!

A Note From Jenn

Though this book isn't named after a particular card, it's quite definitely a book written for The Moon. A card of mysteries uncovered and truths come to light, it's one of the most intriguing cards in the deck! Read on for a full description!

ALSO: Interested in learning more about the Tarot, upcoming book releases, and other bits of arcana and mayhem? Get Connected (heh) and sign up for my mailing list at www.jennstark.com/newsletter!

THE MOON .

The Moon is one of the most mysterious cards in the deck, depicting a large, feminine-aspected orb in the sky shining down over two towers. A wolf and a dog come together (suggesting both the tamed and untamed side of nature), while a crayfish crawls out of the water (symbolizing thoughts or the subconscious becoming real). It's a card that points to mysteries that have not yet come to light, and is considered a card of the occult as well as deep intuition, dreams and the unconscious.

Although often, the Moon implies a malign aspect — deception, illusions, fear and anxiety — that's mainly a warning for the querent to look deeper into the heart of a situation and not accept anything at face value. Don't let fear create false realities that keep you from seeing your true path! Instead, let go of negative self-talk and doubt, and let your intuition guide you. If you draw the Moon, you may learn unexpected truths or be treated to a sudden revelation, and you should definitely pay close attention to your dreams, intuitions and messages during this very fertile time!

Acknowledgments

THE SHADOW COURT was truly an emotional experience for me, as Sara was put through the ringer and lived to tell the tale. Thank you to all my readers for continuing to read my books, which allows me to write these stories for you. I remain truly grateful to Elizabeth Bemis for her beautiful work on my books and my site—especially my gorgeous series covers. My editorial team of Linda Ingmanson and Toni Lee continue their tireless efforts on my behalf as well. Any mistakes in the manuscript are most definitely my own. Thank you to Edeena Cross, Judi Soderberg and Sabra Harp for their insightful, careful beta reads, and to Kristine Krantz, who will one day be so sad when she can follow the bouncing ball on the very first draft. And, of course, thank you, Geoffrey, evermore. It's been a *Wilde* ride.

ABOUT JENN STARK

Jenn Stark is an award-winning author of paranormal romance and urban fantasy. She lives and writes in Ohio. . . and she definitely loves to write. In addition to her Immortal Vegas and Wilde Justice urban fantasy series and Demon Enforcers paranormal romance series, she is also author Jennifer McGowan, whose Maids of Honor series of Young Adult Elizabethan spy romances are published by Simon & Schuster, and author Jennifer Chance, whose Rule Breakers series of New Adult contemporary romances are published by Random House/LoveSwept and whose modern royals series, Gowns & Crowns, is now available.

You can find her online at jennstark.com, follow her on Twitter @jennstark, and visit her on Facebook at facebook.com/authorjennstark.